AF612347

The Consulting Agent: Neutrality Act

Jonathan M. Bryant

English Street Books

ISBN: 979-8-9940191-0-8 (e-book)

ISBN: 979-8-9940191-1-5 (paperback edition)

ISBN: 979-8-9940191-2-2 (hardcover editions)

Book Cover Design by ebooklaunch.com

This publication is Human Authored.

Contents

"No people ever recognize their dictator in advance. He never stands for election on the platform of dictatorship. He always represents himself as the instrument for expressing the Incorporated National Will. . . When our dictator turns up you can depend on it that he will be one of the boys, and he will stand for everything traditionally American."

Dorothy Thompson, February 12, 1937

"Both sides agree that in the event of foreign wars this nation should maintain a status of strict neutrality, and that around the structure of neutrality we should so shape our policies as to keep this country from being drawn into war."

Franklin Roosevelt, July 14, 1939

"There was a time when the mere nonexistence of war was enough. Not anymore. The world is in the odd position of being intellectually opposed to war, spiritually committed to it. That is the leaden note. If war comes, it will be war, and no one wants that. If peace is restored, it will be another arrangement enlarging not simply the German boundary but the Hitler dream. Let me whisper I love you while we are dancing and the lights are low."

E. B. White, August 27, 1939

1

Thursday, July 20, 1939

I should have spotted the black Oldsmobile earlier. It was parked thirty yards behind, and we were the only cars on the block. I'd noticed the car several times, but thought nothing of it. Now I wondered. Was I being followed?

The message from Mr. Hirsch said to meet for lunch at the Standard Club, twelve o'clock sharp. Not wanting to arrive early and appear desperate, I'd pulled over and parked. I had nothing else on my dance card. Along that block of Ponce de Leon, half the storefronts were empty, and uncollected garbage lay in the street. The odor of rot wafted through my open window. Crabgrass poked out of cracks in the sidewalk. After a decade of hard times, economic recovery hadn't reached this part of town. It hadn't reached me either.

I glanced in the mirror again. A driver sat in the Olds, waiting, despite Atlanta's searing July heat. As my mother would say, *Always grab the bull by the horns*, so I got out of my car and began walking toward the Olds. He started his engine, threw it into gear, and pulled out. I slapped his fender as he roared past and earned a startled look from the driver—medium build, dark hair, dark eyes, big nose, soft chin. A couple of blocks further down, he turned right.

I glanced at my watch, walked back to my car, and waited some more. At five before noon, I fired up the Buick and drove down Ponce to the Standard Club. After parking, I sat for a moment, gathering my thoughts.

Astonishingly, the black Oldsmobile cruised slowly past. Damn if the guy didn't look right at me. What the hell was going on?

It was time. Hurrying across the blacktop oven of a parking lot, I pushed the door open and found, thank God, the place was air-conditioned. To the left was the dining room, guarded by a tuxedoed headwaiter behind a chrome and glass podium. He glanced up, and his eyes narrowed. He didn't like what he saw.

I didn't like what he saw either. Mark Twain supposedly said, *Clothes make the man*, and my clothes certainly made me. I wore a light blue broadcloth suit, the summer uniform of Atlanta's business elite. But my suit was old, shiny in the elbows and knees from wear. My shoes, though polished, were literally down at the heels. I needed a haircut, the collar points of my shirt had frayed, and my tie had faded. I was a few weeks short of looking like a bum.

The headwaiter stood taller and sniffed loudly. "May I help you?"

"Sure," I said, handing him my hat. "Take care of that for me."

I stood in the doorway, taking it all in. The dining room was lined with art and fine fabrics, packed with well-dressed patrons. Atlanta's Standard Club had been created by rich Jewish immigrants, so there was a message in the beautiful room for the *goyim*.

Look at this! We don't need to be let into your clubs.

I was one of those *goyim*, and the headwaiter guessed it. "Sir, may I have your name?"

"Mark Morgan," I said. He looked at the list in front of him, frowning.

Harold Hirsch sat at a window table with a bearded man, no food in front of them, so I wasn't late. I headed their way. The headwaiter trailed behind, waving his list, protesting. "Just a moment, sir. Who invited you? Sir?"

Hirsch glanced up. "Ah, Mr. Morgan, I'm so pleased you could join us." He pressed on the table to help himself stand. The headwaiter scurried away.

"The pleasure's mine, Mr. Hirsch," I said, shaking hands.

Years had passed since I'd last seen Harold Hirsch, and those years had not been kind. He was in his fifties, but looked older. He'd lost weight, his once round face had crumpled, and his skin was sallow with a hint of jaundice. Hirsch's hair hung thin and lank to a collar much too big for his neck. He slumped, looking exhausted.

He's dying, I thought.

"This is Rabbi Goldstein," said Hirsch, nodding toward the man who stood beside him. "The rabbi's new to Atlanta."

"Nice to meet you," I said, shaking hands across the table.

Goldstein had bright blue eyes and a dark, dense beard with a touch of gray. Just under my height of six feet, he was slim with a long, corded neck. His beard made it hard to tell his age, but maybe forty, forty-five. He smelt of cologne and wore a smart double-breasted gray suit with red pinstripes and a bright red pocket square. His handshake offset this touch of dandyism: firm and strong, his hands callused like those of a manual laborer or farmer. A confusing mix.

"Rabbi," Hirsch said, "I met Mr. Morgan when he worked at Coca-Cola. He was one of Woodruff's favorites. You know who Robert Woodruff is?"

"The chairman of Coca-Cola," said the rabbi softly. "One of the richest men in America."

"Not just Coke. Woodruff controls Atlantic Steel, Atlantic Coal, the Trust Company Bank, and a myriad of other enterprises. He's the industrial and financial king of the South. I played a central role in building that empire. Mr. Morgan helped build Coca-Cola's international business. His work—often risky work, I might add—earned Coke millions of dollars overseas. Last winter, however, Woodruff discarded him. Threw you aside after working for Coke, what, ten years?"

"Twelve," I said.

"Twelve years." Hirsch shook his head. "You've been ill-used by Woodruff."

The tone of the conversation worried me. I knew Robert Woodruff well. He was not a monster, simply a very aggressive businessman. I even understood why he fired me, and for now, I would lie low. Woodruff was mercurial and had surely forgotten about me, *the problem*. In six months or a year, there would be a crisis in Colombia or Germany, and Woodruff would remember me, *the solution*. To be polite, however, I stayed in my seat.

The waiter arrived, and the rabbi ordered grilled chopped steak. I ordered Dover sole. Hirsch waved the waiter away.

"I'm sorry, gentlemen," he said. "I've not been well, and my doctor has me on a special diet. I'm not supposed to eat out." He gripped the edge of the table again for support and stood. "Mr. Morgan, so good to see you. Listen to Rabbi Goldstein. He speaks for me."

Startled, I stood and watched Hirsch shuffle toward the door. Conversation dropped; curious eyes followed as he slowly made his way out of the room, and then those eyes turned back to look at me.

"Okay, Rabbi, how can I help you?"

He tented his hands and then tilted them to point at me. "Harold tells me you were Woodruff's fixer, that you solved problems Coke had overseas. At least until you got into a poisonous jam and almost didn't get out." He chuckled.

"Fixer wasn't exactly my job title."

"Ah, but titles do not reveal who we really are." He smiled and leaned forward. "The Baptist World Alliance is meeting in Atlanta next week. Perhaps forty thousand visitors, maybe more. Messengers, they call them, from all over the world. This will be good for Atlanta. News reports will appear around the globe. Atlanta will emerge for the first time as a truly international city."

"Rabbis are interested in the well-being of Atlanta?"

"Rabbis are interested in many things, Mr. Morgan. Sadly, there are political problems. Should they exclude Czechoslovakian Messengers because, thanks to the Nazis, that country ceased to exist last March? Will there be conflict over the lack of religious freedom in Spain? Should Japan be rebuked for its war in China and the murder of missionaries? Problems, you see."

I already didn't like this guy, but it was a free lunch, and we hadn't gotten our food. "Those are problems for the Baptists," I said. "I don't really care."

"No, Mr. Morgan, these are problems for us all. All men of good will should care."

He took a sip of water and leaned back in his seat. "Then there's the German Messengers. Tools of Adolf Hitler. Nazi Party members." He leaned forward and lowered his voice. "There have been threats."

"Threats from the Germans?"

"No, against them."

"By Jews?"

"Czechs, Slovaks, and countless others hate and fear the Nazis. Now there's this Polish crisis. It doesn't have to be Jews."

Our food arrived, and we ate quietly for a few moments. My Dover sole was delicious, buttery yet firm, just as it should be. All I lacked was a glass of good white Bordeaux. Then the rabbi pointed his fork at me. "It would be terrible if something violent happened. Violence could crush this city in the eyes of the world. Imagine. Atlanta: a city too backward to host an international conference. Atlanta: a city never too busy to hate. It would take years to recover."

"I see," I said, glancing toward the door.

He put his fork down. "Worse, much worse, would be violence blamed on Jews. If Germans are hurt or . . . killed." He struggled for words, looking down at the table. "It would be a disaster, a pretext for more Nazi persecution. More laws, confiscations, murders, even another *Kristallnacht*, as happened after the murder of the Nazi envoy in Paris."

"Sounds like you need to talk with the police," I said.

The rabbi toyed with the ruins of his chopped steak, which he'd slashed to pieces with his knife but hardly eaten. "The police cannot be trusted. Atlanta's police don't have the best reputation."

"Then a private detective or something. I don't see how I can help."

"You must help, Mr. Morgan. We need your experience, skills, and discretion. We need you to find the source of the threats and head off violence."

"That's not the kind of work I do."

"Hirsch told us you'd say that. But he also insists you're the right man for the job. You speak German. That's important. The job will take a week. For that week, we will pay you seven thousand dollars. One thousand dollars a day. We will also give you five hundred extra for expenses. Seven thousand, five hundred dollars total. If this goes into a second week, we will pay the same. One thousand dollars a day."

The rabbi slid a fat brown envelope across the table. I looked at the envelope, licked my lips, but did not touch it.

"Let me get this straight," I said. "You're hiring me . . ."

"Oh, no, Mr. Morgan, not me. The Jewish Welfare Alliance of New York is hiring you."

"The Jewish Welfare Alliance of New York is hiring me to protect these Nazis?"

"Yes, Mr. Morgan, that is exactly what we are doing."

At the car, I counted it. Enough money to buy a house in a good neighborhood. I counted it again, astonished that it came out the same: seven thousand, five hundred dollars. For a moment, I worried about the implications of so much dough for a strange job.

Too late, I decided; *I shook his hand and took his money*.

After all I'd been through over the past year, something was finally going my way. I'd learned a lot from that terrible year. Worrying about what was right or just was hogwash. You had to look out for yourself. Trusting others was a trap. Trusting my employer had almost gotten me killed. Trusting my wife had led to humiliation and financial ruin. I gladly took the rabbi's money and ignored the strange context.

He'd given me a file with information about the Germans and copies of the threats. I threw the file onto the car seat, tucked the envelope full of money into my breast pocket, and pulled the Buick onto Ponce., heading downtown feeling flush. At the Municipal Auditorium, a sign announced a Louis Armstrong concert next month. I laughed and slapped my hands on the steering wheel. I could buy the best tickets and hear Satchmo in person.

But why go alone? Since my divorce, I'd avoided romantic entanglements and I intended to keep it that way. But I had no romantic interest in Emma Connor; she was just an interesting friend. Maybe she would go with me?

I parked at number ten Pryor Street and hurried up the hot stairway two steps at a time. By the fifth floor, I was sweating rivers. I collected myself, then stepped to her office door.

Emma sat erect at her desk, pencil in hand, a typed manuscript spread out in front of her. She'd angled a fan behind to blow across her back but not disturb the papers on her desk. Emma made a swift mark on the page, then held her pencil up, ready to pounce again. She'd swept her brown hair up into a bun, but small tendrils had escaped, waving charmingly in the fan's breeze. Her ears poked out, her nose was a bit long, and she hid gorgeous hazel eyes behind round wire-rimmed glasses. A navy-blue cotton dress clung to her tall, slender figure. Emma was no Greta Garbo, but she was pleasantly fair with a nice heart-shaped face. More importantly, she was the smartest, best-read woman I knew.

In 1937, when Atlanta was almost bankrupt, the city's Carnegie Library had laid Emma off. But she'd bounced back, joining the WPA Writers' Project, conducting and editing interviews with older Americans. Meticulous, polite, and thoughtful, she introduced herself to the subjects as a spinster librarian. That went over well with the old folks.

I knocked softly on the door frame, and she glanced up. "Mark? Is something wrong? You're flushed and sweating."

"Just what a glimpse of a lovely WPA gal does to me."

"Oh, go jump in the lake."

"It's hot enough to do that, but I'm feeling a different heat."

"You're incorrigible," she said, shuffling papers, but I saw the hint of a smile. "I have work to do. As usual, I bet you don't."

"You'd lose that bet. Did you know that a month from now, Louis Armstrong will perform at the city auditorium? Wanna go?"

She pounced, making a mark on the page. "That's out of the blue," she said, raising her pencil. "I can't really think about it now."

"Why don't we talk about it at dinner tonight? We could hit the Brass Rail, or maybe Herren's?"

She waggled her pencil impatiently, not looking up. "Knock it off, Mark. I know you're broke, and I sure can't afford it."

I patted my breast pocket. "Broke no more, I've got it covered."

She looked up. "Be careful; that's a dangerous thing to say."

I collapsed into a chair across from her. "Got a new job; it pays well. I'll tell you about it tonight."

She took her time, considering. "I have an interview late this afternoon over on the west side. We're booked up with interviews for the next week. And, as always, there's overdue editing work."

"Seven-thirty?"

"Mark, I just can't tonight. Tomorrow, maybe, that might work."

"Tomorrow? I thought WPA meant 'we poke along'? Put it off."

"I can't miss this interview. I've worked for weeks to get it; it's with an elderly ex-slave. But tomorrow night's Friday. We can stay out late."

"Tomorrow, and tomorrow, and tomorrow," I intoned.

She laughed. "I hope your mysterious history is not as violent as Macbeth's."

"What?"

"Your history, Mark. You've never told me anything about your past. You've said almost nothing about your family or about yourself. If I go to dinner with you, that will be the required topic. It's my fee."

I tried to read her face until she smiled.

"So, there's a fee? Does that mean I get to cash in later?"

She blushed, the flush rising to her ears. "Don't get ahead of yourself."

"Okey dokey. I'll pick you up after work tomorrow. We'll go to the Rainbow Roof. Dinner and dancing; the orchestra is supposed to be hot."

"You didn't say anything about dancing."

"Yes, dancing. Live music."

"Swanky stuff. Sure thing, I'll go if you're paying. So, what's this about a new client?"

"Nope," I said, standing up.

"What, you'll make me wait?"

"Turnabout's fair play." I laughed and headed toward the stairs. Back on the street, I fired up the Buick and turned toward the Atlanta Athletic Club. All the cash in my pocket made me feel like a new man—and then it hit me. *Her fee.*

Father told people he was "in sugar," and he was, as were half the Americans living in Havana. We had moved there when I was small. I grew up speaking Spanish with my playmates and the servants, English, and German at home with my family. Father was quiet, tall, and awkward, somewhat like the actor Jimmy Stewart. He collected books—hundreds of books—including many beautiful old leather-bound volumes. As a child, I understood them by their smell; the new ones were oily and fresh, the old smelled musty and mysterious. Father was mysterious as well. He often went on long trips, but never told us why or what he did.

I turned sixteen in 1921, a bad year. Sugar prices collapsed, the flu still raged, and political violence spread across Cuba. Father came home after a three-week absence with a bandaged thigh and a terrible fever.

"Dear God," Mother said. "Rebels must have shot him."

The next day, they took Father into surgery. I skipped my swimming practice to wait at the hospital. The procedure took so long that my mother and younger brother left to get food.

While they were away, the surgeon emerged from the operating room. "It went well," he said in Spanish. There was fresh blood on his smock, and I realized with a start that it was my father's blood.

"A thousand thanks, Doctor," I said. "What caused the infection?"

"A second bullet was in the wound. Thankfully, gangrene hasn't set in, so we did not have to amputate. Our concern now is septicemia. If we avoid that, he should be fine, except walking may be a problem."

"A second bullet?"

"Yes, incredible. He had no idea; how could he? Two bullets in one wound—imagine the chances. Those damn Americans, hundreds of shots were fired. It must have been like war. I read about it in the papers a week or so ago. He's lucky to be alive."

That evening, I went through the stack of unread newspapers that had arrived from the American Club while Father was away, and found the story. A gun battle had erupted just outside Charleston between rival rumrunners. Two men had died. The criminals had disappeared. Police were investigating, but I didn't have to read any further. The pieces fell into place, confirming what I had already guessed.

My father, the quiet bibliophile, was a gangster.

The Atlanta Athletic Club owned a ten-story building in the best part of downtown, with an indoor swimming pool, gymnasium, barbershop, three restaurants, ballrooms, and even sixty hotel rooms for members and guests. I scanned the parking lot for the black Oldsmobile, but saw nothing. Since my divorce, I've lived on the seventh floor. The upper floors were not air-conditioned, and my room faced southwest, so it broiled in the afternoon summer sun. Small air-conditioned offices for members were on the second floor. I locked myself in one and spread the rabbi's file on the desk.

First was a list of the German Messengers' names and the schedule of their arrivals in Atlanta—almost 300 names, an astonishing number of German Baptists.

Many were already here, staying in private homes. The rest would stay at the Henry Grady Hotel on Peachtree, only a few blocks from the Athletic Club. Other documents covered transportation and immigration matters for the Messengers. Finally, there were images of the seventeen threatening letters.

The photos were clear and well lit, all apparently taken on the same desk. Sixteen were well written; they didn't seem to have been penned by fanatical or unhinged people. Most reflected deeply held concerns and made only rhetorical threats. But one addressed to Mayor Hartsfield gave me pause. Typed in capital letters on a single page, he threatened to pursue, terrify, and slaughter the Germans one by one. He would execute everyone guilty of Nazi crimes. The author signed it "THE ANGEL OF DEATH!"

I put the photos down, thinking. I'd been paid a fortune, $7,500, but there was just one letter of genuine concern. That made the arrangement even more curious.

According to the list, Gerald Lowder, an Atlanta businessman, was hosting Otto Erlanger from Essen. I looked Lowder up in the phone book. Cedar-9813. I dialed.

A woman picked up. "Good afternoon," I said. "My name's Mark Morgan. I'm sorry to bother you, but I need to speak with your guest, Dr. Erlanger. Is he there?"

"No, he and Gerald are out touring the city."

"This is important."

"Mark Morgan, you say?" She paused, breathing into the phone. "Why don't you come by the house between five and five-thirty? They should be back by then."

"Thank you. I'll be there a bit past five."

Hanging up, I checked my watch. I had plenty of time. In the basement, I showered and then went to my locker. A cedar box on the top shelf served as my archive and bank, holding the legal documents from my divorce, the title to my car, and forty-eight dollars. That, along with my clothes and the forty-dollar Hamilton watch on my wrist, was my entire net worth. Or had been before my lunch with the rabbi. Standing in front of my locker, I counted the money again, enjoying the feel of the hundreds in my hands: new, smooth, and slippery. I poured them into the box and considered the pile. Seven thousand, five hundred—even just thinking the number made me stand straighter, breathe deeper.

After a few moments, the money looked wrong sitting in the battered old box. Seven thousand went back into the brown envelope. I hid that under my shoes at the bottom of the locker. The remaining five hundred and forty-eight dollars, enough money to buy a good car, filled my wallet nicely.

The suit in the locker was just as worn as the suit I had on. I fingered the fabric, thinking about Muse's men's store just down the street. After all, as Twain said, *Clothes make the man.*

I bought three fine suits at Muse's. The first was a light blue summer-weight broadcloth, very much an Atlanta style. I also chose a white linen Palm Beach suit with a top-quality Panama hat. Both had two-button jackets, none of that double-breasted fashion for me. Finally, I picked a third suit, charcoal gray with subtle pinstripes, the fabric a summer-weight wool. I'm six feet tall and just shy of a hundred and eighty pounds. Astonishingly, it fit.

"Suits never fit me off the rack," I said.

"Look how well it drapes on your shoulders," said the clerk, smoothing the cloth. "We can do a quick alteration of the trousers, and they should fit perfectly. Ten minutes."

"That quickly?"

"Yes, sir. The other suits will take a day. We'll send them over tomorrow."

They finished the alteration, and I looked at myself in the mirror. The charcoal gray suit gave me gravitas. In fact, it made me look a bit menacing. I left wearing the new suit, a matching dark gray fedora, a Prussian blue tie, and new black Oxford shoes.

Dark clouds loomed overhead, and an ominous stillness had settled on downtown. Streetcars, buses, trucks, and autos still crowded the street, but pedestrians scurried for cover. Then suddenly, the storm broke. I ran to my car. Lightning flashed, and thunder boomed as I hurled myself in and started the engine. Heavy, hissing rain fell, overwhelming my wipers. The traffic slowed to a crawl, inching north on Spring Street.

The storm soon moved off toward the east, purple lightning bolts dancing in the clouds. Traffic sped up, and past Brookwood, I gunned it, not wanting to be late. When I glanced in the mirror, I spotted a black Oldsmobile two cars back. *What the hell's going on?*

At a quarter past five, I hit Buckhead and turned left onto West Paces Ferry Road. The Olds continued straight, going north. Relieved, I motored along, enjoying the parklike surroundings of a rich neighborhood. During the teens and twenties, Atlanta's wealthy had moved north, outside the city limits. Many had built imposing estates on heavily wooded rolling land along West Paces Ferry. In the thirties, newer developments sprang up on side streets off West Paces, Northside, and Habersham. There, in somewhat more modest homes, lived many of Atlanta's second tier of businessmen, lawyers, and doctors. Some suggested annexing the area to Atlanta, but I couldn't see that happening. County taxes were cheaper.

The Lowders' home was a large brick colonial in one of the new neighborhoods, on an acre of grassy lot framed by glorious oaks. Shadows from the trees dappled the yard. An enclosed sunporch on the left of the house matched a porte cochere on the right. I parked on the street, shrugged the new jacket over my sweat-damp shirt, and cut across the grass to the front. A Black maid opened the door, grimaced, and showed me into the parlor.

"They're not home yet," Mrs. Lowder said. She was in her fifties, plump, with white hair, a single strand of pearls, and an unbuttoned sweater over an older, fairly formal dress. On the right lapel of the dress, she wore a large gold brooch of a penguin with emerald eyes.

The room was as cold as an icebox. "Air-conditioning?"

"Isn't it grand?" she said, smiling. "Dreadfully expensive, of course, but so worth it." She touched her penguin and smiled. "How delicious to wear a sweater in summer. Please sit, Mr. Morgan. I'm trying to remember; don't you work at Coca-Cola?"

"I did. With the Export Corporation, but I left last year."

The maid brought in a tray with glasses and a pitcher of sweet iced tea. She poured one and put it on the end table beside me.

"Thank you," I said. The maid scowled again and shuffled out.

"I knew your name was familiar," said Mrs. Lowder. "You had legal problems in Ecuador or Panama—well, somewhere down there—didn't you? They even charged you with murder? It was false, of course; I know what those Latin people are like. Then, when you returned to Atlanta, that very public divorce. It made a splash in the papers for a week or so. I'm sorry, but I remember it."

"Peru."

"What?"

"Peru. I was charged with murder in Peru."

"Oh," she said. "So, what did Mr. Woodruff object to? The murder or the divorce?"

"He objected to paying me for the five months I spent in a Peruvian jail."

"But you were innocent!"

"It was a business decision."

Mrs. Lowder considered this. "I'm sorry. Are you a Baptist, Mr. Morgan?"

"I'm not much of anything."

"I see. Well, Gerald's a deacon at Second-Ponce de Leon Baptist Church. His company built the Sunday school addition. Did you know that? Anyway, we're very involved in the church. That's why we're hosting Dr. Erlanger and his wife. Dr. Erlanger's a distinguished Baptist theologian, an important pastor in Germany."

"I look forward to meeting him."

"Yes, well, the wife's a bit of a surprise." She smiled.

We sat in silence, sipping iced tea until car doors slammed out front.

"I do believe they're home," said Mrs. Lowder, standing. I stood too.

A short, heavy, bald man bustled into the room. He wore a cream linen suit stained with sweat, his face red from the July heat. "It sure feels good in this air-conditioning," he said to his wife. After giving her a peck on the cheek, he turned to me. "I saw the Buick out front." Lowder extended his hand. "I'm Gerry. That's a great-looking convertible, what, a '38?"

We shook. "It is. I'm Mark Morgan, and I need to speak with Dr. Erlanger."

"Certainly," said Lowder, loosening his tie. "Otto," he called, "you have a visitor."

A tall, elderly gentleman entered the parlor. Probably seventy, Otto Erlanger stood well over six feet with a long, dour face. His silver hair was brushed straight back without oil, thick and shiny, curving like a wave above his forehead. His appearance, with his long, aquiline nose, long arms, long legs, and black suit, surely made a powerful impression in the pulpit.

"I am Dr. Erlanger," he said in very good, deeply resonant English.

"*Herr Doktor Erlanger*," I said, speaking German. "My name is Mark Morgan. We must speak about a matter of importance."

"What a relief not to hear more English," said a woman in German. A blond followed Erlanger into the room. She was younger, much younger, and a stunner: a dead ringer for the actress Carole Lombard. Wavy honey-blond hair fell almost to her shoulders, framing a strong jaw, a straight nose, and full lips. Red lipstick was her only concession to makeup. Lively blue eyes danced and sparkled under perfectly arched eyebrows. Though short, she stood ramrod straight with squared shoulders and all the right curves.

"*Meine Frau, Anna*," Erlanger said.

"You speak German, Mr. Morgan?" Lowder said in English. "I don't know a word, and poor Mrs. Erlanger doesn't speak English. I'm afraid today's tour was a bit of a trial for her."

"*Was sagte er?*" snapped Anna.

"That today's tour was difficult," said her husband in German, irritated.

"Why we are meeting in such a dismal place, I do not know."

"Anna," said her husband sharply, nodding toward me.

I continued in German. "*Herr Doktor.*"

"Please, dispense with the titles. I am a simple Gospel minister."

"Of course. I must be blunt. There have been some concerns about the safety of German Messengers. There have been threats, some suggestions of violence. I'm trying to untangle these things, make certain you and your fellow Messengers are safe."

"Are you from the police?" asked Erlanger. He almost stepped back a pace.

"No, darling," said Anna, "he is not a policeman."

I looked at her. She locked eyes with me and smiled, showing bright white teeth.

"How do you know I'm not a policeman?"

Anna Erlanger laughed and sat down. "Mr. Morgan, if there is one thing we Germans have learned, it is how to identify a policeman. You don't act like one, stand like one, or speak like one. Your suit is too nice. No policeman could afford a suit of that quality, or if he could, he certainly wouldn't wear it for work. With your size and that face, you could never be an undercover officer. Your heavy brow, wide-set eyes, square chin, and crooked nose. You're too memorable, too dangerous, too . . . dark."

"Anna," scolded her husband. "My apologies, Mr. Morgan."

"No need," I said. "You're correct. I'm not a policeman. And Atlanta hardly compares to Essen, except we have less factory smoke."

"You have been to Essen?" she said.

"Three years ago. I went to help Ray Powers with some Coca-Cola distribution problems. His office is in Essen, and as you see, I know some German. I spent two months there, though much of that time was spent in Berlin, dealing with bureaucratic matters." I looked at Anna and smiled. "Ray taught me to watch for people watching us; undercover policemen following foreigners. You are right; my size and face are too . . . distinctive."

She smiled and covered her mouth with her hand while her blue eyes glowed. Dr. Erlanger's frown deepened. "These are serious matters," he said.

"Yes," I said. "But one can always laugh."

"Where did you learn German?" Anna asked. "Your accent is odd."

"My mother was from Hamburg; she spoke beautiful High German. We lived in Cuba. There, I also learned Spanish. *Mutter* despaired of my accent; corrupted as it was by my father's Southern American English and my playmates' Cuban Spanish. I've worked to improve it, but so far to no avail."

"Your hard face, an exotic childhood, the languages; what an interesting man you must be, Mr. Morgan."

Anna Erlanger was beautiful, vivacious, and playful. The contrast with her grim, elderly husband could not have been greater. I wondered what had brought them together.

"*Doktor* Erlanger," I continued, "there have been threats. How serious we do not know, but there are concerns."

"Who would threaten Baptists?"

"Not because you are Baptist, but because you are German. Many people might object to your presence here—Poles, Czechs, Russians . . ."

"Jews," said Anna.

"Perhaps," I said, glancing at her. "World affairs are tense now, and many people fear there will be a war."

"Oh, there will be war," said Dr. Erlanger, "more terrible than the last war."

"Otto and I disagree on this," said Anna. "On our way here, we came through Paris during the first week in July. It was l*a grande semaine*, and all of Paris was caught up in lavish parties. No one there wants war. They will negotiate a settlement to this Polish problem, just as they did for the Czech problem, you will see."

"There will be war," insisted her husband. "Hitler wants a war, and he's pushing the world toward fire and blood."

"Mr. Morgan," Anna asked, ignoring her husband. "Who precisely is paying for your services?" She smiled sweetly, but I saw the steel.

"Atlanta's business leaders," I exaggerated. "Newspapers across the world will report on the Baptist meeting, and these men want the world to think well of Atlanta."

"Thank you, Mr. Morgan," said Anna. "As my husband will tell you, we see so much hypocrisy, exaggeration, and lying these days. Honest men must be treasured."

"I'd like to know your schedule," I said. "When you are meeting as a group. Whether you brought your own police. I need to speak with them to see what security measures they've taken, so we can coordinate."

The Erlangers glanced at each other.

"Mr. Morgan," said Otto. "If there are security people among us, I do not know about them."

"Otto and the government do not see eye to eye," said Anna.

"I thought all Messengers were Party members?"

"Most are, but I have never joined," said Erlanger. "I do not think it proper for ministers of the gospel to involve themselves in politics. Because of my age, I suppose, they have tolerated me. Or perhaps they think I do not matter."

"Of course you matter," said Anna, taking his arm, the automatic response of a wife.

In the pause that followed, Gerald Lowder leaned into the room. "Sorry to interrupt, but the Erlangers need to dress for dinner."

"Of course," I said. "I've taken enough of your time."

Anna stood and reached into her purse. "Mr. Morgan, here is a tentative schedule. At the luncheon tomorrow, you can return it to me."

She stepped close to give me the schedule, and her perfume came with her: herbal, dark, and rich. A unique scent that was vaguely musky. A surge of desire swept through me, and I stepped back.

Anna smiled brightly, took another step forward, and her fingertips brushed mine as she handed me the schedule.

"Tomorrow, then?" she said.

Odors disturb you too much, Mother often told me. The odor outside Tub O'Bryan's blind pig was, however, disturbing. My car windows were down, and underneath the coal smoke and burnt metal smell of the nearby Atlantic Steel Mill was the fetid stink of dung and rotting meat. The smell of death.

In Atlanta, I'd always kept my nose clean. I didn't want to do anything that might attract the police's interest or connect me to my father's legacy. And because of that, I knew nothing about Atlanta's criminal groups beyond what I read in the papers. Tub was the only person I knew who was involved with Atlanta's "underworld." He'd quit his job as a janitorial supervisor at Coca-Cola to open this blind pig disguised as a grocery store. I watched his business from the car. White steelworkers came by after their shifts to buy bootleg pints of corn whisky. Atlanta had legalized liquor in 1938, but the few licensed bars were expensive and liquor taxes high. Moonshine and places like Tub's were still the choice of workingmen.

As the shadows lengthened, Tub's business grew brisk. Every minute or so, someone went in or out. None were Negroes. Tub served only whites. Near dusk, a police car cruised by. I turned my face away as it passed, but I needn't have bothered. The cops paid no attention to me or Tub's whisky mill. Two years before, an investigation under Mayor Hartsfield had found that forty percent of Atlanta's police force were on the take. Some said the estimate was low.

A barefoot boy in dirty overalls stood by my right front fender, solemnly studying the tire. His message was clear. I got out, caught his eye, and flipped him a dime.

"You'll watch the car, right, kid?"

"A dime more when you get back?"

"Sure thing," I said. The boy nodded and leaned possessively against the hood.

The shop was little more than a shack. Dust-covered groceries lined the shelves. A Royal Crown Cola cooler wheezed rhythmically in the corner. Tub O'Bryan stood behind the counter, handing a paper-wrapped parcel to an older man in work overalls. Glass clinked. Tub was very fat, maybe forty, but the ravages of a hard life made him look much older. Sweat ran down his face and coated his jowls.

"Yes, sir," said Tub, smiling with recognition. "Why, that's a nice suit, Mr. Morgan. A rite nice suit. I could get you some soap flakes that'll keep that white shirt white?"

"We need to talk," I said.

"I'm kinda busy," said Tub.

A door in the back wall cracked open, and someone passed a package through. Tub gave it to a pinched-faced woman in a cheap cotton paisley dress. Eyes downcast, she scurried past, out the door.

"It's important." I flashed a ten-dollar bill.

"Pete," Tub called into the back. "Cover the counter."

We stepped out front together, and Tub built a roll-up. He glanced at the boy guarding my car. "You pay that ragamuffin?"

"Sure." I gave Tub the ten, and he stuffed it into a pocket under his pendulous belly. Smiling, he lit his cigarette and drew on it. "What can I do you for, Mr. Morgan?"

"You know about the Baptist World Alliance meeting here in Atlanta?"

"Who don't?" He blew smoke out his nose. "Egan and the boys been gettin' ready for over a week. Laying in extra, 'specially downtown."

"More liquor? For Baptists?"

"Yep." Tub noticed me shaking my head. "World's an interesting place, ain't it?"

"Have you heard anything about people wanting to hurt Messengers, maybe even kill some?"

"You mean, like hiring someone to shoot one of 'em?"

I nodded. "Or even just to harass 'em, cause trouble. I don't know anything about this stuff. I don't even know where to ask questions."

Tub took a long draw of his cigarette and thought for a moment. "I don't know nothin', and I ain't heard nothin'," he said. "But there's this fellow you oughta talk to. He'll be out at the Emerald Club. Off Buford Highway. Calls hisself Clyde Berger. He sorta provides security there and does other things too. Best I can do."

Tub fished around in his pocket, cigarette dangling from his lip. He came up with a five-dollar bill and handed it to me.

"What's this for?" I asked.

"Hell," said Tub, surprised. "I didn't give you ten dollars' worth. A man's gotta be honest, don't he?"

The Emerald Club on Buford Highway was a nightclub and gambling joint out past the city limits. I'd never been there, and as I drove across town, I realized how little I knew about Atlanta's underside. Throughout my career, I'd done everything possible to distance myself from my family's past. I wanted no part of the world of gangs and crime that had surrounded them. I'd built a different life, a life of my own. Until the disasters of the past year, I'd done well: prep school in Connecticut, then Princeton, followed by a career at Coca-Cola, a wife, and two children. My job at Coke had weathered the worst of the crash, and I was making four thousand a year. A charmed life, even though I had to work hard and travel a lot. Then, it fell apart.

The first blow staggered me. I returned from imprisonment in Peru to find Mabel had filed for divorce. Her lawyers were good. In court, they painted me as a cheating scoundrel, a murderer on the run from something terrible in Peru. My crooked nose, beetle brow, and sallow complexion from long-term illness did me no favors. They put a working girl on the stand, who told salacious stories of frequent, perverse sex. In particular, she said, I demanded sodomy. To help those who didn't quite understand, she described the act in detail, and the jury was appropriately shocked. During cross-examination, my attorney presented travel documents to prove I was out of town when several of these supposed encounters took place. It didn't matter. Newspapers loved the stories, as did the jury.

Mabel won a big settlement, the house, and alimony. She got the kids with child support. There was an editorial in the *Journal* arguing that I should be criminally charged under Georgia's sodomy laws. The divorce wiped me out financially and destroyed me socially. I often wondered what they'd paid the girl.

The second punch was the haymaker. I demanded pay for my time imprisoned in Peru. Woodruff called me to his office. My association with Coca-Cola, he said, was a liability. The newspapers painted me as a criminal and a sodomite. He knew I needed money after my divorce, but he had to think of Coca-Cola first. Then he fired me. Mabel had reveled in that; she even phoned to gloat. In Atlanta, if Robert Woodruff publicly dropped you, you were ruined. All I could do was struggle on and take the lessons about trust and betrayal to heart.

The two-tone tan '38 Buick Special was part of that struggle; a remnant of my previous prosperity and a symbol that I'd not surrendered. The car even had a fine radio, not one of those tinny things that only let you hear rhythm and brass—so I dropped the top and turned the radio up. After the hot day, the night wind in my hair was wonderful. As if timed for the moment, Artie Shaw's "Nightmare" came on, his signature piece, letting listeners know his band's show had begun. Shaw's arrangements weren't always as tight as Bennie Goodman's, but I liked the mellow tone of his clarinet better than Goodman's edgy playing. Soon, I swayed in time with the music as I drove.

The Emerald Club's green neon sign invited patrons to dine and dance. At ten o'clock on a Thursday night, cars crowded the graveled parking lot. The club's heavy, padded green door opened directly into a bar and dining room packed with noisy customers and filled with cigarette smoke. The lighting was green, giving the smoke an otherworldly glow. To the left, a quintet sat on a raised dais, tuning their instruments. I figured the gambling rooms were in the back, out of sight.

The band began to play a ragtime tune with modern jazz inflections. They weren't bad, and the crowd soon noticed. Some got up to dance. Most were young, well-dressed, and ready to burn some cash. A headwaiter erupted from the din and told me it'd be fifteen or twenty minutes before they could have a table ready.

"I'm not here to eat," I said. "I'm looking for Clyde Berger."

"Who?"

"Clyde Berger. I need to speak with him."

"Don't know him." The headwaiter stepped past me, opened the door, and motioned me out. "Next time, Mac, make a reservation."

I stepped out, and the headwaiter closed the heavy door with a bang. I went back to my car and waited, top down, enjoying the band's music. A sedan drove up, crunching through the gravel, and parked. Two couples went inside, the women shrill with excitement. The band began playing Tommy Dorsey numbers, and moths battered themselves against the overhead streetlight. *Tap, tap, tap*; the knocking provided a weird, asynchronous accompaniment to the music from the club. About ten minutes and hundreds of taps later, the headwaiter opened the door and peered out.

"I told you to beat it," he shouted.

"Nope, you asked me to make a reservation next time. I need to see Berger."

The headwaiter went back inside. A few minutes later, a lone man came out. He was about five and a half feet tall, thin, with his hat pulled low, shadowing his face. He kept his hands in his suit jacket pockets as he walked up.

"Who are you?" he asked in a thin, whispery voice.

"Name's Mark Morgan. You Clyde Berger?"

"Why?"

"Tub O'Bryan said Berger might be able to help me."

"Tub, huh?" The man stood for a moment, considering, then walked around to the passenger side and climbed in. Something in his right jacket pocket swung heavily.

"Nice car," he said.

"Yeah, I enjoy it."

"Nice suit too. You looking for my help with a problem?"

"Just checking out threats against some people at the Baptist World Alliance meeting. Heard anything?"

"Don't shilly-shally, do you? Just get right to it." He took out a cigarette case and offered one.

"No, thanks, I don't smoke."

Berger lit his cigarette and inhaled deeply. "A big fellow like you should be more careful. People look at your size, see that face, and well, let's say they make assumptions. The Emerald Club's not a good place for those assumptions."

"I'll remember that."

Berger blew out a long stream of smoke and wheezed repeatedly. He was laughing. After another long drag, he blew out the smoke and grunted hoarsely. "There's been talk around town. What's it worth to you?"

I put a twenty-dollar bill on the dashboard. He nodded toward it, and I laid a second twenty down.

"More folks than you'd think are upset," said Berger, picking up the bills and slipping them into his pocket. He coughed, a deep rattle. "This Baptist thing means extra traffic, extra runs for streetcars and buses, extra trips for the garbage men, extra patrols for the police. Unions hope for some national attention, so the cops have to look out for demonstrations, probably at the cotton mills. City employees want overtime, but the city can hardly pay them as it is. So now you've got forty thousand visitors crowding in, and no one's happy about it."

He paused and glanced around the parking lot. "These Baptists won't do much for the entertainment business. Drinking on the sly is about all they do. Don't chase girls, or gamble, or get high. They may be interested, but they just don't."

I glanced at the full lot. "I don't know; there's probably some Baptists here tonight. They just worry they'll run into someone from church."

Berger wheezed again, blowing smoke out of his nose. He jerked his head, and I heard his neck crack.

"Anybody talking about the Germans, Italians, stuff like that?"

"Funny you ask. They had a column in the paper about all those Huns coming to town. It caught people's attention. Not here, but at a bar downtown, a bunch of Polack rail yard workers passed it around and yapped about busting Nazi heads. Tough men who talked like they meant trouble, but they were drinking hard. You know how Poles are. And some others, Hunkies and Slovaks, have been badmouthing the Nazis. But then, the damn Greeks won't stop talking about the Italians, and we got a lotta Greeks in Atlanta now. Me, I think it's a load of hot air. Men say things when they're drinking, and it don't mean spit."

"Where would I find these guys?"

"Look in the Marietta Street beer joints for the Polacks. Over by the rail yards on the west side. Check around the cotton mills for the bohunks. They might be labor organizers, maybe CIO. If so, they'd better watch out after what the Klan did to the last bunch."

"The Ku Klux Klan?"

"The East Point Klan. Call 'em the 'Wrecking Crew.'" Berger flipped his cigarette butt into the parking lot. "Stretched two of those CIO boys out naked over a log and beat the living hell out of 'em. Used a heavy bullwhip. Tore their asses to shreds. One guy almost died from kidney damage."

"I didn't see that in the papers."

"You won't."

"Would the Klan bother any of these Germans?"

Berger reached into his coat, took out another cigarette, and lit it. With the light from the match, I saw what looked like a harelip. No wonder he liked the dark.

"The Klan's different these days," he said, "mostly anti-Communist, anti-union, anti-Jewish. They're happy with Coloreds who know their place. The Angelo Herndon trial got 'em all riled up, but they paid more attention to his communism than his color. Some of these yahoos sound like Hitler when they yammer about communism and Jews and all that. They'd love to march around in brown shirts and break Jewish windows, jabbering about enforcing morals, and this being a Christian nation. The Klan probably adores these Baptist Nazis."

"You don't think much of the Klan."

"Why? Do you?"

"Look, there are some threats. I'm just trying to see if there's anything to it."

"Why? You're not a cop. You some sort of private dick?"

I paused and watched Berger smoke his cigarette. He cracked his neck again and stared at me. *What the hell am I doing?* I wondered. *A formerly respectable Coca-Cola executive digging into the dung heap?* The answer was simple. I needed the money.

"I'm the consulting agent hired to find out."

Berger drew on his cigarette. "Consulting agent? Ha, that's a new one. And you're working for the Huns? Good luck. You can't protect people from a determined killer. I know that for sure. But I don't think your threats are real unless there's a single lunatic who plans to do it himself. You can't stop a lunatic loner. If anyone were hiring muscle, I'd have heard about it. If they were bringing in shooters, I'd know. That's my turf. Brother, you're on a wild goose chase."

"Your turf? Shooters?"

"Yeah. What'd Tub tell ya I do?"

We sat quietly for a moment. "I can pay for more information," I said.

"Maybe you can, but I don't got any more information. Look, I'm on the level with you, 'cause you seem to be on the level with me. So, give me a phone number. I'll ask around. If I hear anything, I'll drop a nickel, but you better be able to pay."

I took a card from my wallet that read *Morgan Consulting*. I scribbled my room number and the club's phone number on the back.

"They can ring my room."

"Consulting agent, huh," he said, considering the card. "That's rich."

He opened the car door, then paused. "These Nazis always bring their own cops with them. Call 'em Gestapo. Be careful; those guys are God's own sons o' bitches."

2

Friday, July 21, 1939

Years ago, I swam competitively for the Atlanta Athletic Club with some success. Last March, after the divorce trial, when I'd explained I could no longer afford the dues, the Board voted me a life membership. This allowed me to use the pool and rent a room for ten bucks a month. I couldn't have been happier, even though it was a lousy room. Swimming was my respite; I needed it. Swimming put me into a trance, focused only on the stroke, the wall, the turn, and the stroke. While I swam, an idea or a new concept would pop into my head. It was my best place for thinking.

While I was swimming that morning, another guy dove in. Like so many, he started out pacing me. After three or four laps, they'd usually fall back or quit. This guy kept it up, lap after lap. I lifted my head to look; maybe late thirties, muscular, not as tall as me. He lacked the leg length needed for a powerful kick, but he had a smooth overhand. I picked up the pace, felt my joints stress as I added power, and gloried in the thrill. After a couple more laps, he began to lag, dropping back.

One side of the locker room was lined with private changing rooms. The opposite wall had photos of club members in competition. They were dominated by images of the club's most famous member, the golfer Bobby Jones. I finished dressing and found the visitor looking over the photos before he went into a changing room. A few moments later, he emerged and sat down to slip on his shoes.

"Naval Academy?" I asked.

The visitor paused while pulling on a sock and glanced at me. He smiled. "Think so?"

"The haircut," I said, "and your sidestroke. You swim it Navy style, top leg on your scissors kick goes back instead of forward."

"You must be Sherlock Holmes," he said, rubbing his cropped brown hair. I laughed. He stood up, one shoe off, one shoe on.

"I'm Joe Packard," he said, stepping forward and thrusting out his hand. "And you are Henry Mark Morgan."

I shook his hand. "Now who's Sherlock Holmes?"

"It's easy. Your face is kind of unique, and there's a picture of you over there on the wall. The one that says, 'Olympic Trials, 1924.' I swam at Annapolis, but I never did anything like that. No wonder you were kicking my butt."

"That was a long time ago. I got my butt kicked by a guy from Chicago named Johnny Weissmuller."

"Tarzan beat you?"

"No one ever beat Weissmuller," I said. "Ever."

"Yeah, what'd he win, five Olympic gold medals? Easy to forget that now, isn't it, with him swinging around and yodeling in the trees with Jane and Cheetah?"

"Everybody's got to make a living. Besides, Jane's pretty good-looking."

"Not sure what to make of the monkey," he said. We both laughed.

"So, you're visiting Atlanta?"

"Yep, visiting."

"Lots of people in town for the Baptist World Alliance."

"Who knew there were so many Baptists?"

I laughed. "I guess you're not Baptist. Where are you from? You sound like you're from Boston."

"Do I?"

Packard's sudden evasiveness put me off. I turned away to adjust my tie. One of my older ties, and a glance in the mirror showed it had begun to wear at the knot. A collar point on my shirt was frayed as well. It cheapened the look of my new suit. So, I needed to go back to Muse's for new shirts and ties. I took out the envelope with the $7,000 and fingered it before hiding it again. I could buy all the new clothes I wanted.

"You swim every day?" asked Packard.

"Weekday mornings. I'm too lazy on weekends, unless I'm bored."

"I may be in town a while," he said. "Guess I'll see you around."

Atlanta, a city built by trains, had three passenger stations. Terminal Station was on the southwest side of downtown, at the beginning of railroad gulch. Twentieth-century Atlanta had built extensive viaducts above the numerous tracks, encasing, almost embracing the force that gave birth to the city and sustained it. People went down, beneath the streets, to the true ground level, where the trains came in. It wasn't quite underground, but close enough.

Parking at the station was impossible, and crowds packed the doors. Confused passengers swarmed the concourse. Sweating men in department store suits shouted at porters and argued over taxis. The world had sent its Baptists to Atlanta, and they were lost.

I hurried down to the platforms, afraid I might miss their train. The air grew hot and damp, with the stench of diesel, coal smoke, and burnt rubber. The New York train pulled in ten minutes late. Scanning the crowd, I spotted Erlanger and his gorgeous wife with a small group of well-dressed men. One man held a large sign that read "*Deutschland*." Other groups held signs for England, Canada, France, and even Siam. By half past ten, around seventy people had gathered at the Deutschland sign. They made their way up the stairs and out of the station.

I'd not planned well for the next stage. A pair of buses took the Germans to their hotel. Because of the crowds, I'd parked blocks away. I hurried; glad I knew they were going to the Henry Grady. By the time I arrived, the Germans had disembarked and were waiting in front with their luggage. One bus stood there idling, diesel fumes sweeping over the crowd as porters unloaded luggage.

I hung back, watching. A nervous middle-aged man stood on the opposite side of the group. He reached slowly into the brown paper sack he held in his left hand and drew out a green sphere. In a quick movement, he tossed it high in the air over the German Messengers.

"Shit-eating Nazi swine," the man yelled in German.

My eyes followed the arc of the green sphere as it curved leisurely toward the packed group of Germans. It was an odd moment with the loud diesel rattle, Messengers coughing from the fumes, and the long arc of the green sphere over the crowd.

"Grenade!" yelled a German voice, breaking the spell. Two men, probably war veterans, flopped onto the sidewalk. The sphere fell, hitting one German's black homburg hat. It smeared the brim bright green and then tumbled to the ground, splattering the man's shoes. I looked back at the assailant, who had launched more green spheres.

Two young Germans grabbed the attacker. One was short but well built, with a broad face and brown hair. The other was tall and blond. The blond kid kicked the attacker's legs out from under him, pushed him to the sidewalk, and took him by the throat, choking him.

"*Est war Mist*," I said, stepping forward, putting my hand on the blond man's shoulder. "Just manure. No one is hurt."

The dark-haired man backed away, but the blond one continued throttling the assailant. He swiveled his head to look at me. His pale blue eyes were eager, his young face lit with joy. He seemed shocked I'd touched him. I grabbed his arm and applied some strength, breaking his grip on the man's throat. The assailant collapsed, coughing.

"Nazis," the man croaked. "Murderers."

"*Juden*," hissed the blond between clenched teeth.

"I will deal with him," I said in German.

"Who are you?"

"Security." That did the trick. Schooled in authority, he relaxed and stepped away.

"So, Mr. Morgan, you will take care of it, yes?"

I turned to see Anna Erlanger at my shoulder, purposeful and beautiful. Her eyes were like deep blue pools, and her lips were pink without lipstick.

"Is anyone hurt?" I asked.

"No, it was horse manure. Best we go inside, yes?"

"I agree." I reached a hand down. "Come on, buddy, let's go," I said in English, pulling him to his feet. Grabbing his collar and twisting an arm behind, I frog-marched him down the street away from the hotel.

"What are you doing?" the man protested in German.

"Quiet, before those Nazis kill you," I said softly in English. "That blond kid has a crazy look."

I pushed him past the Capitol and Roxy theaters and through the brass-framed glass doors of Davison's Department Store. Salesgirls stared as I marched him in. We stopped at the "White" water fountain.

"What's your name?" I demanded in English.

"Are you the police?" said the man in German.

"Speak English," I insisted. I took a small notebook from my jacket. "Name?"

Again, authority worked. "Mendel Rubenstein."

"Address, Mr. Rubenstein?"

"535 ½ South Washington Street."

I wrote it down. "Who else is with you?"

"I came alone." He had a very strong accent, but his English was clear.

"Who told you when the Germans would arrive?"

"No one. I just happened to see them, hear them."

"So," I said, suddenly switching to German, "you just happened to have a bag full of horse shit with you?"

Rubenstein looked at the paper sack as if seeing it for the first time.

"Who told you when the Germans would arrive, where they would stay?"

"The parade is tomorrow. I guessed they would arrive today. I thought they might be at the hotel near the flag."

"Flag?"

"The big Nazi flag hanging in front of the hotel."

I had not noticed the flag. So much for my detective skills.

The floorwalker approached us, determination on his face. "Gentlemen, may I help you?"

"Just having a little discussion," I said. "Trying to decide what to buy."

"*Ja*," said Rubenstein. "He needs a new tie, but I'm leaving."

He grabbed the paper bag and marched quickly out the door.

"We do have a fine selection of ties," said the floorwalker, peering at mine.

Pushing past him, I followed Rubenstein out and saw him turn right, away from the hotel. I waited for him to walk past the Winecoff Hotel and cross to Forsyth Street before I felt sure he would not double back. Beyond him, the huge Coca-Cola sign in front of the Candler Building glittered in the midday heat.

Then I looked back toward the hotel, and there it was, just as he'd said: a blood-red German flag with its black Nazi swastika in a white circle, lit brightly by the noonday sun. It hung over the center of Peachtree Street, suspended on a wire running from the front of the S&H Cafeteria to the front of the Roxy Theatre. Dense traffic, slowed by trolleys, clogged the street, but the black swastika apparently caused no concern among pedestrians or drivers below.

Then, I saw something more. Standing under the gallery in front of the hotel, wearing a white straw boater, was Joe Packard. The man I'd met that morning at the pool. Packard exhaled smoke, threw down a cigarette, and stepped on it. After looking directly at me, he turned and entered the Henry Grady Hotel.

When I reached the lobby, Packard was gone. So were the Germans. I asked at the front desk about their delegation.

"They've rented the Spanish Room for lunch," said the clerk.

The Spanish Room was on the second floor. Used for luncheon during the day, at night it offered dinner, live music, and a floor show. Shabby and a bit sad compared with the glittering clubs in New York, it was among Atlanta's best. I climbed the stairs two at a time and found Anna outside the club door.

"Dr. Erlanger wants to thank you for your help," she said in German.

"It's why I'm here."

"So, who was he? What did he want?"

I showed her my notebook. She leaned close and studied the name and the address. Her dark, seductive perfume enveloped me, and I closed my eyes.

"A sad little man," she muttered.

"No," I said. "A very angry one. I think you must be careful."

The door behind us opened, and the blond man who had grabbed Rubenstein by the throat came out. The shorter man with brown hair followed him. They were arguing, though I couldn't make out what they were saying. Finally, the brown-haired man called the blond a moron.

"You can go to hell," said Blondie. The brown-haired man spun on his heel and marched away. The blond turned and seemed startled that Anna and I were standing so close together in the foyer. He nodded politely and turned toward the Spanish Room.

"No, Rolf," called Anna. "Please, come here. Herr Morgan, you met Rolf briefly. Rolf is a Messenger from Berlin. Rolf Schulman, this is Herr Mark Morgan."

Rolf was about my height, but slender. His hair was shaved on the sides, but a long hank of oiled bangs folded back above his forehead. His eyes flashed with anger; he was still worked up from the argument.

"Good day," I said, offering my hand.

Rolf did not shake my hand. He stood erect. "You're the American?"

"I told him you were the American watching over us," said Anna.

"Then I suppose so." I continued to hold out my hand until Rolf finally shook it.

"Where is the prisoner?" he asked.

"He won't bother you again." I could see him measuring the statement, wondering what it implied.

"Very good," he said at last. "Your appearance shocked me out front. Of course, it is because you look like Max Schmeling. It startled me, yes, to have the great boxer pulling on my arm. You are quite strong. Do you box?" He chuckled, staring at my crooked nose.

"Only when I have to, but I do swim."

"That is also good. Not so good as boxing, but good. All sport is good. Now, you must excuse me."

Rolf returned to the Spanish Room. I rolled my eyes and looked at Anna. "Do they stamp 'POLICEMAN' on their foreheads?"

"He's an earnest young man."

"So, he's here to protect you?"

"Of course not," said Anna with a pitying look. "Rolf is here to spy on us."

Joe Packard caught me at the front door of the hotel. "Let's talk."

"Only for a moment," I said cautiously. "I have an appointment."

We stepped out of the hotel and turned left, up Peachtree. It was bright and hot; the July sun beat down on my dark gray suit. I stayed with the crowd, moving along the busy sidewalk, waiting for him to speak.

"Anna Erlanger's a real looker," said Packard finally. "And the reverend's a bit long in the tooth. Makes a fella wonder, doesn't it?"

"Why's the Navy here?"

"I don't know what you mean. What I do know is that you need to move on."

"I can't," I said.

"Morgan, what the hell do you think you're doing?"

"This is my job. I'm a consultant for the German delegation."

"Well, you're consulting with some damned dangerous people. I saw you grab Rolf Schulman earlier. That's playing with fire."

"Rolf? You know these people?"

"I know about several of them. I'd say hands off, Henry Mark Morgan. This stuff is way over your head."

With that, Packard turned back toward the hotel, leaving me alone on the bright, hot sidewalk.

I was sick of being told I knew nothing, so I headed to the Carnegie Library. Panhandlers gathered near the entrance, begging nickels and dimes. I pushed past and turned left to the periodicals room. First, I glanced at the newspapers. For once, Germany and Poland did not dominate the morning's *Atlanta Constitution*. It focused on the Baptist World Alliance meeting. I turned to other items.

Eugene Talmadge had decided to run for a third term as governor, but he faced challenges. His well-oiled political machine had splintered, his law firm had collapsed, and, most importantly, he was broke. *Well deserved*, I thought.

When hecklers called out accusations that Talmage had stolen money from the state, he'd said, "Sure I stole, but I stole for you." The Talmadge supporters laughed and roared their approval. Given the opportunity, they would raid the state's coffers too. In their eyes, he was a charming scamp, sending up the city slickers. But in reality, Talmadge was a dangerous, racist demagogue, a threat to decency and common sense. Anything that hindered his winning another term as governor was a blessing in my book.

Page three had an interesting story. The Ku Klux Klan had inducted 400 new members Thursday night and burned a 180-foot-tall cross at Stone Mountain, just east of Atlanta. This happened just about the time I visited the Emerald Club. There was a photograph of the huge, flaming cross and another photo of a smaller burning cross surrounded by robed Klansmen, arms extended in salute. Change the uniform, and they could be Brownshirts burning books.

Disgusted, I folded up the newspaper and turned to my work. The reference librarian helped me find information about the police in Germany. Everything we found confirmed what I knew: secrecy and fear lay at the heart of Nazi power. The Gestapo, the secret political police, came at night, and people simply disappeared. Those few who returned told appalling stories of abuse and privation. No one knew how many tens of thousands populated the concentration camps or how many prisoners had perished there. If blond Rolf had been an American kid, he might have been a baseball pitcher, a soda jerk, or a CCC boy. Instead, he served a terrifying police state.

The Germans also had a spy service, the Abwehr, run by the military. *Time* magazine reported that the Abwehr had prepared the way in for Franco's fascists in Spain, and then in Austria, and in the Sudetenland, in Czechoslovakia, recruiting so-called fifth columns. Provocateurs, saboteurs, spies—they were now thought to have agents in Poland, France, and England. Nazi agents were lining up political support, spying, and stealing military secrets.

"Thank God for the Neutrality Acts," said the librarian as she handed me more material.

"Why do you say that?"

"Keeps us out of this mess. We don't want to be suckered into another war, and these fools are rushing into one. They're all horrible people. Murderous Nazis, lying Frenchmen, conniving British. We can't do anything about those countries. Best if we just let them kill each other. Like we did with Spain. No reason to get involved. There are plenty of problems here in the United States."

"So, you think neutrality is the best policy? Sell nothing to the nations at war?"

She struggled to remain polite. "Where you been, mister? That's what sucked us into the last war. So now the law says we can't sell any weapons or munitions to countries at war. We can't travel on their ships or planes. It all makes great good sense. No merchants of death, no *Lusitanias* sunk. We stay neutral in thought and deed and tend our own garden."

At half past four, I left the library and hit the columned lobby of the Henry Grady. From a pay phone in the row of booths, I called Emma at her office. "We have seven-thirty reservations for dinner and a show at the Rainbow Roof."

"Sounds wonderful. I'll have to go home to dress."

"Okay. I'll pick you up at seven. Wear your dancing shoes. I plan to wear you out."

"Is that all you plan, Mark Morgan?" she said archly.

Surprised, it took me a moment to reply. "See you at seven."

I hung up and sat in the booth for a moment. Maybe that librarian was right; there really wasn't much we could do about the Nazi government's policies. So maybe my job, insuring the Germans' safety, was a kind of neutrality act? Didn't Germans deserve to travel freely and safely like anyone else? Perhaps they would see the even-handed fairness of Americans and reflect on affairs in their own country? Then, I kicked myself. What a bunch of hooey. It was simple; the world is full of awful people doing terrible things. That was the wisdom of the Neutrality Act. Don't get involved with those people; don't try to fix the world. Instead, make some money and seize the day.

Rolf was seated in the lobby, dressed in a thick tweed suit, already sweating. He spotted me when I left the phone booth and nodded. I joined him. "Good evening," I said. He simply stared at me, so I tried again.

"It would help if I knew the security officers among the Messengers. Perhaps we could meet as a group, coordinate?"

Rolf returned to scanning the room. "You understand nothing."

I didn't like it. People kept telling me how much I didn't know. Just then, a group of four Germans came out of the elevator. The same brown-haired man who had reacted swiftly to Mendel Rubenstein's manure attack was with them. Rolf tracked the group with his eyes. When they walked out the door of the hotel, he stood.

"*Guten Abend*," he said, pursuing the group of Germans. A moment later, I followed. The doorman flagged down a cab for the first group. Rolf climbed into a second cab and followed. Just like a movie. I shook my head.

"Where are those fellows going?" I asked the doorman, pressing a dollar into his hand.

"They wanted to see Decatur Street. I told 'em it wasn't much; the real action these days is on Buford Highway, or down by the river, but they wanted to go. Didn't seem to know much English."

"Thanks," I said. The doorman smiled and tipped his hat.

Emma boarded at a quaint bungalow in a shady, wooded neighborhood near Georgia Tech. To my surprise, she wore a beautiful dark blue gown emphasizing her tall, slender silhouette. Even with low heels, she was only a couple of inches shorter than me. She turned to lock the door, revealing two small blue straps crossing her back. Otherwise, she was bare to her waist. A little jolt surged through me. Then a jolt again, when I caught her scent. Usually, she smelled of powder and rosewater. Along with the daring dress came a lovely new fragrance: bright, floral, and rich.

"My God, you're gorgeous," I said.

"Think so?" She smiled and did a little pirouette on the walk. The dress swirled out and fell back in place when she stopped.

"See," she said. "Perfect for dancing."

"Your perfume, it's wonderful."

"Isn't it?" she said. "It belongs to my landlord's wife. It's called *Joy*. Roses and jasmine."

"Wow, I've never seen you like this."

She laughed and swatted me with her clutch purse. "You don't look so bad yourself. Is that a new suit?"

I wore my white Palm Beach suit, white Panama hat, and spectator shoes. "Just bought it. You like?"

"The only thing missing is spats. And maybe a tommy gun." We laughed together, but I wondered if she knew something about my father.

We'd lunched several times over the previous two months and gone to a matinee movie once. This was new: an evening out. But going out with Emma was safe. After what had happened with my ex-wife, I didn't want another disaster involving a woman.

The Rainbow Roof was on the top floor of the Ansley Hotel. Recently refurbished and air-conditioned, it was Atlanta's premier showplace. The ritual was fun; a doorman bowed us into the lobby, where we passed the famous Ansley clock. Up the elevator to the top floor, where a cute hatcheck girl greeted us, along with another girl selling cigarettes. A maître d' led us to our seats in a mirrored room full of recessed lights and streamlined curves. It was packed with well-dressed diners. The orchestra sat on a curved podium with white and chrome accents in front of a round dance floor.

"It's perfect, isn't it?" said Emma as we were seated. We sat three rows back from the orchestra, not too close and not too far. She looked around the room, eyes shining and a wide smile on her face. "So modern. Just like the World's Fair, or something in the movies."

"They're trying to copy the Rainbow Room in New York, only they don't have the revolving dance floor."

"Sourpuss," she said.

I was saved by the arrival of the waiter. I ordered a gin and tonic and asked for the wine menu. After a moment's hesitation, Emma ordered a martini. The dinner menu had only a few choices, so when our drinks came, we ordered our food. I also ordered a nice bottle of French Chablis, and Emma looked at me, surprised.

"You must really be flush," she said.

Everything unfolded in its usual fashion. Light chitchat soon turned into a discussion of books, as it always did at lunch. Emma had found Ernest Hemingway's latest novel, *To Have and Have Not*, tedious and lacking.

"It just doesn't have the fire, the conception, of his earlier books."

"I read it a while ago," I said, "and I don't recall it well."

"My point exactly."

It was too much. "Enough books for tonight, Emma. We always talk about books."

"What?" She covered her face with a hand. "Oh, Mark, I'm sorry. Have I been going on?"

"I just want to talk about something else."

"I get caught up, you know. And I'm nervous."

"Well then, tell me about you."

She blushed. "I'd rather not. I'm more common than you think, Mark, not like the Driving Club crowd you run with."

"You mean the Driving Club crowd that dropped me. I've learned a lot this past year—a hard year. You can't trust people: A guy has to look out for himself."

"Wow," she said. "And here I thought you were a romantic." She smiled and finished her martini.

The wine arrived, and it was perfect: crisp, with a hint of apples. Emma said she had never had French wine before, so I told her about Chablis, the cold weather, the rocky soil, and the resulting stress on the vines. We tasted it together, and I had her describe what she experienced.

"It's sharp," she said, looking at the glass. "I mean, a bit like tart fruit. And there's something else, something almost harsh."

"Some people say you can taste the flinty soil, the austere fields."

"Dirt? We're drinking dirt? How much did this cost?" She picked up the bottle to look at it and laughed.

"That's better," I said. We touched glasses and took another sip.

"Okay," she said, leaning forward, her eyes glowing. "We'll talk about other things. Tell me about your time growing up."

"In Cuba?"

"Okay, Cuba. What was the best thing about growing up there?"

"When I was a kid, the best thing was getting to eat fruit every day. Mangos were my favorite. Have you ever had a fully ripe mango?"

"No, Mark, I'm serious. Tell me about your family."

I took a long swig of wine and then a deep breath. "I'm not sure about this."

"Aren't we peas in a pod, both bound up in bundles of secrets? So, here's a truth. I'm your friend, and you can tell me things. I won't judge you. You'll do the same for me."

"Okay, okay." I took a sip of wine. "My family moved from Savannah to Cuba in 1908, the year Georgia went dry. I celebrated my fourth birthday in Havana; it's one of my earliest memories. We must have already had some money, but my father saw a business opportunity in Georgia's new prohibition law. He began smuggling rum from Cuba into Savannah. Soon, he had a distribution network across the eastern part of the state and then into South Carolina. He was well placed when national Prohibition began in 1920. After that, he probably made hundreds of thousands smuggling hooch, maybe more. It paid for me to go to Princeton."

"My God, that's exciting."

"Emma, my father was a crook, a rumrunner."

"Sure. That came out during your divorce, didn't it? It was in the papers. And then, just before the crash, your father lost everything and died. But you were already here, working for Coca-Cola."

"You knew about my father?" I asked, surprised.

"Of course. Didn't you think I'd research a man before I went out with him? Especially such a dangerous-looking man with a mixed reputation? I'm a librarian, and Mama didn't raise no fool." She grinned, finished her wine, and poured another glass. "Now I know why people rave about French wine. It's the cat's meow."

"The librarian drinks?"

"I like a little touch every now and then. The Connor family came from Ireland after all."

"Recently?"

"Oh, so now it's my turn? No, silly, long ago. They were Irish Protestants."

"So, what about your family?"

"There's not much to tell. I grew up in Macon, where my father had a small drugstore. On the sly, he sold medicinal alcohol; it probably paid for my schooling, so maybe Dad wasn't so different from yours? Just after I graduated from the women's college in Milledgeville, Dad died. His heart gave out. There was no money. I couldn't find a job. My family moved to a farm where we worked as tenants. In the first year, boll weevils ate up our cotton, and we went into debt. We had no electricity, water from a hand pump at the well, and the stink of animals all the time. And the bugs—oh God, the bugs drove me crazy. I couldn't stand it, so I found a way out and came to Atlanta."

"I'm sorry. That your father died, I mean, not that you came to Atlanta."

She smiled. "Seems to be the story of all the people who come here. The smaller towns and countryside are changing; people are leaving for the cities. At least, anyone who wants to be anything. One of my brothers is in Baltimore, one in Chicago, both working at steel mills. Only my little brother is still on the farm."

"What about the other men in your life? Childhood friends, former beaus, you know."

"What about them?" She looked away, not meeting my eyes. "Mark, I'm too tall for most men, I talk a lot, and I don't suffer fools. Everyone thinks I'm so smart about everything, but courtship and men remain mysteries." She looked up again. "Why a guy like you is interested in me is mysterious, too. It frightens me a bit."

"You're a very interesting friend," I said.

Her mouth twisted. "Interesting? Or maybe safer after your horrible ex-wife?" She threw back the last of the wine in her glass and took a deep breath. "Sorry, Mark, I didn't mean to display my demons."

"We all have demons. Mine are worse than you could imagine."

She shook her head. "It must be the drinks. *In Vino Veritas.*" She shook her hair back from her face. "Don't worry, I'm not going to jump off the building or anything. Sometimes those feelings just come out. I've made it thirty-three years. I can make it thirty-three more."

The waiter arrived with our food. Our focus on the meal helped us leave the uncomfortable conversation behind. We tasted each other's dishes. My fish was indifferent, as I expected, but her roasted scallops were surprisingly good. I ordered another bottle of Chablis, and after the waiter poured, Emma took a sip. Her eyebrows went up, and she looked at me.

"It does go with the scallops," she said.

The orchestra began playing, a bit too loudly for us to talk. The music was lush, mostly Paul Whiteman standards, so we got up to dance. Emma relaxed and let me guide her. With my left hand on her waist and bare back, I felt taut strength, smooth muscle and skin. The orchestra's elaborately coiffed torch singer wore a long yellow silk gown and sang well. Her version of "My Reverie" was a showstopper. Emma put her head on my shoulder as we danced.

After four dances, Emma wanted to see the roof garden. Passing our table, she picked up the bottle of wine and her glass. Outside was like stepping onto the rooftop of the city. Flowers in planters lined the perimeter of the roof. A cooling breeze blew from the northwest, fresh and clean. Light flared out in all directions to the distant outskirts of Atlanta. Nearby skyscrapers were lit from below, enhancing their architectural details with deep shadows. We sat on a bench overlooking the city.

"Mark, I'm not used to this sort of thing. The wine, the music, the glamor, the dancing—it all goes to my head. I can't think straight."

"No reason to think. Just have fun."

"Maybe." She leaned back and tilted her head up, looking at the sky. "At least it's not spinning."

I looked up too. "Actually, darling, the earth is spinning." It took her a moment to catch on, and we both laughed.

That would have been the moment to kiss her. She seemed to expect it, and when nothing happened, she abruptly pulled a cigarette from her purse and lit up. The smoke she exhaled vanished with the wind.

"So, tell me about the moneybags client."

I told her about the meeting at the Standard Club, the threats, even Berger's warnings about the Klan. She lit a second cigarette, then a third. She refilled her wineglass. I explained my realization that I could do this sort of investigation.

"I know the right people, I'm good at research, I know the city, and I don't quit."

"My goodness," she laughed. "My guy, the private eye." She toasted me with her glass, swaying a little.

"At Coke, I solved problems, sometimes big problems. Go to Mexico or Honduras, uncover what's wrong, figure out who needed to be promoted, fired, or paid off. I researched government leaders, local businessmen, laws, and trade regulations. Coke profited. All I got was my salary. This'll be different. I'll do the same sort of thing for businesses here in Atlanta, but I'll be my own boss and get paid the value of each job. I'll be their consulting agent."

"Seriously?"

"Hell yes. So far, this is more than I made at Coke in a year. Easy money, too."

"Dad always said to watch out if the money's easy."

"I'm watching," I said.

She looked at me for a moment. "All right, I like it," she said, lighting another cigarette. I looked at it pointedly, and she smiled. "I'm too old and too tall for it to stunt my growth. So, you're a 'consulting agent.' You'll need to put that on your office door."

"If I had an office."

"You will. What else has happened?"

I told her about the manure attack at the Henry Grady, my research into the German police, and about Rolf. Finally, I told her about Anna Erlanger.

"She's pretty?"

"Not just pretty. Glows like a movie star. I'm not kidding, like Carole Lombard. The way she moves, stands, shakes her hair back; it's Lombard, straight out of the movies. Almost as if she's studied her. There is no way to really describe it; you have to see for yourself."

"Not sure I want to." Emma finished her wine. She tried to pour more from an empty bottle. "Here I thought I was the girl in your life."

"Emma . . ."

"Guess not," she said, standing, looking out at the city. "Isn't that just peachy keen? A gorgeous girl and German spies; maybe we ought to make a serial for the movies? And these Nazis are out on the town tonight?"

"They are. The group Rolf was tailing went down to Decatur Street."

"So, what are we doing here? Shouldn't we be there, seeing what the bastards are up to?" She spun slowly to admire the view, then leaned back on the parapet, a bit unsteady. She focused on me. "Can I see the money?"

I took the envelope from my breast pocket and gave it to her. She sat and pulled out the hundreds. Seventy of them. She fanned them apart like a deck of playing cards.

"I've never held this much before," she said breathily. "I've never even seen this much before. Seven thousand dollars. You know, Mark, this could buy a house? A nice house. Or you could start a business."

"I know."

"And you're just walking around with it. What if someone took it?"

"No one'll take it."

"You're a fool. People would cut your throat for this."

"Only if they know about it."

She gathered the bills together, thumped them on the bench to even the edges, and clumsily put them back in the envelope.

"Let's have more wine," she said, handing me the envelope. "And then you can show me Decatur Street."

"You're too drunk for Decatur Street."

"No," she said. "We're both drunk. Perfect for Decatur Street."

Decatur Street had a bad reputation, but I thought it no worse than other parts of town. You could find whores and crooks anywhere; plenty of them were around the Henry Grady Hotel, especially when the Legislature was in session. But because entertainment for Atlanta's Colored community was concentrated around Decatur Street, whites damned it. Negro leaders, desperate to prove their respectability, condemned it too.

Several of the beer halls and clubs offered jazz. It wasn't Harlem or Southside Chicago, but a good band, quartet, or a skilled pianist could usually be found somewhere along Decatur Street. In segregated Atlanta, these businesses served whites only on Saturday nights. But this was Friday, after 9 p.m., and Negroes packed the street, dressed in everything from overalls to evening gowns. Emma, a tall, White woman dressed beautifully, drew stares. Several Negro men tipped their hats to her. After a couple of hours checking the bars and theaters for the Germans, we gave up. They weren't on Decatur Street.

The walk had sobered us both, so we decided to enjoy some music before going home. At The Reno Casino, we sat and ordered Atlantic Ales. The pianist had a strong right hand, and his melodic work was superb, but his left hand was weak. I guessed he usually played in a group with a rhythm section, perhaps a bass, which covered up the weak hand. After a quarter hour of bright, sprightly jazz, he shifted to darker, blues-infused music. That was his calling. Though we'd finished our beers, we stayed, entranced, listening, wallowing in his despair.

Suddenly, two Negroes sat at our table. One looked like a young Cab Calloway, with a thin mustache, light skin, and conked hair. He wore a top-quality dark suit with a solid red tie. The other man, younger, bigger, hair cut close to the scalp, wore a white shirt rolled up at the sleeves and dungarees. Both men put beers on the table. They nodded at Emma, then stared dourly at me.

The Suit said, "I see why they callin' him 'the mug.' Damn ugly, if you ask me. Lady, why's a gem like you tooling around with such an ugly mug?"

"Because he brings me to great places like this," Emma said coolly. "The music's good, and the company's even better." She smiled.

The Suit sat back, clearly surprised by her sharp answer and calm demeanor. The big guy in dungarees laughed and turned to me. "Hey, mister, how come you're so ugly?"

I smiled. "Maybe it's my skin?"

"Maybe we need to take that skin off, see what's underneath?" said The Suit. He glanced at Emma to gauge her reaction.

"Oh," she said, "he's the same color underneath as you. Red-blooded."

Both men stared, and The Suit cracked a smile. "Shit, you got backbone." He lifted his beer in a mock toast.

"We heard you wants to know about them Baptist Alliance people," said Dungarees.

"We do," said Emma.

"We saw plenty today. Rode by in taxicabs, gawking at the sinful city. Junior had some of the girls go sit on the porch in their slips. That slowed the taxis down."

"Germans?" I asked.

"Humm," said The Suit. "Well, four Krauts visited a cathouse on the west side. I guess black stuff's pretty exotic to a German."

"A brothel?" I said.

The men looked at each other. "A brothel," mimicked The Suit in a high voice, wide-eyed. Both laughed. Emma remained silent.

"You don't know who I am?" asked The Suit.

"No, sorry."

"I'm Bill Cadwell. 'Wild Bill' in the papers. And this plowboy here is Junior."

"The *Journal* dubbed him that," said Emma. "The series on vice in the city after the Guyol murder. Said 'Wild Bill' Cadwell ran the prostitution and numbers rackets in town."

"They exaggerated," said Cadwell.

"That's what newspapers do," I said. "I'm Mark Morgan. So, you saw these Germans at the brothel tonight?"

"Naw," said Junior. "That was last night. Them squareheads gone to one of Mr. Green's houses over in Washington Park on the west side. High-class place; bright-skinned girls, young, ain't cheap. Four Germans, no drinking, just nailing dark meat." Again, they glanced at Emma, expecting to shock her. She smiled sweetly.

"Baptist Messengers? You're sure?"

"Shit, man, even ministers got needs. Maybe more needs. They just need a quiet place where no one knows them."

Emma showed no shock. "You hear of anybody wanting to hurt Germans?" she asked. Junior turned to her. "Naw, ain't nothing like that I heard of."

"Junior would know," said the suit. "But that's not why we're talking to you. You see, you're not the only White folks with questions about the Germans. Another guy's been poking around."

"Really? What's he look like?"

Junior furrowed his brow and looked up, clearly trying to remember a face. "Hard to say," he said. "Just white. Nicer face than you; he ain't been all beat up. Younger, short hair. Pushy."

"What'd you tell him?"

"Didn't tell him nothin'. Besides, he got on my nerves with his attitude and Yankee accent."

We headed for my car. The only information we'd uncovered was that someone like Packard had asked around about the Germans. So far, my 'private eyeing' had resulted in a growing conviction that the threats were hollow. Everyone I'd spoken to, people who should know, said nothing was up. If Mendel Rubenstein and his manure were the worst I had to worry about, I didn't have much to worry about at all.

"Sorry you had to listen to all that," I said.

"Mark Morgan, you must think I'm some prude. I've met all kinds of people in my work. Heard all sorts of stories. This, however, was the first time I've met an admitted criminal. It was interesting."

"Well, you showed some moxie, that's for sure. And you paid attention to the information I told you."

"It's a puzzle," she said, "and I like puzzles."

The attendant at the parking lot was a slight, older Negro in overalls with a checkered cloth cap. He shuffled up, looking for a tip. I thanked him, gave him a dime, and said goodnight.

He followed me to my car. "Y-Y-You be the peoples wantin' to know 'bout 'dem Germans?"

"Yeah."

"T-T-They's some mens here wants to talk wif you."

The attendant quickly hobbled away. Hearing gravel crunch behind me, I turned. There were three men. As they moved closer, I saw them clearly in the streetlight: White men, police officers. Two of the policemen were young, meaty, their Sam Browne belts stretched across broad chests. The third was older, tall and thin. He tapped one of my Buick's headlights with his nightstick. "A fine automobile. Be a shame if something happened to it in this bad neighborhood."

"Yes, Officer," I said, confused. Policemen in Atlanta had always been deferential and polite with me, the well-dressed businessman. But these policemen had an air of menace I'd never experienced before. I wasn't sure how to act.

"Good to see officers keeping the peace," said Emma. She crowded a little closer to me, sensing the menace.

"If you find White people down on Decatur Street, you know they've been up to something," said the older policeman. They stood in a semicircle facing us, trapping us against my car. All three held nightsticks. "Now, this fellow here," he continued. "We already know he's no good, bringing a White woman down here amongst all these niggers. We need to talk with him."

"Officers, we just had a beer and listened to some jazz."

"Or, the lady might be shady," continued the older cop.

"I hear dinges will pay top dollar to make it with a White girl," said the biggest cop.

"Yep, that's true," said the older cop. "You been screwing niggers, lady?"

"Officers," I said, spreading my hands, "we're going to get in my car and drive home. Good night, gentlemen."

The older one ignored me and tapped his palm rhythmically with the nightstick. "You never know what you'll find: disorderly conduct, public drunkenness, resisting arrest. In a situation like this, you young fellows need to be ready for anything. It can get rough."

One of the younger cops poked Emma with his nightstick. I grabbed it. That was the trigger. The other youngster swung his stick. I tried to duck, but it connected, glancing upward off my skull. Enraged, I wrenched the first cop's nightstick away. Immediately, the older cop struck my elbow. Agony shot through my arm, and the nightstick fell from my hand. After that, the second young cop hit me on top of my head. I collapsed onto the graveled lot.

"Damn it, Will, that's enough," said the older cop. "Hit a man like that, and you might kill him."

"You bastards," said Emma. "Goddamn bastards."

"Quiet, lady, or you'll get some too."

I stayed on my hands and knees. Pain and dizziness melded into a growing nausea. I vomited, then felt rather than saw the older cop squat beside me.

"A fella's got to be careful in this part of town," said the cop. "These niggers down here are dangerous. We often find White fellows all beat up in an alley—teeth broken, eyes gouged. Why, just last week we found a guy with half his nose cut off. Sometimes fellows get that way from asking the wrong sort of questions, you know, puttin' their noses where they don't belong. Gotta be careful about that. And White women down here, they get gang-raped. Sometimes their faces get all cut up. Every weekend, it seems. These coons are animals."

With that, he and his companions strolled away slowly, their footsteps crunching rhythmically in the gravel. Emma sat beside me, holding my head in her lap. I stayed on the ground, smelling vomit, motor oil, dust, and the warm, coppery odor of my own blood.

3

Saturday, July 22, 1939

I lay stunned on the gravel; for how long, I don't know. Suddenly, a man knelt next to me.

"Hey, fella. Let's sit you up."

"Mark, he's here to help," said Emma.

He pulled me to a sitting position, and my head swam. I bent to the side and retched. The guy gave me a handkerchief. "Don't try to stand yet," he said. He tilted my head to look at it in the dim light. Then he walked away and came back with a towel.

"Hold that on the cut," he told Emma. "Get a doctor to look at it soon; he probably needs stitches."

My eyesight had cleared some, and I saw a guy in a brown suit with dark hair, dark eyes, a big nose, and a soft chin squatting next to me in the dim light. "Who are you?" I asked.

"Name's Jimmy Brown. Saw you were in trouble, and I had to help. Why'd those cops attack you, anyway?"

The towel shifted, and pain poured down with blood.

"Hey, hold it still," Brown said. "So, what was their beef?"

"We've been asking around about German Messengers to the Alliance meeting," Emma said. "They didn't like that."

"Germans? Huh, I thought you two were seeking some companionship, you know, on Decatur Street. Hoped it'd be real juicy, you know, three together. But you-all just wandered around and listened to some music."

I shifted so I could sit cross-legged. "You followed us?"

"Yeah. You spotted me on Thursday, but I'm still supposed to stay on you."

"You're following him?" said Emma. "Why? Who?"

"Uh, uh, uh," he said, mockingly. "I'll be following you some more, so just accept it. Don't try to run. From what I've seen so far, you don't got nothing to hide." With that, he stood and walked away.

I opened my eyes at the sound of a car starting. A black Oldsmobile pulled slowly out of the parking lot and turned north. Soon after, Emma helped me to my car and put me in the passenger seat. I was in pain, woozy from the blow, pressing the towel on the cut, and worried about her driving.

"Didn't know you could drive," I said.

"There's a lot you don't know about me."

When we reached the Athletic Club building, I said, "You're not supposed to come up to my room."

"Bunch of hogwash. Show me where to park."

We went in the side door of the Athletic Club and slowly shuffled up seven floors to my room. Opening the door, Emma flipped on the light, looked at me, and gasped. My new Palm Beach suit was covered in blood. "Mark, my God, that's a lot of blood."

"It's on your dress too."

She glanced down. "Damn. So, what do we do now?"

"Can you clean and bandage my head?"

She found iodine, gauze, and tape in my medicine cabinet and cautiously bandaged my head. "It's not bleeding so much now, just oozing."

"Thank you; now go home."

"How do I do that?"

"Take my car. Clearly, you can drive."

"Okay, but I'll be back in the morning."

"They won't let you in."

"You think I'd go to the front? Give me the key to the side door. I'll come up the stairs just like we did tonight."

After giving her the keys, I mumbled good night, and she left. I tore off the Palm Beach suit. It was ruined, so I threw it angrily into the corner. I took a BC powder, pulled on pajamas, and lay on the bed and pondered. Was this job worth getting beaten, having my nose cut off, or maybe ending up a drooling moron with scrambled brains? What good was I doing, anyway? And what's worse, if I'd died tonight, who would have cared? Maybe Emma? She'd stuck with me through the rough stuff, but I wasn't sure how to read it.

My thoughts turned to the policemen. They attacked us because we were asking questions about the Germans. Just when it began to look like I was chasing a heap of nothing? And then there was the guy following me. Jimmy Brown. Who the hell would want me followed? And why had he helped me? Just like my head, things were spinning out of control.

My room was on the southwest corner of the building. A good location in winter, but in summer, the heat of the afternoon sun lingered all night. I lay beneath the open window, sweating, listening to the booming rumble of the Southern Railway yards half a mile away. The crash-bang of cars coupling, the high-pitched whistles of switch engines, echoed through the night. The trains never slept. Near dawn, I finally did.

I slept lightly, haunted by dreams of running, of men with guns and knives chasing me through an endlessly winding neighborhood in Peru. Nightmares of things that had happened, and of things that had not.

I woke in blinding pain. The top of my head was wet, the bandage soaked with blood. My pillow was the same, and my sheets. Cursing, I stumbled to the bathroom and searched for another powder. Mixing it, I downed the bitter draught in several quick gulps. In the bright light of the bathroom, I carefully removed the gauze.

The cut was leaking blood, and the edges gaped. It needed stitches, but I couldn't go to the hospital. "And how were you injured, sir?" they would ask.

Then, I remembered Doc Terry, the building superintendent. He'd served as an orderly in a field hospital during the World War. I phoned his basement room, and after seven rings, he picked up.

"What?"

"Doc, this is Mark Morgan up in 707."

"Morgan? What the hell? It's six o'clock on Saturday morning." Even on the phone, his harsh cracker twang came through.

"Sorry. Listen, during the war, did you learn how to sew up cuts? I cut my scalp pretty good. It won't stop bleeding, and I can't afford the hospital. Could you sew it up?"

"Oh," he said, his tone softer. "Mr. Morgan. Yeah, sure, come on down. I can sew most anything up. I keep needles and gut in my kit. Even got some cream that numbs the skin."

An hour later, my head had a clipped patch around the cut, ten stitches, and a coating of iodine. It was ugly, but Doc was no prize himself. Gray-haired, maybe forty-five, his cratered, grizzled face looked like he'd seen all that life can throw at a man. He asked no questions about the injury. "Might be more stitches than you need, but I wanted to be sure."

"Thanks, Doc." I gave him twenty bucks, which surprised him.

"You said you couldn't afford no hospital?"

"I can't," I said. "Thanks."

Next, I needed food. While my room was essentially a hotel room with a bath, I'd smuggled in an electric tap, a small icebox, and a toaster. I put two slices of bread in the toaster and scrambled three eggs with a little milk, salt, and pepper. The coffee had only begun perking when the eggs were ready, so I ate the toast and eggs and had another glass of water while sitting at the desk in the corner. The warm, slippery scrambled eggs comforted me. I sat quietly by the window, mouthing each lovely bit, listening to the growing murmur of a waking city.

I poured a cup of coffee, flipped on the radio, and turned on the water heater. The throbbing in my head continued, so I sat and explored the knot gingerly with my fingers. The radio news came on: Hitler screaming grievances. I switched it off.

Somehow, in poking around, Emma and I had touched a live wire. What made questions about the German Baptists so threatening to someone powerful enough to use the cops? Was this what Packard meant when he said I was in over my head? And why had Packard or someone like him been asking questions down on Decatur Street? I climbed into the shower, careful not to wet my head, and stood under the warm flow. Of all things, I suddenly thought about my kids.

Emma arrived about seven-thirty and slipped up the stairs as we had the night before. She was astonished to see the stitches in my head. "Here I was going to take you to the hospital and tell them you fell off a ladder putting in a lightbulb."

"Thanks a lot."

"I've read some about head injuries. You need to rest up today. If you get a really bad headache, you need to go to the hospital."

I almost told her I was thinking about my kids, but decided it was best to say nothing. Instead, I said, "Why did this happen?"

"It happened because something really is going on with the German Messengers. Something important enough to try and scare us off."

"I'm pretty scared," I said.

She laughed. "I don't think much scares you, Mark Morgan. Look, I've got a meeting at the writer's project, and then I plan to go shopping with my friend Sally."

"Take my car," I said.

"Nope. Here are the keys. There's blood on your seats, by the way. You'll have to clean up somehow."

With that, she left.

Mother once told me that marriage was not about love; it was about money. My ex-wife Mabel clearly agreed. When I returned from five months in a Peruvian jail, Mabel cleaned me out with the divorce. Three months later, she married my good old work buddy, Tony Parker. They lived in my old house, with my money and my kids.

I parked in front of the two-story colonial in Morningside Park. It was surrounded by azalea bushes and mature trees. I had planted the azaleas, mown the lawn, painted the fence, and paid the mortgage for seven years. It still felt like my house, but it wasn't. Climbing carefully out of the car, I perched a light blue fedora on my head to hide the stitches. Tony Parker opened the screen door when I was ten feet from the front porch.

"Sorry to bother you, Tony. Just wanted to see my kids."

"Can't it wait?" He stepped outside and closed the screen door.

"There's a parade downtown today. I thought the kids might want to go. They'd have fun."

He looked confused. "I don't think Mabel would like it. Besides, you're not supposed to be here today. Next weekend you can see the kids."

I saw my son Hank in the shadows behind Tony. At nine, Hank was tall for his age, and he had black hair like mine. He no longer looked like a little kid.

"¿Qué pasa, chico?" I said.

"Hi, Dad." He pushed open the screen door, stepped past Tony, and gravely shook my hand. I was so proud of him. I swept him up and hugged him.

"What's shaking?" I joked, putting him down.

"Playing in the neighborhood mostly. Burt Adams and I ride our bikes a lot. And reading. I like the Tom Swift books now."

"That's pretty grown-up stuff."

"Yeah, Mom doesn't like it. But, Dad, he has an electric rifle. I wish I had one."

"You haven't been playing The Bug, have you?"

"Dad!" Hank looked nervously at Tony. The Bug was slang for Atlanta's illegal lottery. A couple of months before, I'd let him choose some numbers. Hank had very seriously given me a dime. A week later, I'd used some of my precious remaining funds to buy a bicycle. The Bug had paid off, I told him.

"Hi," said a soft voice.

I looked up to see Susan with her bright blond hair. She was four now. I'm sure she thinks of Tony as Dad. Hell, maybe he is her dad; she doesn't look a thing like me.

"Hi, yourself."

She pressed against the screen. "Can we go for a ride in your rumble seat?"

"No, silly, Dad's not supposed to be here," said Hank.

"What's going on?" said Mabel, coming to the door. "Oh, it's you."

"Yeah," I said. "Me."

"Children," said Mabel. "Upstairs. Now."

"Mom, I want to talk with Dad," said Hank.

"Henry, come in now. Tony should never have let you go outside." She stepped forward, pushed the screen door open, and motioned my son in. Tony followed and dropped into the background. That's where he always was, lurking in the background. The next thing you know, he's screwing your wife, and she wants a divorce.

I winked at Susan. She burst into a smile and dashed upstairs. Hank followed reluctantly.

"How dare you come by and disrupt our morning. I've half a mind to report you to the court."

"How are you, Mabel?"

"Why are you here?"

"I thought the kids would like to go to the Baptist parade. Could be fun."

"Baptists?" said Mabel. "You must be kidding. My children go to the Episcopal church. And you're only allowed to see them twice a month. This isn't on your schedule."

"Yeah, my schedule. Sorry I disturbed you."

"Mark," said Tony suddenly from the background. "Wanna go grab lunch? We need to talk about your kids' school tuition."

The headache spread across my forehead, and I suddenly felt very tired. It wasn't the injury. "Write me about it, Tony."

I drove away from the house, but my vision narrowed, and the headache grew. I pulled to the side of the road, closed my eyes, and was surprised by a memory.

A couple of weeks after Father's surgery in 1921, I talked with my mother. She was a tall, solidly built redhead, the daughter of a German sugar merchant. Though her English was perfect, Mother insisted that my brother and I speak German with her. Father spoke to us in English. The servants and my friends all spoke Spanish. I thought the babble of languages was normal. We sat in the garden, surrounded by the red hibiscus my mother loved so well. Adella brought her a second cup of coffee.

"Mark, would you like a cup?"

"*Nein, Mutter.*"

"Is this about the new school? It's a fine school in New England. It will prepare you for the best American colleges." She took a sip of her coffee. "Does this worry you?"

"No. I'm worried about Father."

Her eyes dropped to her coffee, and she took a long sip. "Your father will be well," she said. "The doctors assure me he is out of danger."

"This time."

"You must not think like that."

"How should I think?"

"You should be proud of him. The Morgan family is respected in Cuba. The interior minister and even the president have visited our home. You share in that respect, and you share in the wealth. It will pay for you to go to the best schools; you may become a doctor, a lawyer, or even a professor."

"But what he does . . ."

"*Cállate*," she said harshly, switching to Spanish. *Shut up.* Her face flushed; she seldom used what she called the language of servants.

"You are only sixteen; there is much you do not understand," she continued. "Your father is a good man, a kind man." She sighed and looked away, gazing at the garden. "However, there are those around him who are not so good, not so kind."

"What do I tell the other boys at school?"

"Tell them your father is in sugar. It is true, you know. He has made large investments in *Oriente* province. Our income from sugar is substantial."

"I lie?" I said, astonished.

"Certainly you lie." She took another sip of coffee, and then she looked directly into my eyes. "My son, lying is the way of the world."

"Hey, hey, buddy." A hard hand shook me. The memory passed, and I opened my eyes. It was Jimmy Brown again, the man who had helped me on Decatur Street. "Gotta be careful about head injuries," he said. "Worried you was fading out. That can happen, you know. Guy just goes to sleep, never wakes up."

"Thanks." I sat up straighter in the car seat. Glancing in the mirror, I saw the black Olds pulled up behind me. "I appreciate your help, Brown, but what's going on? You're still following me."

He took a moment. "Yep," he said. "I'm supposed to catch you out, see if I can show you doing bad things."

It suddenly dawned. "Mabel," I said.

"Truth is, you seem clean, and that lady you took dancing's a real straight arrow. But I get paid by the hour; it's easy work, and maybe you're digging an interesting hole. I'd like to see what you find."

"Just a spectator, huh? Well, I'm completely lost."

"Yeah, it's hard sometimes, when you don't seem to be finding nothing, but then, you get a break. So, whatever it is you're on to, just keep working 'til you get that break."

"Thanks," I said, and started my car. "I'm headed to the parade, in case you want to follow."

He waved as I drove off—and then it hit me. There was no way of knowing if he told me the truth. He hadn't said anything about working for Mabel. I just made that assumption, but I didn't really know what Jimmy Brown was after.

I watched the Baptist Alliance parade from the sidewalk in front of Regenstein's Department Store. The bright sunshine hurt my eyes, and I feared the headache would return. Boy Scouts, marching bands, and thousands of Messengers streamed by. Four hundred from Texas alone. They had to march from Five Points up Peachtree Street to Ponce de Leon, then east to the baseball stadium where the first mass meeting would be held. More than three miles under a blazing sun on dark asphalt in ninety-degree heat. I wondered how many casualties there'd be. While the delegation from Texas flowed by, I glanced at the terrace of the Henry Grady across the street. To my surprise, Anna Erlanger stood there, watching the parade.

As the last of the Messengers plodded past, the crowd began to break up. I crossed Peachtree to the hotel and hurried up the steps to the terrace. Anna leaned on the rail, gazing north up Peachtree, and didn't notice me until I stood beside her.

"Great God," she said in German, startled. "I did not expect you."

"My apologies. I thought you would march in the parade?"

"Me? Mr. Morgan, I am just the wife, not a Messenger. For Germans, that is a role only for men. Besides, the speeches will go on for hours. I would never be able to stay awake, and it's already hot."

She shook her hair back from her face as she turned to me, just like Carole Lombard in the movies. Suddenly, her brow wrinkled with concern. "Are you in pain, Mr. Morgan?"

"Please, call me Mark."

"As you wish." She smiled. "Mark."

"If this is a good time, I would like to speak with you about some of the Messengers."

"Today, I have nothing but time."

We stepped indoors, into a dark lounge with worn carpet and stained walls. The corridors of the hotel were even worse, lined with yellowed forty-watt sconces and faded wallpaper. Anna was far too pretty for the Henry Grady Hotel.

"Tell me about Rolf Schulman," I said.

"I don't know much about him."

"Gestapo?"

"Probably, or something similar. He's not really a Messenger; the church he's supposed to represent in Berlin does not exist."

"Doesn't exist?"

"There is no such church. One never knows how to read such things. Are the police incompetent, making such an obvious mistake? Or, do they know we know this, and so intend for us to understand what Rolf really is? To frighten us, yes?"

"Too complicated a game for me," I said, shaking my head.

"It's more than a game, Mr. Morgan."

"Who was the other man? The one with brown hair who grabbed the manure man?"

Anna covered her mouth with her hand and giggled. "The manure man. Wonderful. We were attacked by the manure man." Her eyes sparkled, and I felt that tug again. "I'm sorry; that was amusing. As you might imagine, my husband does not make jokes. He is always serious." She paused and twirled a tendril of her hair while gazing into my eyes.

"The man with brown hair?" I prompted.

"Ah, yes. Paul Dittmer."

"Is he a real Messenger, or is he also from an imaginary church?"

"Paul is very real, the youth minister for a large church in Düsseldorf. Not so far from Essen. My husband says they have met before. Paul belonged to a glider club. Very military, you see. I think that accounts for his strict bearing."

"Surely Rolf is not the only policeman? Do you know of others? Perhaps there are members of the SS? The intelligence services?"

"Mr. Morgan, your efforts are wasted. I am simply the wife of a minister who came with him on an adventure to America. These questions make me nervous."

"My apologies," I said.

"No, no," said Anna, standing. "I'm bad-tempered and bored. Who would think I could be bored in America? I can't speak the language; it's steaming hot, and there is nothing for me to do. Over the next week, Otto will be debating ideas while I rot in this squalid hotel and practice my ten words of English. Perhaps I will learn an eleventh word, yes?"

"This hotel? I thought you were staying with the Lowders?"

"We are, but this is our headquarters—so I must wait here during the day for my husband. Solidarity, you see, and to show that I am a proper wife." She turned toward the stairs.

"Anna, wait." She paused. "I could show you the city. There are a few points of interest, some nice things to do. And it's part of my job to learn more about the Messengers."

"You are kind, but it would not be proper."

"Of course it would be proper. Didn't you come with your husband to see the United States? Surely, he would want you to tour?"

"I suffered through one city tour already."

"We could go for a walk, or perhaps you would like to ride?"

"Horses? I love horses."

"Then we'll go riding. I'll arrange it for tomorrow."

"No, not tomorrow. Tomorrow is Sunday, and I will attend church."

That night, I dreamed the dream again that was entangled with memory. I woke sweating, gasping, choking in the dark. Struggling to breathe, to fight off panic, I climbed out of bed and sat in an armchair by the window, trying to calm myself. As I sat there, the memory came back fully, viscerally. But the dream that reflected the memory had grown worse.

The memory was clear. In June of 1938, I'd been sent to Lima, Peru, by Coca-Cola to check out problems at a coca leaf processing plant. Processing removed the cocaine, retaining the other coca alkaloids that were part of Coke's "secret formula." The cocaine was sold for medicinal purposes, while the remaining alkaloids were shipped to Atlanta for use in Merchandise No. 5, an essential part of Coca-Cola's syrup. But production was behind, causing shortages, and the income from the sales of medical cocaine lagged. Worse, the amount of cocaine produced did not match up with the amount of Merchandise No. 5 produced. I was tasked with finding out why.

I hired Enrique, a well-regarded local private investigator, as my assistant. We found nothing openly wrong at the coca processing plant, but we left quite certain that cocaine was being siphoned off and sold into the black market. The factory was owned by a Spanish corporation based in Salamanca, meaning it was probably connected to Franco's fascists. Perhaps it was funneling money to Franco's cause, the fascist cause. In my naivete back then, I thought to do something good by stopping it. Questioning workers, neighbors, and officials went nowhere. I offered money for information, but no one responded. I know now because no one dared. Soon, I grew desperate to find a way forward.

Enrique came to my hotel room late one evening. He paced, took off his hat, and gestured with it while holding it by the crown.

"We have been summoned," he said.

"Summoned? Who summoned us?"

"Don Carlo. We are to meet him at his house in Barranco at three a.m. It's south of the city, on the coast. Many wealthy people have homes there."

"How far?"

"Mr. Morgan, we should not go. In fact, you should leave on an airplane first thing in the morning. I will visit my parents up near Cusco for a few weeks."

"Why?"

"It is not good to awaken Don Carlo's interest. Don Carlo is a businessman, but he is also what you would call a gangster. A very dangerous man."

"So, where's Barranco?"

"South of the city, on the ocean. Rich families have built homes there. My advice is to ignore this summons. I think you should leave Peru by airplane in the morning."

"I think we should go to this meeting." I began to dress.

"No, I will not go."

I went to my suitcase and counted out ten hundreds. "Enrique, I'll pay one thousand dollars for you to take me to this meeting. Just drive. Nothing more."

He looked at the bills hungrily; it was more money than he earned in a year. He snatched the bills out of my hand.

"I will drive, but I will not come inside. If anything happens, I will leave, even without you."

"Agreed," I said.

It took almost an hour to reach Don Carlo's house on Avenida San Martín, and we arrived just before three in the morning. It was winter in Lima; low gray clouds covered the city, and moonlight shone through the clouds as a dim, glowing halo. Enrique pulled to the curb in front of a *Belle*

Époque mansion surrounded by a tall ironwork fence with a single gate. Two men stood by the gate, their hats pulled low, their long trench coats protecting them from the damp air.

"I will stay in the car," said Enrique.

I gave the men my name, and they gestured me through. A butler answered the door and led me into a wood-paneled sitting room lined with family portraits. There, a man waited. Most *Limeños* chewed and spat Spanish at high velocity, but Don Carlo spoke in a cultured, almost languid manner with a *Castellano* accent. The room, his speech, the house, all signaled a well-established, educated, and wealthy *Criollo* family.

After a few formalities and the offer of tea, Don Carlo said, "It would be best if you left Lima immediately, Mr. Morgan. There is nothing for you here."

"Apologies, but my job requires me to resolve some problems."

"I am offering you a great courtesy, showing my respect for your employer. I also respect your devotion to the task, but you will solve nothing. Again, you must leave. If you wish, I will write a letter explaining this for your superiors."

"That won't be needed. I'm staying here until I'm satisfied."

He shook his head, almost sadly. "Then we have no more to discuss. Good night."

Outside, Enrique stood beside the car, shifting from foot to foot skittishly. "Something's not right," he said. "Four men sit in a car down the block, waiting. This at three in the morning."

The butler came to the gate, spoke briefly to the guards, who glanced at us. Then suddenly, one hurried down the street to the waiting car. Its engine started.

Enrique bolted. "Run," he shouted. "Run."

I ran.

The car pulled out behind us. The headlights shone past, lighting the cobbled street, allowing us to run faster. Surprisingly, Enrique headed toward the ocean. Barranco stood on a cliff almost 300 feet above the Pacific, and there was no obvious pathway down. But he wound through narrow streets, getting ever closer to the cliff, the men behind shouting and the car grinding its gears to follow.

Suddenly, Enrique dodged right and vanished. I followed and found he had dropped over a concrete wall onto the precipitous tracks of a funicular that ran down the cliff to the ocean. I followed him, making a terrifying leap into the darkness. We hopped downward, from crosstie to crosstie, struggling to keep our balance, on the edge of a deadly fall. It went on endlessly. The crossties were wet with condensation and slippery. I fell and began to slide, but my trousers caught on something and ripped. Enrique grabbed my hand.

"The car can't follow us here," he said. "We're safe."

I glanced up to see headlights shining into the darkness above the cliff. Silhouetted against the halo of moonlight, dark shapes moved around at the top of the funicular tracks, but none pursued us. We continued more carefully, slipping and sliding. Waves tumbled on the rocky beach below, and the iodine odor of the ocean grew stronger. Suddenly, we reached the bottom, among bathhouses next to a short boardwalk.

"We go north," said Enrique. "In about a kilometer, there is a path up the cliff."

We stepped off the boardwalk and began walking across the pebbled shore. Suddenly, there was a fusillade of shots. Enrique fell. I turned toward the sound; then, something jerked my left leg from under me, and I went down.

Agony. I lay face down on the pebbled shore, my leg twisted under me, the pain growing with every breath. Next to me, Enrique gurgled and writhed weakly. Regular, unhurried steps crunched across the stones. Four men. One bent over Enrique. "He is finished," the man said. Two others grabbed my shoulders and rolled me roughly onto my back. My broken leg twisted, and I screamed.

"*Silencio,*" one hissed. He punched my nose, and choking blood gushed into my throat.

"No, no," said Don Carlo. "Let him scream. There is no one to hear."

"Kill him, Don Carlo?"

"No, he will be the message." A knife flashed, and I struggled desperately. Don Carlo laughed.

"This could have been much worse, Mr. Morgan. I could have taken your manhood." He showed me the knife and pricked the end of my nose. "Remember," he said.

Then, he and the others were gone, and I lay on the rocks by the ocean alone.

With that, I always woke from the nightmare, sweating. In pain, I would reach down to feel if I was whole. In the waking world, I was. But, in the dream . . .

While physically I was whole, mentally I wasn't. Perhaps the dreams signaled insanity? They'd lock me up in the Milledgeville State Hospital, a literal hell on earth. So I never dared to go back to sleep, afraid madness might overtake me. That morning, I sat in the chair by the window. With the first glimpse of sunrise, I stirred and went to the mirror. My eyes were sunken dark pools above my crooked, broken nose. My face was ashen, exhausted. I was a wreck, and though physically whole, in truth, they had unmanned me. I couldn't even cry anymore, for I'd cried enough already.

4

SUNDAY, JULY 23, 1939

The lump on the side of my head had shrunk to a small knot. The stitches in the cut on top looked clean, with no proud flesh or pain when I touched them. I'd been lucky. I dressed the cut and went downstairs to the club kitchen, where the cook let me have some toast and boiled eggs.

"Funny things happening," he said, staring at the bandage on my head. "You hear about that flag?"

"Flag?" I said, slowly chewing some toast.

"Yeah, that Nazi flag on Peachtree—out in front of the Henry Grady."

"Uh-uh," I grunted, peeling an egg.

"Well, looks like some fellas came before dawn and ripped it down. The night porter at the hotel saw 'em."

"What fellows?"

"No one knows. Probably some of these Baptists that don't like Nazis. Word is there's gonna be a big blowup about Nazis and the Jews at their meetin'. They're already callin' for takin' down the Colored section signs. Gonna let the races mix. Sounds like helpin' Jews is next."

I stepped out the back door. It was early, just past dawn on a Sunday, and deliciously cool. I ate my breakfast, enjoying the quiet city. While I respected the move to tear down the Nazi flag, it would make no difference. You can't do anything to change the world.

Returning to my room, I tried to read the newspaper, but I gave up and threw it on the floor. The nightmare hung too heavily, so I dressed and walked to the Henry Grady Hotel. The cook was right; the flag was missing. I wondered if the Germans would notice. Over the next two hours, I saw nothing but Baptists headed to early services. All seemed calm and normal. Then, at about ten o'clock, I thought of Phil Sanders.

I'd met Phil at an Athletic Club tennis tournament in the summer of '33. He was older than me, a small fellow, balding, with a pencil-thin mustache. His jokes and shrewd commentary about politics and life made me laugh. We played tennis several times and became friends. Phil's father owned textile mills in western Georgia, and Phil's three older brothers all worked in the family business. Phil, however, had been cast out. The story was that he wanted to do something else with his life. Others said he just wasn't up to dealing with the rough and tumble world of the mills, that he was too soft.

"The real reason," Mrs. Sidney Barrington Porter had whispered to me at the Driving Club's Nine O'Clocks' ball, "the real reason is Phil Sanders is a fruit, a swish."

Stunned at hearing this from the white-haired *grande dame* of Atlanta society, I'd stared at her, speechless.

"Oh, don't look so shocked, Henry Mark Morgan. How did you think I've kept my place in society so long? I know everything about everybody. I even know all about you." Mrs. Porter had smiled and adjusted her hat.

So, Phil was homosexual, and his family had disowned him. He never seemed especially effeminate; he was just a nice guy. Phil later told me that instead of an inheritance, he'd been given $50,000 and told never to return. To most people, that would be a fortune. Managed carefully, at three or four percent, it would produce enough to get by.

The father clearly had not known his son. Instead of just getting by, the exile proved a gifted investor. Through the dark years of the early 1930s, Phil worked the securities markets like a virtuoso, earning a quarter of a million dollars in just five years.

In 1935, Phil opened an investment firm, Sanders Securities, which only accepted select clients willing to invest at least ten thousand dollars. Wealthy Atlantans quickly learned that he constructed brilliant portfolios, nothing like the plunger's portfolios of the 1920s. He devised several top-performing closed-end funds for his clients, and his business grew rapidly. No one cared about his alleged sexual proclivities because he earned big returns. Rumor said his current personal fortune was well over a million, maybe more than two.

"It was easy," Phil had explained one afternoon after losing to me again at singles. "I started with the market at the bottom. All I had to do was pick good companies. After that, the money came automatically."

Automatically, that is, for Phil Sanders. He always picked good companies while the rest of the world picked losers.

I went to a hotel phone booth and dropped a nickel. "Hi, Phil, this is Mark Morgan."

"Good morning, Mark. Isn't it a bit early?"

"It's almost ten," I said. "All the good Baptists are in church. Look, I need to drop by today and pick your brain. It's business."

"Oh, sure, Mark. Come on out. I'll be around the house because, you see, today is Sunday, and Sunday is the day I don't do business. You know, the day of rest."

"Would eleven be okay?"

"You'll come by no matter what I say."

I dressed in tan trousers and a blue cotton golf shirt. My Panama hat was smashed somewhere in the Decatur Street parking lot, so I put on a straw boater. I tucked the envelope with seven thousand bucks into my breast pocket and headed for the car. Glenn Miller and his Orchestra played on WATL as I drove north on Peachtree.

Soon, I was out of the city and into Fulton County. Escaping Atlanta's 25-mph speed limit, I shifted into third, and the Buick was hitting on all eight. No black Oldsmobile followed me. The breeze through the windows felt marvelous, and I turned the music up.

In Buckhead, I bore left at the Coca-Cola sign above Jacob's Pharmacy. Going north on Roswell Road, absorbed in the freedom and speed, I almost missed my turn. Swerving onto Blackland at the last moment, the Buick handled beautifully. Then I turned onto Tuxedo Road, where huge new homes and estates were being built.

I slowed, crossed Valley Road, and then saw it. You couldn't miss Phil Sanders's new house. Built on a hill, white, concrete, angular, showing plenty of glass and steel. It surely offended the neighbors with their Federal-style mansions and fake Norman chateaux. The thought made me smile. It probably made Phil smile too.

I idled up the long drive and pulled to a stop at the front. Before I reached the door, a Black maid opened it.

"Already a hot day," I said.

"Yes, sir, don't seem to be no other kind lately. Mr. Sanders, now, he's out by the swimming pool."

"Thank you." I stood in the front entry, feeling foolish. The interior was vast, open, with hard shiny surfaces, long drapes, and glass everywhere. I couldn't see a pool, nor did I see a back door.

The maid caught my difficulty. "You haven't been here before?"

"No. Mr. Sanders and I know each other through business. And we play tennis regularly, but I only see him in town. I don't have the money to run with his crowd."

She smiled. "Huh. I don't think his crowd would like the way you look. You look a bit rough, like a hard man."

She led me down a hall and through an open set of glass doors to a patio behind the house. The swimming pool sat farther back. I spotted Phil in the pool, with a huge straw sombrero protecting his bald head. He'd put a chair in the shallow end of the pool and sat covered in water to his chest, reading a book. Except for the sombrero, he was naked.

"Mark Morgan," he said. "How nice to have you visit my humble home."

"So humble." I laughed. "How are you, Phil?"

"Hot. Sitting in the pool like this is the only way to stay cool. The house is supposed to be air-conditioned, but some of the parts were wrong. A $70,000 house, but two missing ten-buck parts have screwed it all up."

"For the want of a nail, a kingdom was lost."

He laughed. "Trust you to be the philosopher. Sit down, please."

"What are you reading?" I asked, finding a chair with shade.

"I saw it on the bestseller list, so I had Miller's Bookstore send over a copy. Steinbeck's *The Grapes of Wrath*. It's about a family trying to escape the Dust Bowl by moving to California. Right now, they're journeying west. I don't think it's going to end well."

"It doesn't. My favorite part is the story of the turtle."

"The turtle?"

"Remember? At the beginning? The turtle trying to cross the road? It gets hit by a truck, flips in the air, and lands on its back."

"Okay."

"Well, the turtle doesn't give up. He struggles to turn over and then starts again on the same journey. Focused, determined."

"Stupid?"

"Maybe, but it won't quit. I like that turtle. A great metaphor."

Phil looked up. "And my friends say you're just another pretty face." We laughed again.

He waded to the edge of the pool and put his book on the concrete deck. "What'd you need to talk about?"

"A couple of things. First, I've got seven thousand bucks. I know that's not the ten you usually require, but I wondered if you could invest it for me and keep it mum."

"So, you're in the money again?"

"Doing a job for Harold Hirsch."

He whistled. "Hirsch? Then you are in the money. Give me the bank account number, and we'll get the money moved over."

I took the envelope out of my pocket and put it on the table by the pool.

"Okay," Phil said, looking at it. "So, a cash deposit. I'll open an account tomorrow. But, Mark, secrecy and cash make me nervous. Especially coming from someone with your family background."

"It's clean, Phil. I don't want Mabel finding out, or she'll claim that it's money I hid during the divorce. There isn't a contract or anything for the work I'm doing. It's all on a handshake. I'm only sorry it isn't more. God knows I owe you."

After the attack in Peru, they'd jailed me on the charge of murdering Enrique. Thinking I was dead, Coca-Cola had let me rot. Only Phil Sanders spent huge sums of money, brought pressure to bear, and kept it up for months. Finally, I had a lawyer, there was a hearing, and I escaped. I owed Phil my life.

"What's Hirsch got you doing?"

"Know about the Baptist Alliance meeting?"

"Of course, they've about closed down the city."

I told him the whole story. Phil digested things for a while when I finished.

"She's pretty, huh?" he finally said. "This German gal."

"Gorgeous. Seriously, she looks and moves like a movie star. Beautiful eyes, perfect skin, a great figure."

"So, you're interested?"

"Of course I'm interested. I'm always interested. And then, there's my friend Emma."

"Ah, yes, the poor, dry, old librarian."

"You should have seen her Friday night. Her dress was great, and her hair looked wonderful; she was beautiful. When those cops jumped us, she stood up to them. Impressive as hell."

"Mark, from what you've told me, Emma's a good woman, and you like her. Meanwhile, you know nothing about this German dame. Jesus, do you read the papers? Germany's a nightmare. Anyone allowed to travel from there must be complicit with the regime."

"She and her husband don't agree with the Nazis. He's not a member of the party."

"How do you know? Because they told you? What the hell is wrong with you? Meanwhile, there's Emma. You know her; you share ideas, interests, have fun together, yet you're obsessed with this *Fräulein*."

"I'm Emma's friend."

"This Nazi Carole Lombard? She's married to a really old bird, you said. Do you think he's too old? Is she getting any? Is that your fantasy—you'll fulfill her desires?"

"You know better."

Muttering, Phil waded to the steps, climbed out of the pool, and wrapped himself in a white terrycloth robe. He pulled a chair over to the shade and flopped into it. "But you're going to think about it anyway."

"I just need to get more information out of her. No plans beyond that."

Phil watched me silently for a moment. "If that's how you want it. What about this Jimmy Brown fellow? The guy who's following you?"

"I don't know. Could Hirsch have hired him to make sure I was doing the job?"

"You said you spotted him before you met with Hirsch, so probably not. My money's on Mabel. I'll ask around, see if I can find out anything."

"Thanks."

"Let me see your head." He moved his chair in front of me. I took off my hat and bent forward so he could look.

"Animals," he muttered, touching the skin around the cut gently. "They could have killed you. Then all the money I spent to get you out of Peru would have been wasted."

"I knew you'd be sympathetic." We both laughed.

"You know," he said, "a lot of the Atlanta Police belong to the Klan."

"Is this another joke?"

"No, it's true. Remember about five or six months ago when the Invisible Empire staged those kidnappings downtown? Robed Klansmen kidnapped six men. They snatched one guy right in front of Woolworth's on Peachtree. Grabbed him off the sidewalk and threw him, screaming, into a car. On Boulevard, they stopped to talk with a couple of police officers while they had the guy tied up and gagged in the back. It was all in the *Constitution*. When Mayor Hartsfield ordered an investigation, the chief of police killed it the next day."

"I sort of remember."

"Well, it made me curious. How could this happen? Why would the police just ignore it? Turns out it goes back to Mayor Sims in the nineteen-twenties. He had a big police scandal, and *The New York Times* dubbed Atlanta's police the most corrupt in the nation. The Klan was a national movement back then. They had something like five or six million members. Sims believed in their program to purify America, a return to old-time values. So, his solution to the corruption was to have Atlanta policemen join the Klan."

"But that must have been what, fifteen or more years ago?"

"Seems like things have changed since then. The national Klan organization is bankrupt. The Imperial Palace, their old headquarters on Peachtree, was sold to the Catholic Church. My God, Mark, you couldn't make this stuff up! The Catholic-hating Klan's former headquarters torn down, and Christ the King Cathedral built in its place. What irony; isn't America a delightful place?"

Phil shook his head and stood. He paced while he talked, his robe swinging around his ankles. "Most Atlanta cops join the Klan when they get hired. They pay the initiation fees and go through the ritual. Of the thousands of Klansmen in Atlanta, a good portion are cops. It's the *de facto* brotherhood for the police."

While I mulled this over, Phil walked toward the house and called to his maid, asking her to bring some iced tea. He came back with our drinks.

"Phil, who runs the police? Or, should I ask, who runs the Klan?"

"Attaboy, Mark, now you're thinking. Officially, of course, the chief runs the police. And above him is the mayor. But Hartsfield doesn't have a good relationship with the cops. During his campaign, he argued that half the force was corrupt. Promised to clean them up, end the shakedowns, graft, and bribes. Fired the old chief and the head of detectives. Most of Atlanta's policemen hate Hartsfield's guts, and they see the new chief as his tool."

"Okay, so it's not Hartsfield."

"Right, and Hartsfield's part of the Coca-Cola crowd, so it's not Robert Woodruff."

"I guess there has to be one thing in Atlanta Woodruff doesn't control."

Phil grimaced. "I'm pretty sure the power company crowd has its finger on the police. They're beholden to Gene Talmadge and his statewide machine. Talmadge is working on a comeback, speaking all over the state, playing on race bigotry hard."

"This is too complicated," I said, shaking my head.

"No, it's simple. Three groups are fighting for control of the city, hell, the whole state. There's Coca-Cola and Hartsfield. There's First National Bank and Governor E. D. Rivers. And finally, there's the power company crowd and former Governor Gene Talmadge. Only one of them probably influences the police. Talmadge."

"But why would the cops, or the Klan, or the power company, or Gene Talmadge, for God's sake, be upset by my asking questions about the Germans?"

"That's what you have to find out."

Back at the Athletic Club, I changed into the blue suit, popped on the light blue fedora, and walked over to the Henry Grady. Most Messengers were back from church and seemed pleased to talk to an American in their own language. I chatted with an amiable deacon from Kiel and a pastor from Magdeburg. When I broached the subject of policemen, both men clammed up and walked away.

A copy of the Sunday *Constitution* lay by my chair. While I watched the lobby, I read snippets in the paper. As usual, the news was not good. Europe was rushing toward the precipice. The Republicans were intent on dismantling the New Deal alphabet agencies, such as the CCC, the WPA, and the REA. Roosevelt could do nothing. A lame duck, his warnings about international fascism and his pleas to change the neutrality laws and enlarge the military were ridiculed by the Republicans. They doubled down on keeping the Neutrality Acts, wanting no involvement in Europe, and jockeying for the 1940 election.

In Georgia, Governor Rivers' "Little New Deal" was mired in corruption. The public school system neared collapse, unable to pay teachers. Unemployment statewide remained above ten percent, much higher in Atlanta, while desperate people flooded into the city looking for work. Facing all these challenges, Atlanta Mayor Hartsfield was focused on fighting a new moral plague—pinball machines.

I almost missed it. But then, the story in the bottom right-hand corner of page seven caught my attention:

Tragic Accident on Marietta Street.

Mendel Rubenstein of South Washington Street was struck and killed by an automobile at the corner of Marietta and Cone. The accident occurred at about 3:00 a.m. Saturday morning. Mr. Rubenstein, who had been drinking, was struck by a westbound car. The car's driver reported that Mr. Rubenstein suddenly fell out of the car in front of him. He described the car as a dark late-model Plymouth sedan. Police say the driver's story is not credible, but have not charged him in the incident.

I sat stunned, then dug out my notebook to be sure. The "manure man" had been Mendel Rubenstein, and he lived at 535 ½ South Washington Street. I hurried to my car.

Washington Street ran south from the state Capitol through one of Atlanta's oldest neighborhoods to Summer Hill, where it shaded into Negro slums. Recent Jewish immigrants had crowded into the run-down houses and apartments of the district. The newspaper estimated ten thousand lived there, but people came and went, so no one knew the true number. Polish, Romanian, Russian, Portuguese, Syrian, and German Jews all together, producing a proliferation of competing synagogues. Not so much a melting pot as a boiling collection of cousins. All, of course, studiously ignored by Atlanta's established Jewish communities.

Mine was the only car that crept down the street. The shops and businesses were all closed. Not due to the Sabbath, which had already ended, but to Atlanta's restrictive Sunday blue laws. Children played outdoors, and bearded men on street corners watched me suspiciously. The address was a turreted Victorian pile divided into two apartments. Several people stood just inside the front door, talking.

"Excuse me," I said. "Is this the home of Mendel Rubenstein?"

There were concerned glances within the group. Finally, one man with a heavy accent and a gray beard said, "Mr. Rubenstein is dead."

Taking a chance, I switched to German. "Yes. I saw the article in the newspaper. That's why I came. To find out what happened."

"Why? Who are you?" he replied in German.

"My name is Mark Morgan. I'm working for Mr. Hirsch and the Jewish Welfare Alliance."

The bearded man was maybe sixty, though his heavy beard made it hard to judge. Dark eyes swept over me, and he smiled grimly. Clearly, I was an outsider. "I'm Max Ostein," he said in English. "What is it you want?"

"Is there a Mrs. Rubenstein? I would like to talk with her, find out what she knows about Mr. Rubenstein's death."

"He was murdered," said Ostein.

"Who killed him?"

"You're not surprised?"

"Maybe not," I said. "I'd like to know more."

"You cannot speak with his wife; it would not be proper. Rachel says they took him away on Sabbath night. Friday night to you. A group of men, large men, who laughed when they saw that Mendel was frightened. They came about eleven o'clock."

"Did she know them?"

"Of course not. Five men. They spoke English. Didn't knock, just burst into their apartment."

"She told the police?"

"The police were not interested. Mendel had been drinking, they said, and he stumbled in front of a car drunk. His clothes were soaked in whisky. It was late at night, they said, and the driver was confused about what he saw."

"Did Mendel drink often?"

"A little wine at celebrations. Never whiskey."

I looked up and down the street. The houses were old but large, divided into apartments. Half a block south, there was a five-story brick apartment building. Hundreds of people lived within sight of the Rubensteins'.

"Surely someone saw this?"

"The Rakanti sisters. They live across the street; Greeks. They heard the car, the loud voices, and thought it odd for a Sabbath night. So they came to the window. They saw the men take him away. Also Levi Messer. He and his son, Adam, were on their front porch talking and enjoying the cool of the evening when the men came. Levi heard Mendel yelling and came down to the edge of the street. Before he could do anything, they drove off."

"What type of car was it?"

Ostein eyed me. "Why do you want to know?"

"If Rubenstein was murdered, we need to force the police to investigate."

He stood quietly for a moment and then nodded. "There were two cars. One, a black Ford, older, maybe a Model A. The other was a dark Plymouth sedan."

"Like the one mentioned in the newspaper?"

"Exactly. These men were strangers. *Goyem*. Mendel had not been here long. He and Rachel are refugees from Germany; they left everything behind. He worked at Rich's; the Rich family has been very helpful to refugees, but he had no friends other than in this neighborhood."

Ostein looked down and toed a loose plank on the porch. I waited.

"For the most part," he said, "we are left alone. I know there are those in America who hate Jews, but they seem to be few. This, though, this frightens me."

"Rubenstein hated the Nazis?"

"Of course. They took away his livelihood, destroyed his family, killed his brother."

"On Friday, he assaulted the Germans in town for this Baptist Alliance meeting. Do you know anything about that?"

"No," he said.

I told him what had happened outside the Henry Grady Hotel. He leaned back, tugging on his beard.

"Perhaps Mendel would do something like that," he said slowly. "Yes, he might have done it. Manure, you say? So, do you think the Nazis murdered him over some manure?"

"Murdered?" said Emma. "But why?"

"That's what I want to know. Why kill the guy? He was no threat."

We sat in the afternoon heat on the front porch of her boarding house. A light breeze blew, cooling us. Rocking our chairs gently, we talked while muted classical music from the radio drifted out of the house. It had all the hallmarks of a normal, lazy, late Sunday afternoon in summer, except for the subject of our conversation.

"The men who attacked us were dressed as policemen," she said.

"Emma, they were policemen."

"And the men who took Rubenstein were dressed in street clothes?"

"That's what I was told. Big men, rough."

"Police, maybe? Just not in uniform?"

"Good question. I'm starting to feel lost, like I'm in the middle of one of those Dashiell Hammett stories. A dozen possibilities, but no way to sort them out."

Emma rocked vigorously, chewing absently on her lower lip. "I think your friend Phil is on to something. Maybe the Germans, the police, and the Ku Klux Klan are connected. That would explain the police attacking us for asking questions about German Messengers, and it would explain the men who took away Rubenstein. Given our limited information, it is the best theory using Occam's razor."

"Whose razor?"

"Occam's razor. Mark, goodness, what did they teach you at that Ivy League school? You know, when choosing between theoretical explanations, the simplest theory is probably the best one? We have to explain why the Klan would attack an obscure Jewish immigrant. The simple answer is that they were asked by the Germans to punish him for the hotel assault. The same if we try to explain why policemen attacked you. Most policemen belong to the Klan, and the Klan may have been told to discourage questions about the Germans. Thus, we can posit a connection between the Ku Klux Klan, the Atlanta Police, and the Germans. QED."

I laughed. "Okay. So, even if the Germans can ask the Klan for favors, I'm still confused. How would that work? These guys are foreigners, and the Klan stands for 100 percent Americanism. They hate foreigners."

"Well, the two groups share similar philosophies, don't they? Particularly about the sources of the problems in our world. Both argue that moral collapse has caused cultural decline. Traditional values have been undermined by rootless cosmopolitans and international trade. They see the Jews as international agents of financial exploitation and decay. Given this, both believe racial purity must be enforced to protect us. And both groups support collective violence to destroy social immorality and to take power. Actually, it makes sense they'd work together."

"But the Nazis govern a major nation. I've visited Germany. It's a highly cultured country, with great literature, science, and music. Klansmen are a bunch of yokels."

Emma took a moment to gather her thoughts. "Many Nazis are prejudiced bully boys like the Klansmen you're thinking about. But not all Klansmen are what you think. You'd be surprised. Important people, decent people, people you would like, have belonged to and supported the Klan. They agree with the Klan's message; fight to preserve the good things being destroyed by the forces of modernism, liberalism, internationalism, and secularism. And Klansmen might see the Nazis as an example of how they can regain power."

"You mean like the 1920s?"

"Why not? Fifteen years ago, the Klan had millions of members and controlled state legislatures across the country, as far west as Washington State. Two governors of Georgia were openly Klansmen."

"How do you know so much about the Ku Klux Klan?"

She stopped rocking and glared at me. "What do you think I do all day? I used to work at a major library. Now I interview people or edit interviews from all across the state. I've read about hundreds of people's lives and talked with dozens of people, from rich businessmen to impoverished ex-slaves. I know what they think, what they've done, what they've seen. I know what they believe about their world and why. Even the best newspaper reporters can't hold a candle to the number of interviews I've conducted, heard, or edited."

"So, working for the WPA is a great education?"

"Damn right," she said belligerently, and began to rock again.

"Talking with Negroes and old people?"

She stopped rocking abruptly. "Mark Morgan, you're bigoted, just plain bigoted. What do you know about being Colored? You have no idea what these people have suffered, how poor they are, the struggles they face. You whine about how hard it is losing your $4,000-a-year job, about how tough times are in this depression, when you live in a fine building with indoor plumbing, own a nice car, and have plenty to eat. You don't know a damn thing about being poor. My God, have you ever had a real conversation with a Negro?"

That stung. I sat silently for a moment. "How did I get into this?"

"By speaking without thinking. Always think first."

"I'm sorry," I said.

"You should be. Most of us don't even notice the Negroes; we act like they don't exist except when we want their work. You wouldn't believe the stories I've heard."

"I'm just upset, Emma. This investigation—it's a mess, a disaster. The Germans, the cops, and now poor Rubenstein. Why did I get involved?"

"Greed," she said. "You're involved because you let an unreasonable amount of money sway your judgment."

"But, I know better."

"Oh," she said. "I understand all too well. I felt it Friday night when I held that money in my hands. Enough to make you secure for years. Always a place to live. Always food to eat. No more uncertainty, no more fear. That kind of money has real power."

We rocked a bit more and slowly calmed down. The heat of the afternoon brought on a summertime lassitude. We watched people walk by as we listened to bird calls and the occasional rattle and bell of the trolley over on Marietta Street.

The screen door opened and closed, and a short, heavy man with thinning gray hair stepped onto the porch. Well past fifty, he wore an old-fashioned brown three-piece suit despite the heat. A gold watch chain ran across his ample belly into a vest pocket.

"Good afternoon, Miss Connor," he said.

"Professor Wimberly. Good afternoon to you, sir." Emma gestured toward me. "Professor, this is my good friend, Mark Morgan. Mark, this is my landlord, Professor Orin Wimberly."

I stood and shook hands. He took a pipe from his jacket pocket, placed it between his teeth, and began the long process of lighting it. "Sit down, sit down," he said around the pipe and the smoke. When it was drawing to his satisfaction, he smiled down at us. "Ah, so you are the man who took Emma dancing?"

"Yes, sir."

"You'd best treat Miss Connor well. She's our surrogate daughter."

"Professor," chided Emma.

"Yes, sir," I said. "I will treat her as well as she allows."

Emma made a face at me.

"Good, good," he said, puffing smoke.

"Do you teach at Tech?" I asked.

"I do, I do," he said, fiddling more with the pipe. "Physics and mathematics." He pulled out a gold pocket watch and glanced at it. "Well, I'm off. Have to check on the lab, you know. Don't dare leave students to their own devices, or they'll blow themselves up."

He walked slowly down the steps and headed toward campus, pipe in his teeth. Emma smiled. "He always says he has to check on the lab. I think it just gets him out of the house, away from Mrs. Wimberly for a while."

"Seems like a nice guy," I said.

She rocked a bit more, then halted abruptly. "When do you see the blond bombshell again? The one that looks like Clark Gable's new wife?"

"That's what's bothering you?"

"I just want to know."

"Well, I'll probably see her tomorrow. I need to talk with her about some of the German Messengers. She may help me untangle which ones are spies or policemen."

"You're a fool, Mark Morgan. You should trust none of these Nazis. Remember, it's not just men who work for the Gestapo."

5

Monday, July 24, 1939

The trolley out to the Ponce de Leon Ballpark was packed and slowed by traffic. By the time we arrived, the meeting had begun, though hundreds still poured through the gates. Banners above read, "A free Church in a free state," and "All believers have a right to equality in Church." Inside, several men checked credentials. One was young and wearing a black suit with a lapel ribbon that read "Usher."

"My name's Mark Morgan," I said, handing him a business card. "I'm consulting with the German Messengers while they visit Atlanta, and Dr. Otto Erlanger asked me to attend briefly today. To get the lay of the land."

"I don't know," said the fellow, wiping his forehead with a handkerchief. "It's gettin' pretty crowded down there."

"I don't need a seat. I'll stand up here with you."

"How long you gonna stay?"

"An hour or so. I want to see where they sit and how events proceed."

"Yeah, buddy, well, it's not just hot up here; things are heating up down there. You might have chosen an interesting day. When folks got here this morning, all the signs for the Colored section were gone. The leaders want Messengers to mix with no regard for race. Breaks a city ordinance, but the mayor said to allow it."

"Really?"

"Yeah. All men are brothers in Christ. I don't have a problem with it, but there's plenty who do."

The ballpark where the Atlanta Crackers played wasn't Yankee Stadium, but it seated over 20,000. Organizers had doubled the capacity by filling the playing field with chairs and benches. I pitied those sitting on the field under the blazing July sun. The stage up front had a canvas roof over it to shade the bigwigs. A voice boomed from huge amplifiers, and there was an echo under the stands. I stepped forward until I had a full view of the throng and could hear more clearly. The usher followed me.

"Where do the Germans usually sit?"

"Down there on the field, to the right of the podium. There are hundreds of 'em. When this Brit finishes, one of the Germans will speak." The usher handed me a program. The current speaker's topic was "Christianity and the Totalitarian State."

"Tyranny and evangelical Christianity cannot exist together," boomed his voice. He denounced the governments of Japan, Italy, Romania, and the Soviet Union for their oppression. After that, he turned to Nazi Germany. Condemning the oppression of Jews and limits on free speech and assembly in Germany, the speaker read a proposed resolution.

"We condemn all racial animosity, and every form of oppression or unfair discrimination toward the Jews, Colored people, or the subject races in any part of the world."

There was a stir in the crowd, both boos and cheers.

"Told you it was heating up," said the usher.

Otto Erlanger rose. Even from so far away, his thick white hair and height stood out; an authoritative-looking fellow. He moved toward the stage, followed by Rolf, the secret policeman. Two other Germans joined Rolf, and they waited at the side of the stage while Erlanger hesitantly climbed the steps.

The speaker gestured toward the Germans, then concluded his speech by saying, "Surely there are enough Christians in Germany to reach the soul of Hitler. And in Italy to reach the soul of Mussolini, and in Russia to reach the soul of Stalin . . ."

"If those guys even have souls," quipped the usher.

The Brit stepped away with a standing ovation.

"Dr. Otto Erlanger from Essen, Germany," said the announcer. Erlanger moved toward the microphone but waited silently as the crowd continued to clap and cheer the Brit's words. Then, in his deep, resonant voice and perfect English, Erlanger spoke.

"I have been asked to respond to my beloved brother in Christ. On the conditions for Baptists in Germany today." He paused, gazing across the audience, then glanced at the Germans standing by the stage. "The best approach for this gathering—the Christlike approach—is to maintain a position of neutrality. Render unto Caesar that which is Caesar's. We must follow the laws of our countries and continue to spread the gospel where and how we can. Political neutrality is crucial to spreading the gospel. Political conflict accomplishes nothing. Political agitation accomplishes nothing. Such things only impede our work of spreading the good news. I admire the United States and the Neutrality Act. Such laws are the best way for the world to avoid war. As for my work in Germany, while I am not a Nazi, there have been no limitations, no threats, no problems for me as a minister. This is the truth of Germany today."

A few in the crowd clapped. Erlanger glanced over toward the three Germans who stood next to the stage. The man in the middle nodded. Erlanger continued, "For a fuller response, I introduce Pastor Schmidt from Berlin." And with that, he stepped away. One man came to the microphone, and the other two walked Erlanger away from the platform.

Schmidt offered a complete denunciation of the Brit's speech, but I was more interested in the stir among the Germans when Rolf led Erlanger away. They climbed to the Messenger's exit, and I dropped back into the shade of the stands as he passed. Rolf spotted in the darkness under the stands, smiled, and mimed shooting me with a pistol. He put his hand on Erlanger's back and pushed him through the exit.

"The organizers didn't expect such strong words about fascism and race," said the usher. "But the Messengers have pushed for it."

"Has it been like this every day?"

"It's been building. Most speakers argue Baptists must pursue peace. Support religious freedom, political freedom, and democracy. Speakers from Hungary, Romania, and Germany have said that's too political. That the world has mistaken ideas about the conditions in their countries. But you can tell who's winning. They've already desegregated the meetings."

I thanked him and turned to follow Erlanger. At the gate, a young woman handed me a broadsheet, the title of which read, "If Christ Came Back to Germany." I tucked it into my pocket. Erlanger and Rolf were walking east on Ponce de Leon, so I followed. Rolf held Erlanger's arm and pulled him along to the streetcar stop, where they waited. I paused, anonymous on the crowded sidewalk, until they boarded an inbound trolley.

I caught the next in-town streetcar. It was only half full, so I took a seat and pulled out the broadsheet. A German who rejected Germany's race laws wrote it. She condemned those who said they believed in Adolf Hitler, expressed pity for those who hid their beliefs, and admired those who fought the regime. "I think," she wrote, "Jesus would make a pilgrimage out to a concentration camp where a man named Martin Niemoeller sits in a dark cell because he dared to fight for Christ in the open."

Was my cynicism about the meeting misplaced? I thought of the Baptists as obsessed with banning alcohol and dancing. But here were Messengers from sixty countries taking up the cause of justice and freedom. Trying to make the world a better place. It gave me pause.

Back at my room, I was still mulling over the Baptist meeting when I thought. Why not talk it over with Emma?

It was half-past eleven, so I phoned her office.

"Lunch?" she said. "Okay, at the Henry Grady?"

"No, not there. I think the Rathskeller in the basement of the Ansley Hotel would be better. Get me away from all these Germans; they're wearing on me."

"Sounds good. Meet at quarter past twelve?"

"Sure," I said.

I was mistaken about the Rathskeller. At least a dozen Germans were there, undoubtedly attracted by the name. It was under the lobby, the low ceiling held up by hefty brick pillars, every bit a cellar. But the food was American fare, not German. Even the beer was American, much to the Germans' vocal disappointment. Emma arrived a little late, flushed from hurrying in the heat.

"Too many darn people on the streets; it was hard to walk through the crowds," she said. Sitting opposite me, she had a view toward the door. We were considering the menu when she looked up and said, "Oh my, is that her?"

I swiveled around. Anna Erlanger, with three other men, waited for a table. As usual, Anna shone brightly.

"You're right, she looks like Carole Lombard," said Emma. "Why isn't she at the ballpark?"

"She's not a Messenger; her husband, Otto, is. I heard him speak briefly this morning."

"Odd she wouldn't go to the meeting and support him." Emma's eyes followed Anna as she and her companions took a table. "Uh-oh, I think they recognized you."

"Listen," I said. "There was the oddest thing at the ballpark. After a British speaker condemned totalitarian regimes, especially that of Germany, Erlanger gave a rebuttal. He called for Baptist neutrality on political issues and respect for the laws of their own countries. Some German fellows, including Rolf, the secret policeman, watched him closely while he spoke. Erlanger kept glancing over to them, as if seeking approval. Afterward, Rolf led him out of the meeting. He didn't handle him gently."

"That's odd," said Emma, "considering he's a prominent minister in Germany."

"It's even odder because when I first met him, Erlanger had nothing good to say about Hitler. Said Hitler was leading the world toward fire and blood, if I remember right. A war more terrible than the World War, he said. His wife, Anna, disagreed."

"Husbands and wives often disagree. So, what's good on this menu?"

A waiter took our orders, and we chatted.

"What a great time we had at the Rainbow Roof," I said.

"It wasn't so great afterward. How's your head?" Without my hat on, everyone could see the shaved patch and stitches. Suddenly, Emma's eyes went wide.

"Mark, good afternoon. I didn't know you'd hurt your head," said a voice I knew in German. Anna stood next to me. She'd come over to our table.

Emma smiled thinly as I stood up.

"No, Mark, sit, sit," said Anna. I sat, and Anna sat with us.

"What's she saying?" asked Emma.

"She is just saying hello," I explained, "and asking about my head."

"Emma Connor, this is Anna Erlanger," I said. Anna flashed a supercilious smile for only a second. Clearly rude, but Emma rallied.

"Mark heard your husband speak this morning," she said.

"What does she say?" asked Anna.

"I went to the ballpark this morning. Your husband responded to a British speaker's criticisms of Germany. It surprised me, given what he said about Hitler when we met at the Lowders' house. Hitler wants fire and blood, I think he said."

Anna looked at me. "Was Rolf Schulman there? Wilhelm Kunst?"

"Rolf was. I don't know Kunst."

"Kunst is a Messenger from Hamburg. You wouldn't like him."

"Well," I said, "Rolf escorted your husband out of the meeting after he spoke. Seemed to have him on a tight rein, in fact."

"Mark, what are you saying?" Emma asked. I began to explain, but Anna interrupted me.

"Rolf is worse than we feared. He has already threatened several Messengers. All must follow the party line, he says. Any variation, and they and their families will be punished. Otto said Rolf threatened to do vile things to me if he didn't cooperate, do exactly and speak exactly as directed."

I translated for Emma, who sat back in her chair. Emma said, "Tell her that's because Nazis are vile."

"So, this girl thinks Germans are vile?" Anna said before I translated. She looked Emma up and down. Emma wore her WPA work clothes: a dowdy green blouse, black skirt, glasses, no jewelry, her hair in an untidy bun.

"Mark," said Anna in German, "I'm surprised a man like you would even sit with such a woman. Skinny, big ears, no fashion sense. She looks just like Olive Oyl in the Popeye cartoon. Just as shrill too."

"What did she say?" said Emma.

Anna leaned forward, looked Emma in the eye, and said clearly, "Olive Oyl."

I walked Emma back to her office. "I almost punched the witch. I know what she meant; you don't have to soft-pedal it."

"I honestly don't understand," I said.

"Oh, Mark. She was staking her claim. Women use words, not punches."

"But she has no claim on me. I mean, our relationship is professional. Nothing more."

Emma chuckled. "That's what you think. How you got this far in life while remaining so clueless about simple things astonishes me. For whatever reason, she wanted you to look at me and think, Oh, Emma does look like the skinny, flat-chested, babbling, and problematic Olive Oyl. Far better to be with glamorous Carole Lombard."

"Why on earth? I'm not her beau. Besides, if she wants something, she's not likely to get it by insulting my friend."

"Being called Olive Oyl isn't so bad. Remember, whenever Sinbad, or whoever grabs Olive, she fights back. She's spunky, even if she needs Popeye to rescue her all the time."

"All that distracted me. Listen, when Rolf led Erlanger out, he held him by the arm, as if dealing with a prisoner. Anna said Rolf has threatened Messengers, demanding they toe the government line. Maybe I can get her to tell me more. Maybe warn her too. Phil thinks the Nazis are behind the Rubenstein killing. She needs to know that."

Emma paused at the elevator. "Mark, something feels completely wrong about this woman."

When I walked into the Henry Grady, the desk clerk motioned me over. "You're Mr. Morgan, aren't you? There's a message for you."

It was from Anna, and used "Du," the more familiar, rather than the formal.

"Dr. Erlanger asks you to join us for dinner this evening. There will be other Messengers there eager to meet you. The dinner will be at the restaurant called Parsifal, Peachtree and Tenth Street, at seven o'clock. Looking forward to our time together. Anna."

What an opportunity, I thought. A chance to listen and learn more about these Germans. And, Emma was right; I wanted to spend more time with the stunning Anna.

I left a note accepting the invitation and then went back to my rooms at the Athletic Club. Moments after I arrived, the room phone rang.

"You should get an answering service," said Rabbi Goldstein. "I've been trying to reach you all day."

"I've been out, can't do this from my room."

"Where can we meet?"

I glanced at my watch. It was almost two-thirty. "Your call. I have dinner plans tonight."

"The Arcade Restaurant?"

"Is three soon enough?"

"Meet me at four," said the rabbi before hanging up.

The Arcade was nearby on Luckie Street. I dropped by the library to check the daily papers and found nothing more on Rubenstein's death. When I walked the few blocks to the Arcade, I had to push through crowds on the sidewalks and dodge crazy traffic. No wonder Emma had complained. Most of the Baptist Messengers were from small cities and towns, and Monday afternoon was time off while the ballpark was prepared for a grand Baptist pageant that night. These folks were out to gawk at the big city.

The Arcade was crowded, and I had to wait for Rabbi Goldstein, who showed up ten minutes late. "Impossible traffic," he said, sitting and glancing at the menu.

He ordered a smoked salmon sandwich, and I ordered an RC Cola. "So, where's the fire?" I asked.

The rabbi took a letter from his coat pocket. Addressed to the manager of the Henry Grady Hotel and printed in large block letters, the author gave an ominous warning:

I WILL KILL THE GERMANS ONE BY ONE. GOD SAYS I MUST WARN YOU. THE ANGEL OF DEATH!

"A new letter from this guy?"

"Charming missives from a charming fellow." Again, there was a hint of an accent, but I couldn't put a finger on it.

"Do we move the Germans from the hotel?"

"Where? No hotel in Atlanta has room."

"The police should see this."

"No." He pushed the message toward me. "Show it to the German security team. Who are the policemen and spies among them?"

"Rolf Schulman is probably Gestapo. Apparently, he has threatened Messengers with punishment if they step out of line. Paul Dittmer may be another, though my source insists he's a legitimate Messenger. Kunst, Hess, perhaps others. I'll know more tonight."

The rabbi waited silently for a moment after I stopped speaking.

"That's it?" he said, his tone rising.

"For now."

"My God, man, you've had over three days. You should know all of these Germans. Among three hundred Nazis, there must be at least a dozen secret agents, policemen, and spies. The Germans live in a world of informers and police."

"Perhaps they merely spy on each other?"

"Of course they do. They're Nazis, after all. But they're always surrounded by police." His sandwich arrived, and he took a bite. "Let me tell you what you will do," he said while chewing angrily. "First, identify all the security agents among the Germans. That's essential. Find out who's Gestapo, who's Abwehr, who's from the SD."

I took a long sip from my RC and watched Goldstein bite into his salmon sandwich again. Chewing, he looked up.

"The Abwehr is not a police organization," I said. "It's German military intelligence; they're spies. I don't know the SD."

"Sicherheitsdienst, thus SD. Internal counterintelligence and political security for the Nazi Party, part of the SS. You at least know what the SS is, don't you?"

"Yes, I know what the SS is," I said, switching to German.

"Good," said the rabbi, also in German. "Then you know what you must do. Find these spies. Tell me who they are. In particular, I want to know which ones are SD? Find the SD men; that is the most important. It is quite simple."

The rabbi bit his sandwich violently, wrenching out a portion of smoked salmon and chewing vigorously.

"How do I contact you?

"I will call you at your room number tomorrow morning at nine o'clock. You should have the information. We paid you well. Too well, it appears."

"That's what you really wanted, isn't it? You wanted me to identify the German police and spies." I put a quarter on the table and stood.

"I need the names," repeated the rabbi.

On the street outside, I almost laughed, but that's when it hit me. Because I'd worked so hard on my own German, I was good at noticing accents. The rabbi covered it well when he spoke English, but in German, he spoke with a British accent.

Parsifal was a restaurant in the developing uptown, out past the Georgian Terrace Hotel. A second-generation Bavarian family owned it and served authentic food. Cheap prints of knights and castles and damsels in distress decorated the walls. A glass case held old, shabby books by Schiller and Goethe. There was a cartoonish mural of the Alps on the back wall. You didn't go there for the art.

There were nine of us. Anna and her grim husband. Rolf Schulman, of course, and Paul Dittmer. Among those I had not met, Horst Hess was from Munich and gloried in the menu. He was in his twenties and wore a cheap brown department store suit with a gray Homburg hat that did not match. Despite this, there was something rather engaging about him.

Nothing was engaging about Wilhelm Kunst. He was past forty, tall, with a crooked nose and broad shoulders. From Hamburg, he dressed with a sophisticated air, but carried himself like an aging street tough.

Artur Sandoval was quiet. A minister from Mannheim, he was born in Hungary and spoke German with a heavy accent.

Finally, there was Peter Goss, a thin, blond man, boyish, almost childlike. From Berlin, he seemed ill at ease, constantly removing and polishing his round gold wire-rimmed glasses.

Anna wore a black dress that contrasted beautifully with her hair. Unlike the dresses I'd seen previously, this one tightly followed her form and displayed a hint of décolleté. Eye shadow and a touch of lipstick were her concession to makeup; that and her deadly perfume, stronger now, dark, and wicked. The men at the table struggled to keep their eyes off her, but her husband ignored her, never touched her. His only contribution to the conversation was to insist we pray before the meal. Otherwise, he sat silently, watching.

"This menu is very good, very homelike," said Hess. "I will order for all; you must trust me."

"Let us hope the food is as good as the promise," said Kunst, staring at me. "And you, Mr. Morgan, why are you here?"

"Dr. Erlanger and I invited him," said Anna.

I smiled and spread out my hands, with my palms up. "What could I do when invited by such a beautiful woman?"

There followed an endless parade of würst and cabbage, pork and potatoes. Huge steins of beer arrived, and only Anna and Otto Erlanger abstained. Teetotal Baptists were evidently not the norm in this group. Hess, who pronounced the food and beer excellent, told a feeble joke, and the table chuckled. Muted conversation followed. No one said anything about politics, religion, or asked questions about Atlanta.

I tried to start conversations, but it was difficult. When I asked about the conference, I got only brief answers. I had to ask directly which committees or subcommittees each man served on. Rolf Schulman seemed confused by the concept, and Kunst shook his head in exasperation.

"I understand there were some fireworks at the ballpark today," I said.

"Fireworks?" said Hess. "I heard nothing."

"Horst," said Dittmer. "He means the controversy. The Alliance President, the Britisher, raised questions about the Führer's racial policies."

Suddenly, Dr. Erlanger spoke. "Remember the parable of the Samaritan woman at the well. Even the despised are included in God's kingdom."

"Enough," said Kunst, glancing at me. "This is to be a pleasant meal. No religion, no politics."

"No religion? Isn't that why you Baptists are here?" I said.

"We are here to eat," said Kunst.

Everyone turned to their food, and silence reigned. Frustrated by the reticence of my dinner companions, I decided to shake things up, see what popped out.

"I remember a joke I heard in Berlin," I said. "Back in '36."

"Yes, yes, the joke from Berlin," said Hess loudly. He had drunk more beer than anyone and seemed to be the only person determined to have a good time.

"Goering was driving Hitler down a road through a farming district at night. They were speeding because they were late for a Party meeting. They came around a curve and hit a pig, killing it. Goering stopped the car."

"'What should we do?' Goering asked."

"'We have said we are friends of the farmer,' said Hitler. 'You must go tell this farmer what has happened and settle up. Here's some money.'"

"So, with that, Goering took Hitler's money and went up the hill to the farmhouse. Hitler waited and waited. Ten minutes passed, twenty minutes, then thirty. Finally, forty-five minutes later, Goering staggered back to the car, drunk."

"'Hermann, what happened?' asked Hitler."

"'I'm not sure, my Führer,' Goering said. 'I went to the door, and when the farmer opened it, I said, "Heil, Hitler. The pig is dead." He pulled me into the room, broke out the schnapps, and we have been dancing to the radio ever since.'"

No one laughed. Anna covered her mouth with her hand, but her eyes showed shock. Peter Goss looked terrified. Hess glanced at Kunst, clearly deferring, waiting. Finally, Kunst spoke.

"This you would not hear in Berlin today," he said.

"It's only a joke. We tell many jokes about President Roosevelt, and even more about his wife. It hurts no one."

"Perhaps in America," said Peter Goss quietly.

"But not in Germany?" I asked, feigning innocence.

"Mr. Morgan," said Kunst, "Adolf Hitler has saved the German people. We were falling into chaos, perhaps even communism, before he exerted his will. Now, we are building a new, greater Germany."

"How is it new?"

"There is order," said Rolf Schulman.

"A cleansed Germany," said Kunst. "This is hard for an American to understand, but your society is polluted. You have no meaningful culture and are producing a mongrel people."

After that, there was silence. I had let the air out of the balloon, but I had also learned some things. Kunst thought Rolf Schulman was a dunderhead. Dittmer was quiet, controlled. Peter Goss feared everyone, as did Hess. Anna was silent, an outsider. All ignored Dr. Erlanger, which explained his sour expression. Most importantly, Wilhelm Kunst was top dog.

Dinner came to a dismal close. Before leaving, I went to the bathroom. Goss stood at the sink, washing his hands.

"Mr. Morgan," he whispered. "I must speak with you tonight. Will you please come to my room, number 609? Later, maybe midnight?"

"609," I said, meeting his eyes. "Midnight."

The Erlangers took a taxi to the Lowders' home. The others taxied to the hotel. I drove back alone. The lights of the theater district shone brightly, perhaps trying to attract adventurous Baptists to a late movie or show. I waited at Lane's Drugstore next to Loews Grand Theatre with three hours to kill. Sitting at the counter, I grabbed the evening newspaper and drank coffee while I read.

The theaters weren't having much luck. Baptists were the wrong crowd for a late show on Monday night. Soon, I was the only customer in the shop. The counterman kept my cup full, and we chatted about some stories in the paper. He said he'd be happy if he never saw another Baptist again. We laughed. At midnight, I thanked the counterman, left a two-dollar tip, and crossed to the Henry Grady.

The sixth-floor corridor was dark, with mahogany-colored wainscoting, worn gold carpet, and dim lights in yellowed sconces along the wall. The odors of stale tobacco and ammonia cleaner lingered. At 609, I knocked. Goss opened the door and looked up and down the hallway.

"Inside," he said. "Please."

I stepped in, and he closed the door. Faded, flowered chintz curtains covered the windows, pulled tightly closed. Two small matching prints of flowers hung on the walls, and a stain in the shape of Africa decorated the ceiling. At least lying on the bed looking at it might be entertaining. The door to the bathroom was open; no one lurked in there. Goss motioned toward the desk chair.

"Sit, please," he said, whispering. He was just under my height, but very slight. His eyes blinked rapidly behind his glasses and darted around the room.

"Mr. Morgan, I do not want to return to Germany. I would like to stay in the United States."

A little surprised, I took a moment to answer. "Stay here? Don't you have family, a church, at home?"

"No." His hair was long on top but cut short on the sides. He ran his fingers through his thick hair nervously. "Well, of course, there are my parents. But I am not married."

"And you are not afraid for them? What about your church?"

"This is more important than my parents. I must stay in the United States."

"There are laws, limitations on the number of immigrants, and that sort of thing. I don't know much other than staying in America can be complicated."

"But aren't you with the American security? I heard you tell Dittmer that on Friday. Like the FBI, yes? Surely the FBI could help me. I know things. Important things. Things you could not imagine."

"Are you Gestapo? Abwehr?"

He looked down, fumbled in his jacket that hung on the back of a chair, and finally came out with a silver cigarette case. There was just one loosie in it. He took his time lighting up.

"I am supposed to say I'm *Sicherheitsdienst*, SD—but I'm not, really."

"If you aren't, who is?"

"Everyone." He must have seen my doubt. "No, it's true. Everyone at dinner—they are all Abwehr or SD. Competitors, you see; the two groups do not work together. Except for Dr. Erlanger. Like me, he is forced to cooperate."

"Rolf Schulman is SD, not Gestapo?"

"Schulman is SD."

"Why are you supposed to say you are SD?"

"Wilhelm Kunst," he said. "Kunst forced me to help him. Here, I will show you."

He put his cigarette in the ashtray, picked up a large steamer trunk, and put it on the bed. Opening it, he pointed.

"I did not need so much room for my clothes." He picked up the cigarette and drew deeply, then put it back in the ashtray. His hand shook. "They made me use this trunk. Look, there's a false bottom."

I stepped forward to look. He moved a small lever. The corner of the trunk's floor lifted slightly. Goss grabbed it and pulled the floor out. Underneath was a large space, perhaps two by five feet, and about six inches deep.

"See," he said. "They hid it here."

"Hid what?"

"Money. American dollars. Lots of it." He took out his wallet and showed five one-hundred-dollar bills. "When they collected the money, Kunst gave me these. He said it was my reward for serving the Reich."

I inspected the bills, then handed them back. "This space was full of hundred-dollar bills?"

"Nearly. There were also two pistols and other small items."

I looked at the trunk and wondered how many hundred-dollar bills would fill about four cubic feet. A lot, I decided. "Who took the money?"

"Kunst. He and Schulman. They took it all away. This was in New York."

"Why you? Why did they have you bring it?"

"Kunst learned I intended to leave Germany. This was the price of not reporting me. Perhaps they thought to sacrifice me if the money was discovered?"

"I don't understand," I said. "How could they make you do this?"

Goss seemed to reach a decision. "I'm a scientist, a physicist. For the past three years, I worked at the Kaiser Wilhelm Institute with Otto Hahn and Lise Meitner. Our research revealed frightening possibilities, so Lise and I decided we had to leave. She is now in Sweden."

"Why didn't you go to Sweden?"

Goss sat on the bed. "Normally, leaving Germany would be easy. I would just attend a scientific conference in Holland or England and simply not return. Many friends left Germany that way. But I waited too long. The government now controls foreign travel by scientists. Too many were leaving, you see. Attending such conferences is now forbidden." He reached for the cigarette, but found only a dead nub. "Then a friend told me about this Baptist meeting."

"Go on," I said.

"The regime might prevent scientists from traveling, but they encourage attendance at other types of conferences. This makes them appear tolerant in the eyes of the world. In that case, I could just be a simple Messenger going overseas, not a scientist. I pooled my savings; I sought a needy church in Berlin and paid them to elect me Messenger. After that, I planned it right so I would never have to return to Germany."

"A clever solution."

"Perhaps too clever. Somehow, someone knew. This is how Germany is now; someone always knows. Not long after I made arrangements with the church, Kunst appeared. This is how they work, yes? He threatened to expose me if I didn't cooperate, send me to a camp, a KZ. You know what this is?"

"I know about the concentration camps. Is Kunst from the Gestapo?"

"No," he said. "I already explained that he is SD. The Gestapo would have simply arrested me. I'd be in Dachau or Sachsenhausen now, where work would make me free." He smiled grimly and opened his cigarette case, only to find it empty. He snapped it shut, irritated.

"So, Kunst knew you were a scientist trying to leave?"

"No, he does not. All Kunst knows is that a Baptist Messenger named Goss made plans not to return to Germany. That is illegal in itself. He offered me a deal. Instead of arresting me, he would have me transport certain items for him. If I did all that he asked, when we finished in America, he would allow me to go my own way. Now I no longer think he will honor the deal. There is something not quite right."

"Who else knows you're here?"

"No one in Germany. I wrote to colleagues in Sweden, Denmark, England, and the United States. In the United States, I wrote to Richard Roberts at the Carnegie Institution in Washington and Enrico Fermi in New York."

"You sent letters? Didn't you think the police would read them?"

"Of course. But I said nothing in them about physics, and I was careful not to reveal my intentions. Also, Peter Goss is not my real name; I purchased the papers of a dead church member. Meanwhile, as far as the Regime knows, the real me is on a hiking holiday in the Alps. If I don't return, who knows what happened? Perhaps I crossed to Switzerland?" He smiled broadly, expecting me to join him.

"What is your real name?"

Goss smiled broadly and shook his head.

"How will the recipients of your letters know you were coming to America?"

"We have worked these things out, we scientists have. You may contact Fermi; he will explain."

"And you wrote to England?"

"I wrote to colleagues who did graduate work with me. They are now at the Cavendish Laboratory. They wrote back, urging me to come, promising friends of theirs who could help."

"You wrote this in a letter?" I asked, astonished. "Just the addresses alone would have told the police something was up."

"The letters went to cutouts, and I used code. We have done this for years to communicate. We are not fools."

"Any code can be broken," I said. "It's just a process of mathematics."

"It would be very hard to break this code. Physicists know a bit about math."

"So, why haven't you run to England, to these men you wrote?"

"On the ship, where could I run? In America, Kunst and the others watch me closely. There has been no chance to escape. Until now. This is the time, and you are my chance."

The telephone rang. Startled, Goss jumped up and stared at it. Finally, on the third ring, he answered.

"*Ja?*" he said carefully. He listened, concern creasing his forehead. "It is very late, and I am already in bed. Perhaps in the morning?" He listened for a moment. "Very well, but I must dress. I'll be there in ten minutes."

He hung up, went to the closet, and began pulling out clothes. "I must leave. They will kill me."

"Who will?"

"Kunst, Schulman. You must help me, Mr. Morgan." He grabbed my arm, pulling me close. "Help me," he begged.

"You told them ten minutes? We'll go now."

He grabbed his toothbrush from the bathroom and started collecting his clothes.

"No. You don't have time." I handed him his jacket and stuck my head out the door. The hallway was empty. I spotted the entrance to the stairwell.

"Let's go," I said, pushing him into the hallway.

"But what about my things?"

"No time. Go."

We rushed down the hall and opened the door to the stairwell. It was dimly lit, but the first thing we saw was Rolf Schulman.

"My God," said Goss. He turned and fled down the stairs. I stood frozen. Schulman didn't move. In fact, he would never move again. He lay in an untidy heap on the landing, his throat cut from ear to ear.

6

TUESDAY, JULY 25, 1939

Atlanta police headquarters was possibly the ugliest building in the city. Built during the Romanesque Revival period, fifty years of soot and grime coated it. The architects had put grim Italianate bastions on either side of a tall tower and mixed Romanesque entryways with Gothic columns and Moorish arched windows. All in red brick and white stone—an appalling mélange of the worst Victorian architectural fashions.

The small, windowless holding room was in the east bastion. It had stained plaster walls, a scarred wooden table, and four chairs bolted to the floor. A shaded light hung from the ceiling. The door was locked; I'd tried it. At least I wasn't cuffed to the chair.

I waited, paced, and thought. Around 3 a.m., a thunderstorm broke with such violence I could hear the pounding rain even in the windowless room. A few minutes later, two dripping plainclothes detectives opened the door. They were not happy.

"Raining out?" I asked.

"Funny feller," said the first in a strong mountain accent. His eyes were brown, muddy, tired, set in a narrow face with sharply defined cheekbones. He dropped a heavy file ostentatiously onto the table. "Sit your ass down."

I sat. The second detective closed the door and stood in front of it. The first flipped open the file. I waited. At one point, he grunted and marked a page. Finally, he reached the end and looked up at me. He clenched his jaw.

"I'm Detective Garrett Hancock. My partner here is Bill Rawson. You're in deep trouble, Mr. Morgan."

"Aw, hell, Garrett, give the fellow a chance."

"A chance? Bill, you know how serious this is."

"Come on," said Rawson, moving over to the table, speaking to Hancock. "At least give the guy a chance to tell us the truth." Rawson looked at me and smiled.

"We already know he's a liar. Who gives a damn; he murdered a German Messenger, Schulman. Cut his throat, nasty stuff. A jury'll send him off for life if he's lucky. If not, the chair. Hard to tell with juries these days."

"The chair!" said Rawson.

"Yep, Morgan here is already famous. Remember all that stuff last year? The drama about him seeing that prostitute? He's a sodomite. Remind the jury of that, and we won't have to do much to get the conviction." Hancock slapped the file closed, leaned back, and smiled.

"Mr. Morgan," Rawson said, grabbing my arm. "That's all you need, isn't it, just a chance to tell the truth?"

"Sure," I said.

"See," said Rawson. He gave my arm a squeeze, then a quick, encouraging nod. I nodded back. They waited. I said nothing.

"We've got to do this by the book." Hancock frowned. "A foreign national attacked and murdered at a downtown hotel. A visitor, a man of God, killed in the most brutal way. Hell, that's the chair for sure, yep, for sure."

Rawson was horrified. "Tell him about it, Morgan. That Hun bastard insulted you, didn't he? Made you angry at dinner. So you got even. Any man would do that."

"No," I said.

"You had an altercation with him last week," said Hancock. "He laid hands on you in front of that good-looking blond broad. Hard to get over that, isn't it?"

"There was no altercation."

"Well, damn it, then, what happened?" snapped Hancock.

So, I told them. The same story I'd told at the hotel. They interrupted, made me jump around in the chronology, but it was the same story. It was easy to keep straight because I simply told the truth. I failed to mention only one thing: Goss's story about fleeing Germany because he was a scientist. That I kept to myself. So, in a sense, I lied by omission. It would have made my mother proud. The perfect little lie, surrounded by truth.

"When I opened the door to the stairwell," I said, concluding the story, "I saw Schulman. He was on his back, with a leg folded under him and his head tilted back. Dead."

"How'd you know he was dead?"

"Because his head was half cut off. When Goss saw it, he panicked and ran down the stairs. I gathered my wits and knocked on the first door at the end of the hall. I told the guy in there to call the police."

"Where's this Peter Goss now?" asked Hancock.

"I've no idea."

"Are you trying to tell us this Goss fellow did it? Or that some mystery man killed Schulman, and you just found the body?"

"I have no idea who killed him. Goss didn't do anything. He was terrified."

"Strange you headed for the stairs, not the elevator, when you left his room."

"Not really. Goss didn't want to be seen with me."

"Why? What was the problem?" Hancock smirked. "We know you're a friend of Phil Sanders, and what you wanted from that working girl. Maybe you and Goss had a really friendly meeting?"

"Nothing like that," I said. "There's some conflict going on among the Germans. I don't really understand it. Goss wanted to leave the hotel and didn't want to be seen. You should ask the Germans about it."

"What the hell happened to your head?"

"My head?" I touched the shaved spot and sutures. "That was an accident."

"What," said Hancock. "When you were fighting with Schulman?"

"I never fought with Schulman. And the cut's old, look at it."

"Uh-huh. The Germans want your hide. Wilhelm Kunst says he knows you killed Schulman. Said you had it out for him, had words at dinner earlier. Some joke you told."

"Look, I just found the body. Bad luck on my part. Schulman wasn't the nicest guy in the world, but I had no reason to kill him. Besides, there were two odd things about the body. First, his head was almost cut off."

"According to you."

"But there wasn't much blood on the landing. So, I'm guessing Schulman wasn't killed there, was he?"

"Yeah," said Hancock. "You moved him after you killed him."

"A second thing. He'd been dead for a while. I'm no expert, but he didn't look like he'd just died."

"Big guy like you, it'd be easy as pie to move the body, and your dinner ended at nine. You reported Schulman's body after midnight. You had more than three hours."

"I want my lawyer," I said.

"The guilty always want lawyers." Hancock frowned. "Tell me more about this other guy, the one who disappeared after running down the steps?"

"Peter Goss. I don't know much about him. A Messenger from Berlin."

"So," said Rawson, "did he kill Schulman?"

I had to pause and think. Had Goss somehow killed Schulman before I arrived? "I don't think so," I said. "He was too frightened. I don't know what happened to Goss, but I'm worried about him."

"Maybe you killed Goss too?" Rawson said.

I stared at him, astonished. His eyes coolly met mine.

"Don't be ridiculous," I said.

Hancock flipped open the file. "You're an interesting guy, Morgan. Unemployed for months, but you had hundreds of dollars in your wallet. You're wearing a new suit and shoes. You drive a swell Buick. Hard to figure out. You were an athlete, belonged to fancy clubs, and you used to work for Coca-Cola. Then you lost it all, didn't you? Your nasty divorce was all over the papers. Now"—he held up a piece of paper—"your ex-wife wants a restraining order so you won't harm her, her children, or her new husband. She says she has evidence that you are violent, that you are morally corrupt, and not fit company for her children."

"Jimmy Brown," I said.

They looked at each other. "How do you know Jimmy Brown?"

"He's been following me. Who is the guy?"

"Brown? He used to be a pretty good cop. Now he's private, and he thinks he's some sort of white knight."

"So, he came up with evidence that I'm morally corrupt?"

They glanced at each other, then Hancock said softly, "You know, you're wanted for murder in Peru."

"Those charges were dropped," I said.

"No, Mr. Morgan, they weren't. That's one reason we have a file on you. The charges in Peru stand. After a hearing, you were released into the custody of the US Consul pending trial, but fled the country. Now, I can understand doing that, but if the Peruvian government sought extradition, we'd have to send you back. We're good neighbors and all now."

"Peru?" said Rawson. "Isn't that where they use the strangling machine?"

"I think so," said Hancock. "The Garrote. I hear it's tough to watch. The condemned kick a lot, wet their pants."

"I bet it's even tougher for the guy they're choking." Rawson laughed and slapped his thigh.

Hancock really looked into my eyes for the first time then. I had to admire him. Despite the weak Mutt and Jeff routine with Rawson, he'd played around until he found the right screw to turn. Being sent back to Peru was the stuff of nightmares, the one thing I couldn't bear. The idea terrified me, and he saw it. Good interrogators don't use torture, don't even need to touch their subjects. They just find that small point of leverage and insert the pry bar.

I took a few deep breaths to calm down. "Not in Peru," I finally said. "There, they just shoot people."

"Oh, really," said Hancock. "How do you know that tidbit?"

"I sat in jail there for five months. Listened to them shoot a few people in the prison yard."

"Aw, that's so sad," said Hancock.

"Look, all I can do is tell the truth. I was doing my job watching the Germans. Later, I talked to Goss, and then I found Schulman's body."

"I don't buy your story about the German protection job," said Hancock.

"Just call Mr. Hirsch. I'm sure he will confirm what I told you."

The two men glanced at each other. "Harold Hirsch is sick," said Hancock. "They say he's not able to take any calls, but we'll try today, anyway."

"Then contact the Jewish Welfare Alliance."

Again, the two men looked at each other. Finally, Hancock said, "There's no such thing as the Jewish Welfare Alliance."

I dozed off in the holding room until the squeak of a key in the lock woke me. Blearily, I glanced at my watch. It was seven-thirty in the morning. Hancock and Rawson came in. Sunlight flashed in the corridor behind. A moment later, another man—tall, probably about fifty, with graying hair, wearing an expensive charcoal pinstripe suit—followed. Finally, Joe Packard stepped in.

"I guess we both missed our swim this morning," said Packard.

"The coroner says Schulman died between nine-thirty and eleven p.m.," said Hancock. "The body was fresh; he got good temperatures, so the time is solid. The fellow at the drugstore confirms you were there drinking coffee from nine to about midnight. Luckily, you gave him a big tip, and he remembered you."

"The unexpected rewards of good deeds," said Rawson.

"I still think you're lying about something," said Hancock. "I can smell it. I'll get the evidence, Morgan; then, you're cooked."

Rawson and Hancock left. I looked at Packard. "So, do I just leave?"

"Not yet," said the man in the charcoal suit.

The suit was Special Agent Flexner of the Secret Service, and the deal was simple. No extradition to Peru if I did what Packard and Flexner wanted.

"This is privileged information," Flexner said. "If you reveal any part of it to anyone, we will no longer intercede on your behalf with the Atlanta Police. Got it?"

I was exhausted and just wanted out of the room. "Okay, I got it."

"Good. So, here's the short version. Excellent quality counterfeit US currency keeps turning up around these Germans," said Flexner. "The deceased man . . ."

"Schulman," said Packard.

"Schulman had ten one-hundred-dollar bills in his wallet, almost perfect bills, but fake. Similar bills were passed in New York and Washington. The Germans were in each city shortly before the bills appeared. Overall, we've found thousands of dollars' worth of identical counterfeit along the East Coast."

"You would think the Bureau of Engraving did these bills," said Packard. "But an expert can tell. The best clue is that the paper they used isn't quite right. Close, but not close enough."

This was quite a twist, and I took a moment to shift gears. "Who's behind it?"

"We don't know," said Packard. "It doesn't take a government to make good counterfeit."

"How does a guy from the Office of Naval Intelligence know about counterfeit?"

"What?" Packard tilted his head sideways. "Agent Flexner and I work for the Secret Service. The Secret Service is in charge of stopping counterfeiting."

I looked at the floor. Once again, I'd gotten it wrong. I took a deep breath. "Why would they bring counterfeit money to Atlanta?"

"We'd like to know," said Flexner. "At this point, we don't know with certainty that they brought it. So far, all we have is the fake money follows these Germans."

"Printing stuff this good isn't cheap," said Packard. "We'd like to know why it was made, who it's going to."

I thought for a moment. "How much of this sourdough would fit into four cubic feet?"

They were silent. Packard drummed on the table with a pencil. Finally, Flexner asked, "Why is that pertinent?"

"Goss showed me a false bottom in his trunk. I'm surprised you didn't find it. I'm sure it's still in his room. He said it was full of cash when they arrived here. I think the total space was about four cubic feet."

Flexner pulled out a pencil and did some figures on a piece of foolscap. He showed it to Packard, who appeared shocked.

"How much?"

Packard glanced at me. "Depends on the types of bills. If all hundreds, maybe as much as ten million."

"Millions? Why would they need millions?"

"Good question," said Packard. "Be even better if you helped us find an answer."

They let me go just before noon. It was hot, humid, and low clouds covered the city. Rain puddles lined the poorly drained street, and the threat of rain lingered. Dazed and exhausted, I started toward Five Points to catch a trolley uptown, pondering my actions. I'm no paragon of virtue, but deep down, maybe I believed in something. More than just getting what you wanted? Perhaps justice? All I knew was Mendel Rubenstein's murder clawed at me. He was just an innocent man fleeing injustice. I wanted to find the killers, to make them pay. And to do that, I needed to continue watching the Germans, which was exactly what the Secret Service wanted. After I walked a couple of blocks, mulling this over, a voice called from behind.

"Morgan? Mr. Morgan?"

I turned and saw the Cab Calloway look-alike, Bill Cadwell, waving at me. "Wild Bill" Cadwell, identified by the *Journal* as one of the most corrupt men in Atlanta.

"Mr. Morgan, we need to talk."

"Okay, talk."

He chuckled. "Not here." He pointed across the street. "There's Leon's Deli. They make great potato salad, fresh every day. Why don't we get some lunch?"

Police headquarters was only two blocks away; it was noon, and the street and businesses were crowded. The situation seemed safe. "Sure, a sandwich would be good."

"They didn't feed you in the lockup?" he asked as we waited in line to order at the outside window. The window marked "Colored."

"Why? Do they usually feed you?"

He smiled. "I wouldn't know. Never been there."

We ordered pastrami sandwiches and potato salad and sat at a picnic table in the alley behind the deli. There were several other tables. I was the only White person there.

"So, what's this about? You've got some information about the Germans?"

"Naw." He took a bite of his sandwich and chewed thoroughly before answering. "What I've got is a German."

Stunned, I put my sandwich down.

"Yeah. Some friends found him wandering around last night. He doesn't know much English. Asked for you. Seemed to know your name real good."

"I'll be damned."

"Probably what'll happen to all of us," he said. "Look, you want this squarehead?"

I thought for a minute. "What if I don't?"

Cadwell's face fell. "Then, I guess we take him back to his hotel. He sure as hell doesn't want us to do that; he screamed bloody murder when he figured out we were taking him there. Took out his wallet to pay us off, shocked we'd already taken the money out of it." Cadwell chuckled and took a sip of his Coke. He pointed at my plate. "You're not eating. Dig into that potato salad; it's real good."

I put a spoonful into my mouth, and it was excellent. I ate another couple of bites while Cadwell worked on his sandwich.

"Okay. What do you want? Money?"

"Why, I want to be your friend, Mr. Morgan. And Mr. Green wants to be your friend too. You see, Mr. Green, he's grown a little concerned about you visiting around town so much. You've been out to the Emerald Club, been poking around on Decatur Street; we hear tell of you in all sorts of places talking to all kinds of people."

"Did you guys pay someone to follow me?"

He tilted his head. "Don't need to. You're easily noticed."

"Who's Mr. Green?"

"Humm. You might think of him as the Bug Man."

"The Bug Man is supposed to run the illegal lottery in town. I thought he was something the police made up, not a real person."

"Now you're on track, except Mr. Green is very real," said Cadwell. "He just wanted me to ask you a few questions. He wonders whether you're representing a competitor. Twenty years ago, your father organized *La Bolita* lottery in Savannah and Jacksonville. Mr. Green is worried that the Cubans might be thinking of moving in on Atlanta. He'd like to know your intentions."

"My father's dead," I said.

"Ah, but *La Bolita* isn't. Now, given recent events in your life, Mr. Green suspects you might have some money troubles. A man will take risks when he has money troubles. Ever since Eddie Guyol was murdered, things have been a bit tense in town."

"I don't have anything to do with *La Bolita*, Bolito, Kino, or any other numbers racket. Guyol's lottery—what'd they call it, the Home Game? I had nothing to do with that either. Anyway, they caught the guy who shot him, that Fluker fellow."

"Yeah, well, Fluker was framed. Cops had to cover up some things. But the business has been topsy-turvy since Guyol was offed."

"I broke with my father years ago, before his death. No business connections to Cuba. No reason to get into the lottery business."

"Wonderful, just wonderful. We'd hoped to hear that. But we'll be watching, makin' sure that proves out." He smiled and wiped his mouth with his handkerchief. He'd eaten all of his lunch while mine was mostly untouched. "Go ahead, Mr. Morgan, eat up."

I took a bite of my pastrami sandwich. "So, what about this German?"

"Oh, I was just angling for leverage. But since you have nothing to do with a lottery, why, I'll have that German here in a jiffy. Gratis."

"I'm glad there's no problem."

"Me too, Mr. Morgan, me too. This is good news, because if you did try to bring in a lottery, I'd have to kill you. That would be a shame, frankly, and stressful."

"Might be more stressful for me." We laughed together warily.

"You know, I think you're growing on me. Calm and controlled, even when threatened. I might need someone like you one day. Let me know if you are interested. You can find my number in the book."

"You're in the phone book?" I said, astonished.

"Of course. I'm a legitimate businessman." Cadwell stood up, nodded to another table, and walked out of the alley. I marveled at how well-spoken he was, not at all what I expected in a Negro gangster. While I wondered, a bewildered Peter Goss wandered into the alley.

"Mark, what are we going to do with him?" Emma said.

It was almost cool in the marble lobby of Number Ten Pryor Street. As we talked, Goss looked around, checked out the directory, and measured out the length of the wall.

"Obviously, he can't stay at your boardinghouse. I guess we'll have to rent him a room, someplace away from downtown where he can lie low. Otherwise, the Germans will kill him. He's a refugee now; he wants to escape the Nazis."

She shook her head. "Are you sure they want to kill him?"

I spoke to Goss in German. "Peter, my friend is worried about finding you a place to stay."

"Oh." He smiled. "Tell her I do not require much. I will be no trouble."

"Do you really think you are in danger?"

"What do you think?"

"He's in danger," I told Emma.

"So," said Emma, "will I be in danger?"

I hadn't even thought of it that way, and she could tell. Anger flashed. "So, you want me to leave work to find a room for him? I can't even talk to him. I don't know any German."

"I think he understands more English than he lets on. Isn't that right, Peter?"

"*Ja*, sure," he said.

"It's between terms, so there are probably lots of rooms for rent near Georgia Tech. Let's get a newspaper and check the classifieds."

She chewed a little on her lower lip. "No, I have a better idea."

We drove to Emma's boarding house. The professor was at the lab, and Mrs. Wimberly was doubtful. "A student's room? Why would you think Orin will let him stay? Who's this fellow again?"

"A German refugee," Emma said.

Mrs. Wimberly pushed back her graying hair and put a finger to her chin. "Well, he'll be at the lab until four. You could ask him."

"Emma, I have to get back downtown," I said.

"Go on, then. I'll speak with the professor. We'll find a place for Mr. Goss."

I drove back to the Athletic Club. It began raining heavily as I trotted from the club to the Henry Grady. At least it left me feeling a bit cleaner after the police lockup. At the back of the lobby were dark wooden telephone booths with articulated doors. I sat in one, soaked by rain, and closed the glass door. Fumbling with the phonebook, I found the number, dropped my nickel in, and dialed.

"The Temple," answered a woman.

"Good afternoon. My name's Mark Morgan, and I work for Harold Hirsch. I wonder if I could speak with the Chief Rabbi?"

"Rabbi Marx isn't here; he's visiting the hospitals today. In fact, he plans to visit Mr. Hirsch. I hope this isn't bad news?"

"No, no," I said. "I'm just trying to find Rabbi Goldstein. Might you have his phone number?"

"Goldstein?"

"Yes, I'm sorry, but I don't know his first name. Mr. Hirsch introduced us at the Standard Club."

"Sir, we work regularly with all the rabbis in Atlanta and across the state. I don't know anyone named Goldstein. There's a Rothstein in Savannah. Could that be it?"

"What about an organization called the Jewish Welfare Alliance?"

"The Jewish Alliance? Is that what you mean?"

"Goldstein clearly said the Jewish Welfare Alliance."

"Wait a minute, I have an idea." I waited several minutes, and then her voice returned. "I found it, Mr. Morgan. We have a new book listing Jewish organizations across the country. There's a Jewish Welfare Alliance in New York City. Do you think that might be Rabbi Goldstein's organization?"

Thank God for efficient secretaries, I thought. "Yes," I said. "That sounds like it. Do you have an address and phone number?"

She gave me an address on Fifth Avenue. "I'm from New York City," she said. "That address is in Rockefeller Center, you know, where Radio City is. They must be a wealthy organization to afford the rent; I'm surprised I've not heard of them before."

"Maybe they're new. I can't thank you enough for your help."

"You're welcome. How's Mr. Hirsch doing?"

"All I know is that his condition is serious," I lied.

"That's what they said last night. It's so tragic. Such a wonderful man."

I thanked her again and hung up. So, the Jewish Welfare Alliance had an address in Rockefeller Center. I'd been to Rockefeller Center, new and unfinished, when I'd returned from Germany in 1936. I'd visited the Rainbow Room and marveled at the conception of such a vast development.

While I pondered placing a long-distance call to New York, angry German voices filtered into the phone booth. Through the glass, I saw Paul Dittmer and Wilhelm Kunst. The normally taciturn Dittmer was shorter than Kunst, but anger seemed to swell in him. His face was red, and veins stood out on his neck. I cracked the door so that the light in the booth turned off, leaving me hidden in shadow. It also allowed me to hear their conversation.

"You have ruined everything," hissed Dittmer in German. "This is not Berlin."

"I did what was best."

"You fool," Dittmer said. "You act like a back-alley thug."

"It was necessary," said Kunst.

"Have you forgotten our goals? We must avoid attention; we need secrecy. Now, thanks to you, the police are involved. They are looking at us. They interviewed me this morning."

"They know nothing," Kunst said. "Remember, these are incompetent American police, not German. I told them I feared Morgan; he appeared to be violent. Rolf and Morgan had several heated arguments, I said. Just small exaggerations, and now the police have arrested him. On the whole, I think it worked out well. The American spy is gone; we needn't worry about him anymore. No one has asked any questions about the Jew. So, in truth, I have removed two problems."

"I disagree. We can't risk being caught in lies. One American spy is nothing. At least we knew who he was. More importantly, he was inept. Now there may be others watching us, more skilled watchers. Maybe Morgan killed Schulman? We don't know, do we? Now you tell me about killing this Jew! He was no threat, just a sad, foolish Jew. You have risked everything to gain nothing, and I will write a report to that effect."

"Write all the reports you want, he was just a Jew," said Kunst. "Your superiors are not my superiors. Sometimes I wonder if our goals are the same?"

Both men stared angrily at each other, then seemed to realize they stood in a hotel lobby surrounded by people, many of whom spoke German. They glanced around nervously. Dittmer turned and started toward the elevators.

"Paul," said Kunst, "I did what was best. But now we have another problem. Goss is missing."

Dittmer stroked his hair nervously. "Has he run? Did the Americans arrest him? I don't like these uncertainties, Wilhelm."

"We will find him."

"So, we are done?"

"There is another meeting tonight," said Kunst. "You must come. I think you will find that they are sound. I am convinced we have found our men. They already helped us with the Jew. When you meet them, you will agree they are solid."

"Perhaps." Dittmer turned, and they walked toward the elevators together. Kunst bent toward Dittmer, speaking in a low voice that I could no longer hear. They boarded, and the door closed.

The lack of sleep was taking its toll. My head lolled and suddenly snapped upright, and then it happened a second time. The doors to the coffee shop were propped open, giving a view into the lobby. I could keep watch from there while I had a cup of java.

"Black coffee, please," I told the counterman. "And keep it coming." By the time I finished the first cup, I felt empowered. I could do it. I would not fall asleep. I would make the right choices. I would figure this thing out.

The next cup only reinforced the sense of well-being. Remarkable stuff. The jukebox played Martha Tilton's performance of Johnny Mercer's hit "And the Angels Sing" in her breathy, sexy voice.

"Hello, Mark." Another breathy, sexy voice. It was Anna, now sliding onto a stool next to me. She looked more like Carole Lombard than ever, only better. Her eyes were devastatingly blue, her lips slightly parted and bright red. A broad light blue hat cocked at a rakish angle and a matching summer dress made her look fresh and clean and ready for a picnic. Corny or not, the music was perfect. I briefly wondered if she'd chosen the song. Then I remembered she didn't speak English, so it was likely she didn't know the lyrics.

She touched my hand gently. "They told us you found Rolf," she said.

"Yes."

"Did you kill him?"

I turned and looked into her eyes. "Why would you think that?"

"That is what Kunst told us. He said you were the killer."

"Not me, angel."

She squeezed my hand. "I knew that," she said. "Rolf and his kind are evil. As a good German, I am used to pretending this is not so. I've learned not to see what I see. Do you understand? Not seeing what you see? Even talking about it disturbs me, but this is America, and you can talk of such things, can't you? So, I will not be frightened. Not anymore, not with you around."

"What do you know of Kunst and Dittmer?"

"Paul Dittmer?" She touched my hand again; this time, her fingers wrapped around and held it. Her hand seemed impossibly small. "I have met Dittmer before. He's a youth minister, but I don't know him. Kunst, I don't know at all, except I don't like him. Clearly a policeman, the bullying kind. Dittmer and Kunst know each other, so perhaps Dittmer is also police?" She looked into my eyes. "You were right to tell that joke last night; we saw behind the masks. I don't think Hess matters. Rolf was merely a policeman, poor man. Dittmer is controlled, thoughtful. Goss is scared, a mouse. But Kunst frightens everyone. He frightens me."

"Goss was right to be frightened," I said. "Did Kunst kill Rolf Schulman?"

"Why would Kunst do that? Goss and Schulman worked for him."

I drank some coffee and pondered how she knew that.

"Anna, Goss was not one of them."

"How do you know this?"

I told her about the conversation we had in Goss's room, his desire to stay in the United States. I told her of his running away. At the last moment, I decided not to tell her about his claim to be a scientist, or that I knew where he was.

"Mark, you are a child. Telling me these things makes me part of them. I could go to prison."

"No one will know but us."

She glanced around the coffee shop. "To stay in America would be a crime, I think. Do you believe Goss? Or perhaps he's a spy who would steal American secrets? A spy would surely lie?"

"My mother once said, 'No one tells the truth in this world.'"

"If that's true, she contradicted herself."

The counterman refilled my coffee and poured some for her.

"Did the police ask you about Goss?" she asked, taking a sip.

"He's missing. They don't like that. They accused me of killing Goss and Schulman."

"Police," she mused, sipping more coffee.

I finished my cup, and the counterman poured more. He winked at me and nodded toward Anna. "It's a grand day, ain't it, buddy?" he said.

"Sure is," I said, looking at Anna. She was so bright, so beautiful; it was exciting just to sit with her.

"I need to follow Kunst tonight," I said. "He's going somewhere important."

Anna's eyes met mine, and she smiled. After a moment, she brushed her hair back with her free hand. In motion, animated, teeth and eyes flashing, she was extraordinary.

"I'll go with you," she said. "Tonight."

Kunst didn't appear until dark. He and Dittmer caught a cab out front. We waited with a cabbie half a block down the street and followed. Anna sat next to me, tense, straining at the bit.

We passed the Exposition Cotton Mills and the stockyards. Just before the waterworks, they turned left onto Huff Road. There was no other traffic. A few residents of the tumbledown shotgun houses lining the road sat on their front porches enjoying the cool of the evening. Kunst's car turned left again.

"Go straight!" I said quickly.

We drove past their turn and watched the other taxi until it was out of sight. The driver stopped, and Anna and I got out. We were under one of the few streetlights on the road.

"Wait for us here," I told the driver.

"In this neighborhood?"

I took out a twenty and tore it in half. I gave him one half and held up the other. "You get it when we come back."

"Plus the fare?"

"Plus the fare. Turn it around so you're headed back toward Howell Mill and stay here under the light."

"Will do, brother."

We crossed the road. To our right, down a steep hill, were railroad tracks. In front of us was an old factory complex.

"Mark, what are we doing?" Anna asked in German.

"They went down a dead-end road. It leads to the old Van Winkle Machine Works. The factory is mostly closed down, just lots of big, empty buildings."

"A place good for secret things, yes?"

I nodded.

The old machine works stood next to an important Atlanta rail junction. All trains to or from the northeast and the northwest passed through. Because trains slowed to navigate the area, hobos jumped on or off trains there. The papers called it "Hobo Junction." Hobos, the empty buildings, and the poverty of the neighborhood made for an area full of vagrants and petty crime.

The fence had been cut several times, and we had no trouble finding a wide gap. As we made our way across a graveled lot overgrown with weeds and tufts of grass, we heard the distant chuffs and bangs of trains in the rail yards, the songs of frogs in the trees, and the low murmur of men down by the tracks. The men appeared as shadows, gathered around a glowing campfire. The smoke drifted up the hill, forming a dark streak against the soft glow of city lights reflected by the low clouds.

There were also lights ahead among the sprawling factory buildings. The building on the far left was well lit, probably the office for whatever work still went on in the old factory. Suddenly, Anna leaned close, her breath warm on my ear as she whispered. "There's the taxi."

Up to this point, I'd felt safe, but as we approached, caution awakened. "Let's be careful. Stay here and watch. I'll slip forward and see what's in that building. Can you whistle?"

"Yes," she said, puzzled.

"If you see anyone, whistle twice. Quietly."

"But they'll hear me!"

"Maybe. But I'll be warned."

"I want to go with you."

"No, this way is best. Sit down; at night, you can see better if you get down low. Look for movement silhouetted against the clouds. The light from the city will help."

"Mark."

I knelt close to her so I could hear. Suddenly, her hands were on my cheeks, and she kissed me. Her mouth opened, and our tongues entwined. I broke away, breathless.

"Be careful," she said.

A light bulb in a steel cage over the building's door illuminated a sign: *Machine Floor #3.* I crawled to the first window, trying to avoid direct light, and peered in. About thirty White men sat on benches surrounded by large drill presses, lathes, and other machine tools. A few wore suits and ties, but all wore white shirts, even those in dungarees. Kunst was talking, smiling, his hands moving, but I could hear nothing. Dittmer sat beside Kunst at the front of the room, looking uncomfortable.

Two windows down, I saw a broken pane of glass. Crawling through the thick, wet grass, I reached the wall below. I could hear Kunst speaking excellent English.

". . . a problem we shall deal with when it appears," he said. "You'll always have your independence; we will not interfere. We are only here to help you. We share the same goals, the same ideals for the future, but it is your future to build."

"The mayor's election is coming up next year," said an American voice. "Hartsfield's not popular. He could be beaten."

"The governor's election is coming up too," said another. "Rivers is corrupt, a liar, with his commie 'Little New Deal.' Gene Talmadge'll win next year."

"Ol' Gene's the right man," said a third. "He'll stop the Reds. He fought the New Deal, and that Jew-lover Roosevelt tried to destroy him. We gotta support Gene."

"No," said another. "General Moseley's the man for governor. He's prepared for it. He gave up his army career to save the country. He understands the Jewish threat, the race problem."

"You know best," said Kunst. "Make the choices, and then act. You must become a true political party and appeal to the people. Become public, unmask, show you're not afraid."

"*Der ist* danger in moving too fast." It was Dittmer. He spoke English with a heavy accent and at a laboring pace. He would not be convincing in comparison with Kunst's smooth presentation. "Be cautious, build your strength, before you become public."

"No," said Kunst. "Act now—this is the world-historical moment. Like a woman, she must be taken the moment she is ripe; otherwise, she will reject future advances. Take her now! If our *Führer* has taught us anything, it is that when a historic opportunity appears, one must act boldly. Strike with overwhelming force! Take charge of history! We can give you money, more than enough to build your party, but you must act."

I heard two soft whistles, so I dropped flat on the ground. Three men were walking up the paved road, chatting and smoking. I lay still, trusting the light from the windows would blind them so they wouldn't see me in the shadowed grass. Then, rain began to fall.

There was more conversation in the machine shop, but I couldn't make it out. Chairs and benches scraped, pushed back as men stood. If they came outside, they would spot me lying on the ground below the windows. I had to move quickly.

The three men out front were talking and laughing. One thumped on the cab's roof, waking the driver. "Hey, buddy, let us in out of the rain."

I wiggled forward along the base of the building, trying to get beyond the light from the windows. Just as I reached the edge of the darkness, one of the men by the cab saw me.

"Hey, you! Stop!"

I didn't stop. I stood and darted into the graveled lot. Behind me came grunts of surprise and heavy footsteps. Then, instead of sitting still, Anna stood. Damn. I had to lead them away from her.

I cut left, down toward the tracks, running hard in the rain. Surely she had the sense to go the other way, back toward the road and our cab. I dodged through several piles of junk, seeing them only at the last moment, frightening in the wet, dark night. Some rebar sticking out of a chunk of concrete caught my new jacket and ripped it down the left side. That swung me toward a pile of enormous concrete sewer pipes. I ducked into one.

Two sets of running feet crunched past, headed down toward the hobo's fire by the tracks. I jumped at hearing a voice behind me.

"This is my place. Come any closer, and I'll cut you."

I glanced behind and saw a dark, huddled shape in the sewer pipe. "Sorry, friend. It's raining. I didn't know you were in here."

"Find your own place; this one's mine."

I crawled out and trotted toward the hole in the fence. To my left, far away, I heard my pursuers yelling at the hobos down by the railroad tracks. Sparks flew as they kicked the fire, scattering it.

"What fun," said Anna.

I hadn't heard her until she spoke. She jogged up beside me as I trotted toward the fence. She ran with ease and athletic grace. I held some of the wire aside as she slipped through.

The cabbie waited where we'd left him. I grabbed the door handle and turned to Anna, standing under the bright streetlight. Her light dress was completely soaked, plastered to her body. I could see all of her; the shape of her breasts and hips, the erect nipples, even the navel in her belly. She could have been naked. I stared, frozen.

She glanced down at herself and laughed. "Later, Mark. Now, we must go."

I opened the door of the cab. She brushed against me as she climbed in.

"Back to the Henry Grady," I told the driver.

"Sure thing, buddy," he said, leering at Anna before we started to move.

She grabbed my hand and began to laugh loudly. I laughed with her, then stopped when she put my hand on her chest. I could feel the swell of her breast and her heart pounding beneath.

"What fools," she said.

"I tore my jacket. I think it's ruined." I'd worn my new dark gray suit. She ran a hand up the jacket, then slipped it through the tear to rest against my ribs. My breath caught for a moment. "There was a man in the sewer pipe holding a knife. He threatened me."

"A knife!" she said, and then laughed again. "Isn't it delicious? Isn't it fun breaking the rules?"

She grabbed my hand again and put it on her thigh, perilously high. I felt the top of her stocking through the thin, wet dress. I exhaled slowly and smiled. Light from streetlights flashed across her face and body, a stirring show.

At the hotel, I gave the driver the other half of the twenty, plus his fare. Peachtree was brightly lit. The bright theater marquees, the neon signs, and the parade of cars all matched our excitement. Outside the glass doors of the hotel, she stopped, and when I turned to see why, she stood on her toes and kissed me.

"*Ich will dich*," she whispered. *I want you*. She pushed her hips firmly against me, pulled my head down, and kissed me again. I reached around to hold her, but suddenly she froze. I followed her gaze.

Her husband stood in the lobby, just inside the door. Tall, dour, and dark, he was talking with a group of men. He'd not seen us.

"My God," she said. "I must go."

And she left me.

"*I want you*," she'd said.

I lay on my bed in the heat, struggling to sleep. The vision of Anna obsessed me. Seeing her under the streetlight, with the wet dress painted to her body, every detail visible. I groaned, flipped over, and slammed my fist into the pillow. What was I doing? I could have, should have, stayed away. Now that was impossible. Not rational feelings, not love, not friendship, but raw feelings: need, desire, lust.

"*I want you*," she'd said.

Eventually, I fell asleep and dreamed. Anna and I were in a beautiful hotel room overlooking the sea. I kissed her, and then we were tumbling, rolling, in confusion. A pause, that breathless moment of awkwardness before the first consummation. In the dream, I was able, erect and rigid. Exhilaration swept through me, followed quickly by a climax so shocking, shattering, and powerful, it jolted me awake.

I sat up. In the darkness of my room, I discovered that the climax had been real.

I got up to wash. After a glass of water, I sat in the dark, listening to the railroad yards, dozing a bit. The noise of the trains was strangely comforting. The slamming of iron upon iron, the chuff of steam. At least other people were engaged in a normal world.

My world was anything but normal.

7

Wednesday, July 26, 1939

At 2 a.m., the telephone rang. I fumbled while picking it up.

"Where the hell have you been?" The rabbi, of course.

"I've been doing my job."

"Your job is to do what I say. We have to talk."

"Okay. Come by my place. I'll make coffee."

"No," he said. "Not your place."

"Look, Atlanta's not New York. Even radio stations shut down at midnight here. A few drugstores might be open, but for the most part, they roll the sidewalks up after ten."

"Pick a place, a busy one."

"There's a Lane's Drugs across from Union Station. They have an all-night coffee shop."

"Half an hour," he said and hung up.

The odor of over-fried meat and burned bread assailed me as I pushed open the door. A dozen tired travelers sat at the steel counter, sipping coffee or picking at an early breakfast. Scuffed linoleum showed the way further back, where Goldstein and a woman waited in a booth. He no longer looked a dandy. His beard was tangled, his jacket mussed, and he appeared smaller, unkempt, and tired. By contrast, the woman was very large and immaculately dressed. She had dark, soft brown eyes and a perfect mouth that smiled when I walked toward them. Probably around thirty years old, she was attractive, well-kept, and fat, like Kate Smith, the singer and radio star.

"Good morning," she said. "I'm Miss Eleanor Jones. So sorry about the time and all that, but I so wanted to meet you." She had a posh British accent.

"Am I meeting with the rabbi?"

"Oh, don't mind me," Miss Jones said. "Rabbi Goldstein and I often work together. What he knows, I know."

"I see. And how are things in New York?"

"New York?" asked the rabbi.

"Rockefeller Center's nice, but the rents must be high."

Eleanor Jones laughed, a pleasant, mellow sound. "Relax, Jacob," she said. "It's evident why you chose him."

The waitress came, bringing Rabbi Goldstein a Coke and a grilled cheese. "I missed dinner," he grumbled.

Miss Jones and I ordered coffee.

"What do you do at the Alliance?" I asked her.

"Ah. The Alliance." She glanced at the rabbi, but he was absorbed in his sandwich. "Well, I don't officially work with them. My current project is helping people escape the Nazi regime. It's frightfully expensive, and often families cannot afford the costs. So I solicit donations to help."

"These refugees come to the United States?"

"A few, but that is difficult. There are strict quotas. As you can imagine, Germans are leaving in droves. Most go to Holland. Some, those with the wherewithal, go to Switzerland or South America."

The waitress returned with coffee. I took a sip and scalded my tongue. It was hot. Not much more could be said for it.

"Miss Jones, thank you. In two minutes, you've helped me understand more than I ever did talking to the rabbi." She smiled.

"You don't need to understand anything," said Goldstein crossly. "Just do what you're told. Do you have the information I paid for?"

"Some." I glanced at Miss Jones, and she nodded. I told them about the dinner, named the men present, and said that Goss had since disappeared.

"Another refugee." Miss Jones shook her head. "Is he dead?"

The waitress asked if we needed anything more, then put the check on the table. I waited until she was out of earshot.

"Goss said he wanted to stay here. I don't know anything more. But, more importantly, Rolf Schulman is dead."

"Who's dead?" said Miss Jones, shocked.

"Schulman. Late Monday night. Someone killed him."

"There was nothing about that in the paper," said Goldstein.

"Yes, strange, isn't it? His head was almost cut off, and they left him in the stairway of the hotel. A murder like that should be front page. I'd started to doubt that there was anything to the threats—then this happens."

"Dear God," said Mrs. Jones.

"Yes. Funny thing, though; there was almost no blood. We have a very violent but also a very neat murderer."

"How do you know all this?" asked the rabbi.

"I found the body."

Miss Jones looked worried. "Are the police involved?"

"They had me locked up until noon." I glanced at my watch. "Yesterday now."

"Jacob, this is terrible."

"Perhaps," said the rabbi. "Do they have any suspects?"

"They wanted to pin it on me, but that didn't work out. If I were the police, I'd look at Kunst. He seems like a man who could kill and feel nothing."

"A killer can also feel a great deal," said the rabbi, wiping his mouth with the back of his hand. "It depends on why he's killing."

"The police let you go?" asked Miss Jones.

"A witness placed me elsewhere when Schulman was killed."

"Well," said Miss Jones. "One thing is clear. You must find Goss. Perhaps I can help him. He wants to stay in the United States, you say?"

"Is Goss what you wanted all along?" I asked.

The rabbi stared at me with flat, emotionless eyes. Miss Jones glanced over and shook her head. She turned back to me. "I simply would like to help him. He's now a refugee."

"I see," I said. "That's all? Maybe find him a place in England?"

"There's no hope," said the rabbi. "The Germans will kill him."

"Not if we help." Miss Jones waved a hand in the air. "So, where do you begin looking for Goss, Mr. Morgan? What will be your process? Where will you go?"

I glanced at the rabbi, his mouth still chewing, then back at the woman. They were probably British agents. *They don't trust me; they don't trust each other, and I can't trust them.*

"What's so funny?" asked the rabbi.

"Nothing is funny; rather, this is all absurd. You've never been straight with me, never told me what you really want, who you really are, so I've wasted a lot of time. Now you want me to find Goss. But you must know that the only way for me to find him is to follow Kunst. Following Kunst will be dangerous. If I screw up, someone might get killed. Like me."

"So, is Kunst Gestapo?" she asked.

"I'm not certain of anything."

"What's your best guess?"

"Kunst is SD, not Gestapo. If he's SD, then he is treading on Abwehr turf. The SD is supposed to do Nazi Party security in Germany, not espionage overseas." I described the argument I'd overheard between Dittmer and Kunst, and Kunst's statement that Dittmer's superiors were not his superiors.

"Are you sure that's exactly what he said?" said the rabbi.

"Of course. It is exactly what he said. So, if Dittmer is Abwehr, then he and Kunst have different bosses. They are potentially in conflict, competitors."

"Bravo." Miss Jones pantomimed clapping.

"But does all that make a difference?"

"Oh, it makes quite a bit of difference. What of the others?"

"Schulman was SD. Hess might be Gestapo; he has the aspect of a well-fed but somewhat dull policeman. Dittmer must be Abwehr. Sandoval, I can't decide. I don't think Dr. Erlanger is involved."

"Anything more?"

I told them about following Kunst and Dittmer to the meeting at the machine works, but I held back Anna's presence.

After a pause, Miss Jones spoke. "You've done well. Better than Jacob led me to expect."

"Hardly," said the rabbi. "He lost Goss."

"You did not ask him to keep track of Goss."

"If Goss ran," I explained, "it'll be impossible to find him. More than a hundred passenger trains pass through Atlanta every day. He could be anywhere by now."

The waitress came back to fill our coffees and stared pointedly at the unpaid check. It was a welcome distraction. Clearly, Miss Jones was going to ask me to do more. When the waitress left, I said, "I've done what you asked. I'm finished. They're on to me, and it's too dangerous for me to continue."

"I had a bad feeling about you from the start," said the rabbi.

"Jacob, he has done what you asked. If we ask for more, we should pay more." She smiled at me.

I finished my coffee and checked my watch. It was almost 3 a.m. "I have to go."

"One moment, Mr. Morgan," Miss Jones said. "Would you be willing to take on a new job? Related to, but separate from, the last one?"

"I'm not interested."

She bent forward and lowered her voice. "Would another five thousand interest you?"

Astonished, I blurted, "Who are you people?"

She just smiled. I hadn't expected this. If they paid, I would have twelve thousand dollars, enough to completely change my life. I could buy a house and start a business. My deal with Packard and the Secret Service meant I had to trace the counterfeit anyway. That meant following the Germans. Why not get paid for it?

"All I have to do is find Goss?"

She glanced at the rabbi. He nodded. "Yes," she said. "He needs to be rescued."

Definitely easy money, since I already had him. Still, I had to play my role. "What if he's dead?"

"Then, that's the end of it." She smiled.

"If he is dead, you'll pay me?"

The rabbi squirmed. "No. Why should we pay if Goss is dead?"

"Why should I look if he might be dead?"

"Your point is valid," Miss Jones said. "So, yes, we will pay you for finding him. Five thousand if he's alive, a thousand if he is dead."

"I want a thousand now."

"This is the type of man he is," said the rabbi, spreading his hands.

Miss Jones held out her hand. Reluctantly, the rabbi handed her his wallet. She counted some bills onto the table, covered them with a napkin, and pushed the pile toward me.

"That's seven hundred dollars. When you have found Goss, whether he is alive or dead, and the rabbi confirms it, we will pay you the remainder. Is that acceptable?"

I scooped up the cash and said yes.

I slept almost five hours, but woke with a start from a horrible dream. Peru again. The nightmares were happening more often. In this one, I was jumping from crosstie to crosstie down an endless funicular track into darkness. At the bottom, I knew something terrible awaited. Groggy, I wandered over to the window. It was almost eight; birds were singing, as was the morning traffic. Knowing it was too late to go back to sleep, I made breakfast: toast, jelly, and an egg. Then I headed down for my swim.

Packard was in the pool, but I ignored him and swam a shortened routine. I was tired, and the exercise didn't help. Two other members joined us while I swam. One, Mitch McGowan, swam like a shark. Packard waited for me by the pool when I finished.

"Must have been one hell of a party," he said, peering at me.

I ignored him and watched Mitch, who was still swimming. "I think he'd give you a run for your money, Packard."

"No, I'd take him in the turns."

I watched some more and decided Packard was right.

He glanced down at my left shin. "That's a bad scar. Almost looks like a bullet wound."

"It was a bullet wound."

He was quiet for a moment. "Aren't you just full of surprises. You find anything?"

"You want to talk here?"

"Sure," he said. "Isn't that what guys do, talk in the locker room?"

"Maybe in the Navy." I retreated to a cubicle to dress.

"Don't you shower off after the pool?" he asked through the door.

"Chlorine is my cologne." I heard him laugh.

I came out dressed in my new blue suit. My last new suit. I sat down to put on my shoes.

"So, spill," he said.

I did, telling him about the meeting at the machine works. "They talked about politics, maybe a new political party." I told him nothing about Anna.

"You've got to find out more about these meetings."

"I'm working on it."

"Have you seen any of the funny money?" he said.

"I wouldn't know how to recognize it. Kunst suggested he had money, but I didn't see any cash."

"Follow them again tonight."

"Maybe," I said. "Listen, do you know anything about the German police, German espionage?"

"Espionage?" he said. "You mean like that movie, *Confessions of a Nazi Spy*?"

"I thought that story was real."

"It is. But I know a little more than the Hollywood guys. Try me."

"What's the difference between the Abwehr and the SD? The Abwehr is military intelligence, and the SD is internal Nazi Party security. Here, though, they seem to be doing the same thing."

"You are catching on. Yeah, Abwehr's a very professional group, with strong traditions going back to Imperial times. The SD is sort of Hitler's private anti-spies, with a reputation for violence and corruption. They're supposed to focus on loyalty within the Nazi Party. If they're sending agents overseas, then we have a new problem. That's one for the FBI. It's not my job."

"Maybe I should go see another picture, that one at the Roxy. *Secret Service of the Air*. Find out more about your job."

"Ha. They've made two of those, you know. A young guy named Ronald Reagan plays a Secret Service agent. He always saves the girl. Not how it goes in real life."

I stayed in the locker room until I saw Simon, one of the Black janitors. Simon was a big man, older, tall, and very dark, stooped from years of labor. Like most Blacks, he lowered his eyes when talking to whites, but he carried himself with pride.

"Morning, Simon. How would you like to pick up a couple of sawbucks?"

He looked at me shrewdly. You didn't survive long as a black man working in a white club in segregated Atlanta without an excellent sense of social order and propriety. "I'm not supposed to take tips, Capt'n."

"Not a tip, and this won't get you in trouble. Don't you bring extra clothes to work; keep 'em in your closet?"

"Yes, sir, Capt'n. They always said I could do that."

"You haven't broken any rules. I just want to rent your clothes for a day."

He looked at me, measuring me, clearly concerned I was trying to cheat him or make him an object of mirth. "I don't know about that, sir," he said carefully.

"Simon, I'm serious. I think your clothes would fit me, and they would help me today."

"Do I get the clothes back?"

"Yep. I'll return everything this afternoon."

He couldn't help but step out of his Jim Crow role. "Look, Mr. Morgan, these ain't very good duds. I keep 'em here in case I gotta paint or do plumbing. They ain't worth twenty dollars."

"That's perfect." I pulled out a Jackson and handed it to him. He looked at it for a moment, then tucked it in a pocket and went to get the clothes out of his closet. He handed the pile to me.

"And your cap?" I needed something to cover the cut on my head.

He handed me his checked cloth cap. I thanked him and promised to return the clothes. "I'll pay to have them cleaned."

The clothes—a checked flannel long-sleeve shirt and a pair of worn blue jeans—were a bit big for me. That was good; it made me look like a man who's lost weight, maybe hungry, some poor palooka needing a job. I owned casual clothes, but they announced my social class. These were workingmen's clothes.

I cinched the belt tight so the jeans wouldn't slide down over my hips. The cap didn't fit, but I pulled it on regardless. I slipped on my battered brogans, down at the heels. Hard to believe I used to wear them with a suit. Admiring myself in the mirror, I rolled up my sleeves. My watch, always there, didn't fit, so I put it in the locker with my wallet. Now I looked like a scrubbed-up workingman—a bit tough with my crooked nose, heavy brow, and square chin. I tucked some small bills in my front pocket and was ready.

The sun was up, quickly heating the city. I grabbed a bus down Peachtree, and then at Marietta Street, I changed to a trolley headed out to Howell Mill. Most of the traffic was in the other direction, people going into work, so I had the streetcar to myself.

Atlanta was a city of deals, of management and commerce, mostly practiced in the skyscrapers and private clubs downtown. Railroad logicians, corporate managers, salesmen, and lawyers dominated, channeling the power of the railroads, guiding the city's economy. But there was also industry. On the west side, a long swath of factories crowded around two important rail junctions and several massive railroad yards. From Atlantic Steel in the north to the Exposition Mills in the south, clustered Atlanta's most important factories. The streetcar reached the core of this industrial district. Leaving the trolley, I walked up Howell Mill past the White Provision Company to Huff Road.

The shotgun houses of Blandtown looked worse by daylight, some falling down, others unpainted. No one sat on the stoops talking. It was a Negro neighborhood, the homes of men and women who worked lesser-paid, segregated jobs. The men served as janitors and laborers, the women as domestics and laundresses. At the Exposition Cotton Mills, Black men could only work outside, manhandling the heavy bales, while whites worked indoors and were paid more. In the stockyards, it was much the same. The adults were at work, and only a few small children and grannies sat on the porches. No one cared when I crawled through a hole in the fence around the Van Winkle plant.

The works appeared more sprawling by day. The weather had cleared, and a bright blue sky arched overhead. Well-maintained buildings stood out, the others tumbledown, and a water tower loomed above it all. Further south, smoke from the Exposition Mills' ancient coal boilers fed long black plumes into the sky. The crash and bustle of the railroad shops sounded in the distance; the stern hoot of a steam engine or the klaxon honk of a newer diesel echoed up from the yards. Cattle lowed in the stockyards, a somber note, accompanied by their barnyard smell and a whiff of offal.

I crunched across the graveled lot slowly, headed for the office. Van Winkle had sold out some years before, and the plant was now run by a Texas company. From the look of things, they weren't doing very well. I knocked and stepped into the office. In the corner, a woman typed on an ancient black Remington. A man came to the counter.

"Can I help you?" he said, his eyes taking me in. I hoped he noticed that, despite my hard face and shabby clothes, I was clean and smiling.

"Ah shore hope so, sir," I said, drawing out my accent and wiping my forehead. I snatched off my cap and held it in both hands, an act of supplication, crushing it nervously. "Wondering if y'all have any kind of work?"

"What sort of work, fella?" He looked at my hands, my shoulders, then stared at the stitches on my head.

"Well, sir, I can do most anything. Used to work for the railroad; I can line up track, pick, and shovel. I can drive a truck, and I've got a driver's license. I worked a while at Fulton Cotton Mills; show me how and I can run any kind of machine."

"What happened to your job at Fulton Mills?"

"Oh, I made some money and tried to go back to farming. Things didn't pan out; you know how it is. Now I'm back, but they're not hiring. So I'm lookin' 'round."

"We need trained machinists. Men with experience who can handle the lathe or a drill press. Can you do that?"

"Not right off. But, like I said, I'm a quick learner. Just let me try."

"Well," said the man, taking out a paper form and a pencil. "Thank you for your honesty. A lot of men lie, saying they can handle machine tools. Just takes a few questions to catch 'em. So, I'll be honest with you. The only work we have is for machinists, and there's not much of that. We don't hire apprentices, and we don't need laborers right now. Fill out this form, and we'll let you know if something opens up. But business is right slow, and I don't expect anything this month."

"Thank you kindly, sir," I said, doing my best to look disappointed. "Do you know of any other work around here?"

"Maybe in the stockyards, but that comes and goes; it ain't regular. Seems like you're looking for a steady job?"

"Yes, sir." I stepped up to the counter and filled out the form using the name William Smith and the downtown YMCA as an address. "It's just, I saw all them lights on last night. Hoped maybe you was running a night shift. I don't mind a night shift."

"Lights?"

"Yes, sir, buildings back that away. Lights was just blazing. I thought for sure you must have a big job going, maybe needed men."

The woman stopped typing. "There was a meeting, Mr. Wilson. The Pioneers. They wear those white shirts."

"Oh, yeah," he said.

"A meetin'?" What kind of meetin'?"

The woman typist looked up at me. "One of the workers' meetings."

"You got a union here?" I lifted my pencil from the paper. "I don't hold with no union, saw what happened in '34."

"No, no, no," said Wilson firmly. "No union; we don't allow that kind of thing. Management doesn't have anything to do with those meetings. The group pays to use the building. The police tell me they're okay, even though they are interested in politics. Isn't that right, Jo Ann?"

"Yes, sir, politics," said the typist, not looking up. She put a new sheet of paper into the typewriter and slammed the carriage return lever hard. The typewriter almost jumped off the desk.

"Well, thank you," I said, putting the pencil down and sliding the paper across the counter. "I need somethin' real bad, so please remember me."

"Everybody needs work." He picked up the form and put it on a thick pile on his desk.

I stepped out of the office and wandered a bit. I counted fifteen large buildings, but only four or five seemed to be in use. A few workers moved about, and in one shop I heard the regular thump of a single-cylinder steam engine, just like in the Cuban sugar mills. Machine floor #3 was idle. The chairs and benches still sat in a semicircle. It had the look of a place used regularly for meetings.

"What the hell you doing?" said a harsh voice.

I turned to see a large White man in a blue short-sleeve shirt and black pants. He was bald, barrel-chested, and held a baseball bat.

"Nothing, friend, nothing," I said, holding up my hands. "Just come to ask about work. They say there ain't none, but let me fill out a paper. Just looking 'round in case they call me, wonderin' if'n it be a good place to work."

"You're not supposed to do that."

"Well, I was just looking. Didn't mean nothing."

"You from down by the tracks?"

"No, sir. Livin' at the Y. Lost my job, looking for anything. You know of any work? I'll work hard. I'm strong."

He relaxed. "Brother, far as I know, there's no work 'round here."

"Well, do believe I'll go see if there's anything at the Exposition mill. Hate to waste the dime I spent on the streetcar. Will I get there faster walking along those tracks?"

"You sure can. Luck to you."

"Thank you kindly." I walked downhill through the piles of junk that were so frightening in the dark. I passed the large concrete pipes, but they were empty. The fellow sleeping there must clear out at dawn. I looked back at the mill works. It felt like I'd run a great distance in the dark, but it was only about three hundred yards. Night changes everything.

The rail junction behind the mill formed an enormous Y. The left arm of the Y headed northwest to Chattanooga, the right arm northeast to Charlotte. The base fed into downtown Atlanta. Sidings led off to various industries and warehouses. Down a steep bank lay a cindered flat next to the junction with the scattered remains of a campfire.

Across the rails, between the arms of the Y, a forest of oaks and pines ran up to Huff Road. Following a well-worn trail, I found the first hobo shack. It was built of packing cases and firewood, a shed a man could crawl into to stay dry, nothing more. There were other shelters, a true Hooverville of lean-tos, tents, even crates, scattered through the woods. A good fifty yards in, a White man sat by a hut built from scrap lumber and oil drums.

"I've got a gun," he said.

"Just passing through."

"Blow your head off. You keep away."

I made a big detour around him and went deeper into the woods. Another tramp was sleeping under a lean-to; I didn't disturb him. A teenage boy, weaving drunkenly at ten in the morning, urinated into a bush. Farther back, I came upon a shack with a tin roof. A man was painting the walls with brown stain.

"Morning, brother," I said.

"Morning."

"A fine house."

"Built it myself."

"That stain will make it last. You must not be planning on moving."

"Nope," he said. "Been here almost six months. Don't see as I'll be moving on for a good while. I like the weather."

"Hey, does that fellow back there really have a gun?"

The man looked at me and put down his brush. He had a strong face, a chiseled chin, and shaggy salt-and-pepper hair. He was older, in his fifties, and wore glasses and torn brown overalls. Unlike the others, he'd shaved recently. "Bucky?" he said. "Naw, Bucky's not right in the head. He don't have a gun, but he thinks he does."

"Why's he so touchy?"

"Well, he and a few other fellows found some chickens yesterday."

"Found? Where?"

The fellow laughed. "You think I'd tell you? Anyway, they had a party; they built a big fire and roasted the chickens on it. The fire was big enough that the rain didn't bother it, so they stayed there, eating chicken, sharing a snort, and having a good time. Bucky's all right as long as no one frightens him, if you know what I mean?"

"Sure."

"Well, two of those damn factory bulls come down and rousted them. One of 'em kicked Bucky in the ribs. They hit another fellow in the mouth and busted his lip. After something like that happens, Bucky'll stay in his place and guard it for two or three days before he feels safe."

I sat down, legs crossed, and eased back the too-tight cap. Sunlight filtered through the leaves, and dappled light danced with the breeze. It wasn't so hot in the shade. A train clanked by on the tracks below, wheels squealing across a switch.

"Not a bad place," I said over the racket from the train. "Those fellows up at the factory bother you much?"

"Didn't use to. These last few weeks, though, it's gotten rough. Bulls we'd never seen before came down and chased all the darkies out of here. Let us White fellers stay, but told us to keep out of the factory. Now, they have someone watching the place all night. Used to be you could sneak up there, maybe find something to sell. Not now. Guess it started with the meetings."

"Meetin's?"

"Yeah." He sat down facing me. After settling in, he took out a pouch of tobacco and a paper and began to roll a smoke. "Want one?"

"Naw, too expensive to keep up."

"Got a light?"

I shook my head no. He took a box of matches from his pocket and popped one with his thumb. "Hate to waste one on a cig."

"Yeah."

He took a deep drag and blew out the smoke. "You're not on the rails, not tramping, are you?"

"Nope. Came here to ask about work."

"You look kinda rough, but you're too clean for a tramp. Seeing your nose, though, I wonder what happened to the other fellow?"

"I lost that one," I said, touching my crooked nose. "My name's Mark."

"I'm Al Smith. Folks here call me 'Mr. President.'"

"He lost," I said, laughing.

We shook hands. "Yeah, I guess we're all losers. I used to teach school in San Angelo, Texas, but the oil business crashed, and they let all us teachers go. That was back in '32, and I couldn't find work, so I started to roam. The Santa Fe ran through town, so I hopped a freight. I grew to like it."

"Why are they having meetings up at the factory?"

He took another drag of his cigarette. "Don't know about your politics, but they started out as anti-union meetings. Nothing official, but I think the Klan was behind it. They've been fighting hard against the unions, especially the CIO, all summer. Came down here and preached the gospel to us. No communism, no unions, no Jews, no race mixin'. It was kind of funny, listening to them talk to hobos about unions. You gotta have a job to join a union."

"I didn't know the Klan was still around."

"Then, brother, you must not be from here. CIO's been trying to move into the cotton mills and the Klan's been fighting them. Cops are with the Klan, and the owners turn their heads the other way."

"Are they hurting people?"

"The Klan? Mostly just beat on folks. Rumors say they've killed some fellows, not just Colored. If I hadn't built this house, I might have moved on. Now I'm stuck here. Property will do that to you." He smiled fondly at his shack.

"Been to any of these meetings?"

"Early on, thought it would be interesting. I did go to college once upon a time. But it was dime a dozen talk about Jews, unions, and communism. Sin, socialism, and race mixin's bringing the country down; that's why we're having hard times. They talked about organizing to purify America. Call themselves the Pioneers; they all wear white shirts. They're a political group. Sort of like the Fascists and Black Shirts in Italy, or the Nazis and Brown Shirts in Germany. Maybe you heard of the Silver Shirts up in North Carolina? Anyway, they say programs like the ones in Germany would end the Depression."

"What do you think?"

He drew on his cigarette and blew smoke out of his nose. "Most just want to strut and push folks around. You know the type. A few talked about leading America away from Communism, the New Deal, and all that. Build a completely White society. So, they wear white shirts, get it?

A couple of the guys are good speakers; they get the audience all riled up." He drew on his cigarette again. "One of 'em wants to run for mayor. And they think this General Mosely fellow should be Dictator of the United States."

"Dictator? Jesus. And mayor? They talked about that?"

"Like I said, there's a lot of stuff about politics, not all of it straight. They called Mayor Hartsfield a nigger lover. Can you believe that, Hartsfield, a nigger lover? Even I know better, and I'm not from here." He chuckled, smoke jetting out of his nose. He finished his cigarette, carefully stubbed it out, and tucked the butt into a corner of his tobacco pouch.

"Many folks at these meetings?"

"At first, a lot, maybe sixty or so. Don't seem to be so many lately. Now what you hear is committees, you know, committee this and committee that. It's all a bunch of hot air; it won't amount to spit. I used to teach history. If history shows one thing about American politics, you gotta have lots of money to play. Lots of *do-re-mi*. And these fellows don't have a dime."

Bingo, I thought.

It was after noon when I called Emma's office, but she was out. Then I called her boarding house, but no one answered. I wondered what was happening with her and Goss, where he was living. I guessed I'd have to wait.

Phil Sanders's office was just a couple of blocks away, in the Rhodes-Haverty Building, so I called him. We met for lunch at the Grill Room.

"Glad you called," Phil said. "I need some entertainment today. I'm bored. Everyone's shorting the market, expecting war in Europe and a crash."

"Don't you? Expect war, I mean."

"You betcha. Oh, the market's dropping. Then, one day, everyone will remember how much money we made in the last war. After that, the market will soar too high. It will be impossible to time it, so the only solution is to buy the dip now and hold on for a wild ride. Some of the gains will be solid. By the time this war ends, you'll double, maybe even triple, your money."

"No bonds?"

He smiled. "At two and a half percent? War will bring inflation. Don't you remember 1919?"

"I was in school. We were worried about the Spanish flu."

"Well, bonds were almost worthless. Terrible inflation, something like one hundred percent." He took a drink of water. "Is that what you want me to do with your deposit, put it in bonds?"

"No, I trust you to make good choices. I just want to understand more about what you do, I guess."

"You have to know the companies you pick, have to research them, and prove the numbers the company publishes. A lot of companies cover up the real condition of their business. Sure, the new SEC rules are supposed to make everything transparent, but there's a host of ways to bend 'em. I'll teach you how to sort through them if you want. But that's not why I came to lunch. You're my best chance for something interesting today, this odyssey you're engaged in with the Germans. So, how's it going with the *Fräulein*?"

"It isn't." Immediately, images from the vivid sex dream flooded back, causing me to catch my breath. Phil noticed and gave me an oblique glance.

"There's nothing there," I insisted.

"Sure. You talk to her in German, don't you? Maybe that's the problem? German's such a screwed-up language. Sounds like someone grinding coffee. I tried to learn some once, but I gave up on it as an unholy mess."

"It's not any worse than English."

"Then, why do they wait until the end of a sentence to tell you the verb? Why do they stick all kinds of words together, creating monsters you can't decipher in a week with three dictionaries? Worse, they use that god-awful, unreadable alphabet."

"They think the Gothic alphabet is more German; it reflects their culture."

"You mean that's what the Nazis think. It's another reflection of their insanity. How can the world's best composers and scientists also be the world's best militarists? They want war; they enjoy war. It's in their nature."

"Jesus," I said, "what the hell is wrong with you today?"

"Sorry." He took a breath. "I had dinner last night with Jonathan Coen and his wife. She has cousins trapped in Germany, and the Nazis won't let them leave. Until last night, I hadn't realized how terrible things are over there. I'd only been thinking about Jews as a vague group, not as individuals. The Coens have tried everything. Now they're told that if you grease the right palms, you can get people out. They want me to help. A lot of money has to be transferred to a bank in Switzerland. Twenty thousand dollars. Some people with experience in doing this joined us, including an English woman who looked just like Kate Smith."

"Eleanor Jones?"

His eyes widened. "How did you know?"

"She works with the guy who hired me for the German job. The rabbi. I met her the other night."

"No joke? Boy, that's strange."

"Well, you may have just answered one mystery. How does the rabbi have so much money?"

"You think they're scamming the Coens?"

"Who knows?" I said. "I don't know her, but I know I don't trust him."

Our food came, and we ate as Phil continued to make small talk. "The *Journal* says there were 57,000 people at the Baptist pageant last Monday night. And that British woman speaker was dead-on, saying totalitarianism first works to destroy the mind."

My mind was whirling. A British woman and a rabbi trying to find a German scientist? People who know how to buy people's freedom from the Nazis? Who were they?

The Grill Room was packed, and I needed to talk with Phil in private. After lunch, we walked down the hall to an empty card room and settled into the leather-covered armchairs. Phil took a cigar from his inside jacket pocket, a fine Cuban. He smoked nothing else.

"I set up the account you wanted," he said, waving the cigar. "And I know you don't smoke, but too bad; this is a great cigar." He smiled, rolling the cigar in his fingers. "Tell me, how are the Huns doing?" He chuckled. "Anyone try to kill them yet?"

"Two people are dead."

He laid the cigar down unlit. "Dead? Are you serious?"

"Yes. Murdered."

"God, how have they kept that out of the papers?"

I told him everything that had occurred since we had last talked: Rubenstein's death, my visit to the Jewish neighborhood, dinner with the Germans, the counterfeit cash, finding Rolf Schulman dead, my arrest, and the deal with Packard. Even about Peter Goss and his desire to remain in the US, and that I'd asked Emma to hide him. Finally, I mentioned Anna saying she wanted me. When I finished, he stared at me.

"Shit just follows you, doesn't it?"

"What do you mean? I think I've done pretty well."

"Done well? You've been wildly reckless. It's only luck you haven't been killed, or aren't sitting behind bars. Now you've put Emma at risk? You should be horsewhipped for that. My God, Mark, two men have been murdered!"

Phil remembered his cigar, picked it up, and carefully cut off the end. Then, with two matches, he got it drawing. I didn't mind the break; besides, the cigar aroma was nice.

"I'll be surprised if Emma ever talks to you again."

"It's not that bad. No one but you knows about this."

"Anyone who saw Goss at her office knows. Anyone who sees them on a streetcar."

"It was the only thing I could do." I met his eyes and realized he looked sad, not angry.

"Mark, did you get anything in writing from the police, the Secret Service, or the district attorney about this deal?"

"I didn't think of that."

"Have you talked to a lawyer?"

"Of course not."

"For a smart guy, you can be incredibly stupid. You need to see a lawyer now. Get a promise, in writing, from the district attorney and from the Feds, to protect you from any charges, or worse, extradition."

I thought about it. "Who should I see?"

"I'd suggest Duke Webster. He's friends with the DA and does a lot of criminal work. Stay away from the silk-stocking firms; they'll just milk you."

"Okay, I'll call Webster."

"No, I'll walk you over there now. It may be too late, but you have to try."

"Too late? You think I'm in danger?"

"Goddamn right. The cops are after you, the Germans are after you, and maybe even mysterious government agents are after you. The Klan is even involved. I'm surprised you're still alive, especially since you're hanging around your known residence. The smartest thing would be to hop a westbound train and never come back."

"I can't do that."

"Well, maybe that wouldn't be so safe. If the Nazis figure out what you know, they'll follow you to the ends of the earth. You realize what they're doing, don't you?"

"I think so. The Germans plan to support the Pioneers' political ambitions. Lots of cash will let them run a candidate for mayor—maybe even for governor—or they can buy candidates running for office."

"Yep," he said.

"So what? Backward yahoos ranting about Communist Jews and racial purity. It'll be a joke. No one will buy that drivel."

Phil blinked at me in amazement. "What do you think Gene Talmadge rants about in his speeches? What do half the members of the state legislature preach about in their campaigns?" He pointed his cigar at me. "Sometimes I wonder if you really understand this city, this state, hell, even this country. You lived in Cuba too long, then went to Princeton. I don't know which is worse, but somewhere you lost touch with this reality."

"Come on, Phil, people know better than to believe that nonsense."

"Do they? Look at Germany. The world leader in medicine, science, and engineering. Think of their music, poetry, literature, and universities. Yet, they elected the Nazis. Elected them! Now they roar their approval after every pronouncement by Hitler, even as he leads them toward war. God, have people forgotten so soon what that's like? Millions died in the World War. Millions. It's enough to make you abandon hope for mankind."

"America's different," I said. "Germany lost the World War, felt oppressed by the peace treaty and economic collapse. Hitler offered a way out. Democracy, republics, and liberal thought seemed to have failed, and he convinced them only he could save Germany."

"You could be describing the South."

"The Civil War was long ago."

"Was it?" he said. "Come on, Mark, what's been the best-selling book over the past two years?"

"Book? I don't know."

"*Gone with the Wind.*"

"That's just a novel," I said.

"People believe it, and now they're even making a movie about it. In the novel, after the South loses the war, we suffer under a vengeful and corrupt Yankee dictatorship. The book is not really about the Civil War. It's about oppression and suffering during Reconstruction, of an honorable White majority oppressed by the deluded Black minority, the federal government, and carpetbaggers. The heroes are southerners fighting Negro and federal domination."

"It's a novel, right? It exaggerates for dramatic purposes."

"You and I know that, but most people don't. They take it as history, in part because it reinforces their experience. The South is economically disadvantaged, culturally backward, and a virtual economic colony of the North. I see it every day in my work."

"Oh God, not the '*Sahara of the Bozart*' stuff again."

"To some degree, H. L. Mencken was right, you know that. But the problem's bigger than Southern backwardness. There are good reasons for resentment against the northern states, against the federal government. Look at the unfair freight rates charged by railroads that penalize Southern products. The Interstate Commerce Commission approves those rates. Add that to the economic and cultural disaster that the South has been since the war. Boll weevils, sharecropping, lintheads, tramps, lynching, snake-handling Holy Rollers, demagogues, my God, it's an endless list of misery and backwardness."

"You sound like one of those Erskine Caldwell novels."

He didn't laugh. "Mark, sometimes it's downright depressing being a Southerner. As the president says, we're the nation's number one economic problem. The only wonder is that we haven't had a revolution, and I don't mean Communism."

Phil's argument was unsettling. I hadn't really taken the political threat seriously. Would a group like the White Shirts attract average Georgians, average Americans? Even the name was ridiculous. I stood and began to pace. "What could the Germans want? What could they hope to gain?"

"Take their perspective. War's coming to Europe; everybody knows it. In the last war, Germany defeated Russia, and probably would have made an advantageous peace with France and Great Britain if we had not entered the war. US involvement made all the difference, and they were forced to accept a humiliating peace. Based on that, what must they do to ensure victory in the next war?"

"Keep us out, of course."

"Maybe you did learn something at that college?"

"But, Phil, that's not an issue. We learned from the World War. The United States is committed to neutrality. Look at the Neutrality Acts and other laws. There is no way around it; we won't join this war. Trying to influence our politics might backfire and hurt Germany."

"You need to read more, Mark. We were just as committed to neutrality in the last war, but our economic ties to Britain and France drew us in. The same will happen this time." Phil stood up and grabbed me by the shoulders to stop my pacing. "So, an uninvolved America benefits Germany. Given that, what would be their best course?"

"You tell me," I said, feeling resentful about the lecture.

"What if the United States was in political disarray, fell into chaos? Or, even better, what if a substantial political movement here shared Nazi ideas? Would we abandon the Neutrality Acts? Could we go to war with Germany? And even if the political effort fails, the Nazis might build a cadre of supporters as a fifth column, even saboteurs, if we declared war."

"That's a grandiose fantasy," I protested.

"When are the Nazis anything but grandiose? A committed fascist would think they're doing us a favor. Saving us from Communism, racial degradation, and degeneracy—bringing order to our society."

"I don't know."

"Okay. None of us really knows. But while you're thinking about it, let's go see your lawyer."

Duke Webster agreed to represent me, but he wanted three hundred bucks up front. It's never a good sign when a lawyer wants money up front; maybe he's not sure you'll be around to pay later. A bit after six o'clock, I left Webster's office. Peachtree was packed with traffic; horns honked, and waves of heat from the cars and concrete distorted the air. The Henry Grady shimmered three blocks down the street.

The lobby was busy, with Baptist Messengers on their way out to dinner and guests arriving to dine in the Spanish Room. I sat in the corner and watched the crowd, hoping to spot Kunst, maybe follow him. I was sure he'd go back to the machine works, and I expected him to take some counterfeit with him. After eight o'clock, I began to worry. Had he already passed the money to the Pioneers?

I stepped out front, watching the traffic crawl along a twilight Peachtree Street through the theater district. Flashes from the overhead electrical connections of the trolleys composed an irregular counterpoint to the bright lights and neon of Atlanta's version of Times Square. The sharp odor of ozone and electrical motors mixed with the smell of car exhaust. The smell was familiar—the smell of my city. I turned south and ambled toward the Athletic Club, feeling at home.

When I reached the intersection at Ellis, I waited to cross. A black Plymouth turned in front of me and stopped. The passenger door opened. A lean man in a white shirt and khaki trousers got out and smiled hugely.

"Hey, brother, looks like you need a ride." He motioned me toward the Plymouth.

I sensed a presence behind me. Mostly, it was his smell: cigarettes and sweat, mixed with sour vinegar on his breath. He'd probably had collards with dinner. His hand touching my left shoulder was gentle, but the sharp blade probing me above my right hip was not.

"Be a shame to lose a kidney," he said softly. His harsh cracker accent and vinegar breath enveloped me. The knife point broke my skin. I felt a trickle of blood.

Guided by the man with the knife, I climbed into the back seat. A large fellow in a white shirt waited there. He stuck a blunt barrel into my ribs when I slid up next to him. The man with the knife climbed in, pressed me against the gun, and closed the door. We headed west on Ellis, and the bright streetlights showed that all were wearing white shirts. Then I recognized the driver. The young policeman named Will, the one who'd hit me on the head in the Decatur Street parking lot.

"You was warned," he said, glancing at me.

The man with the knife was my height but thin, with a bulging Adam's apple and bulging eyes. He was smart, watching my hands, the knife still pressed on my right side. The big guy held the pistol across his body with his left hand. I wondered if a shot would pass through me and hit the guy with the knife. I didn't care to find out. The big guy was larger than me, fat, but had massive forearms and shoulders. His head was balding, the remaining hair trimmed close to his skull above a bulbous nose and heavy jowls. Probably another cop. He reached to the floor and picked up a pint bottle.

"Drink up, buddy," he said, pushing the gun into my side more firmly. I unscrewed the cap and took a swig. Harsh odors assailed me as the cheap whisky burned the back of my throat.

We stopped at the intersection of Spring Street and Ellis, where a policeman stood on the curb, watching the traffic. The car windows were open, so I shouted, "Help, kidnapping!"

The knife dug into my side, breaking the skin again. The policeman bent down to look into the car. Will waved at him.

"How's it going, Tom?"

"Oh." The cop looked startled. "Didn't know there was a Klavern tonight. Aren't you supposed to gag the initiates?"

"Not Atlanta. Forrest Park. And he was quiet until now."

"Yeah. Okay, go on." He thumped the top of the car, and Will pulled onto Spring Street, headed north.

"That was stupid," said The Knife. "I could'a killed you."

"Take another drink," said the big guy. I took a small sip, and then a second small sip. Big Smile leaned over the seat and pressed a revolver into my forehead.

"Gotta do better than that," he said. "Drink up." So I drank deeply, and then again. Soon, I'd drunk more than half the bottle, and the harsh whiskey churned in my belly.

"Shouldn't a last drink be better stuff?" I said, then belched.

"Yeah," said the big guy. "You're real tough. Hold still." He tied a bandana over my eyes.

"What's this for?"

"You don't need to see where we're going. It could be bad for your health."

As soon as the bandana was in place, the car turned left. We made more than a dozen turns after that. I counted, but that didn't mean I had any clue where we were. My head spun from whiskey on an empty stomach, the two puncture wounds hurt, and I was thoroughly lost. Finally, we came to a stop, and Big Smile got out of the car. We waited. After a few minutes, he returned.

"What'd they say?" asked The Knife. "Do we take him to the fish camp?"

"Nope. Special service. You stay here."

The Knife poked me again before getting out of the car. He spoke softly before he closed the door. "You're a lucky fella. I was gonna fillet you for the fishes, nice and slow."

The door closed, and I slid closer to it as the car pulled away. The big guy with the gun pressed it against me. "Don't try anything cute," he said. I nodded and carefully felt around with my right hand for the door handle. Suddenly, the big guy's fist smashed into my head. My face slammed against the window glass.

"I told you not to get cute."

Dazed, my nose burned as if on fire, and blood trickled down behind the bandana. We made several more turns, idled at a stoplight, then began driving at a steady pace. The big guy was no longer pressing the gun into my side; he'd shifted away from me. A moment later, he doused me with the remaining cheap whiskey and put his feet against my hips. The car door flew open, and the big guy booted me out. We weren't going very fast. I hit the pavement hard and rolled. Skin came off my elbows, hands, and knees. Angry, I jumped to my feet and ripped off the bandana. Just in time to see the car that hit me.

8

THURSDAY, JULY 27, 1939

I'd known worse pain, or at least I told myself that. I tried to sit up, but couldn't breathe, so I lay back. As long as I took shallow breaths, I was better. I dozed in and out. Each time I woke, my headache was worse. Maybe a hangover from the cheap juice. One of the times I opened my eyes, I saw a nurse.

"Mr. Morgan?" she said, leaning in close and speaking loudly. "Do you know where you are, Mr. Morgan?"

"Grady?" I croaked.

"That's right," she shouted. "You're at Grady Hospital. You had a snootful, Mr. Morgan. Do you remember why?"

"I can hear you. Of course I remember why. The car."

"That's right, Mr. Morgan. You stepped into oncoming traffic on the Spring Street viaduct. Spring Street! At night! You could have been killed."

"Did I break any ribs?" I asked, breathing carefully.

"I'll let the doctor tell you about your injuries, but I think you're going to be fine. The car didn't hit your head, just your hips and chest. You might even get out of here tomorrow, but boy, you're going to hurt for weeks. Think about that the next time you drink."

"May I have some water?"

"Here you go," she said, putting a straw in my mouth. I sucked greedily.

"Thank you for taking care of me," I said.

"It's my job, but you should take care of yourself."

"I'll try," I said, and slept.

When I woke, light shone through the window. I couldn't tell whether it was morning or afternoon. I waited. The room had four beds in it, but the others held quiet patients. My hip and side burned, as if punishing me. After some time, a very young nurse bustled in, not the one I'd spoken with earlier. With bobbed blond hair and freckles, she looked like she belonged in high school. "Sweetie," she said brightly, as if speaking to a child. "Are we awake?"

I groaned. "Damn right I'm awake."

"Oh, that's good," she said, fussing with my pillow. She took my pulse and looked in my eyes. "Dr. Edison is making his rounds. You'll be able to talk with him." She smiled and hurried out of the room.

The light outside grew brighter until it was near mid-morning. Finally, the door opened, and a young doctor and the same young nurse came in together. She smiled at me brightly, nervously. The doctor looked at a clipboard.

"Hello, Mr. Morgan," he said, not looking up. "I'm Doctor Edison, a resident here at Grady."

"Pleased to meet you," I said.

"Uh-huh," he said, looking at the chart. "Well, let's see how you're doing." He put down the clipboard, stepped over, and listened with his stethoscope for a few minutes. He shone a light in my eyes, snapped fingers by my ears, and looked at the top of my head.

"How'd this happen?" he asked, touching the stitches on my crown.

"A cop clubbed me."

"Really? Well, it looks like those sutures can come out. I'll do it when I finish the exam. You're going to have a big scar; it wasn't done by an artist."

"No, it wasn't."

"Your nose was broken too. I set it straight, but you'll have trouble breathing for a while because of the packing and the swelling."

"It was broken before. You probably improved how I look."

He smiled. "Maybe. You seem accident-prone, Mr. Morgan. Were you drinking when those accidents happened?"

"None of them were accidents. Neither was this."

"I see. Not an accident. Well, this time you went too far." He placed his hands on the left side of my chest and pressed. Agony.

"There's not much we can do for these ribs but tape them and let them heal in their own time. Three are broken. We took an X-ray while you were unconscious. Because of all the blood from your nose, we feared a lung was punctured. Pictures showed you're fine. Thankfully, you're in good physical condition; you must exercise a lot. As long as you're careful over the next few weeks, the ribs ought to knit cleanly."

"I usually swim in the mornings."

"With these ribs, you won't swim for a while. Just raising your arm over your head will hurt, but pulling down will be agony. Lay off the swimming for now. In a couple of weeks, you might try."

He pulled back the sheet, exposing me below the waist. The star-shaped puncture and long scar from the gunshot and compound fracture covered my left shin.

"That's an old injury," I gasped, trying to pull the sheet back over myself.

"We knew that," said the doctor. His eyes met mine, sympathetic. I glanced at the young nurse. Her eyes were big, horrified.

"It happened a year ago, the same time as my nose."

"Neither was treated properly."

"I was shot in the leg. It shattered the bone."

"Well, I need to examine your hip, Mr. Morgan. I'm sorry. I should have warned you. I want to look at your hip, nothing more. It's terribly bruised." After he checked my hip, he pulled the sheet up to my chest, tucking it around me. "Do you need us to contact anyone? Your family, an employer?"

"Call Phil Sanders." I gave them the number.

"Do you have the means to pay for your care here? Or do we need to put you on the charity?"

"I can pay. Check my wallet; there should be enough. If not, Phil will pay."

"Okay. As far as I can tell, you're going to be fine. Thankfully, you have no significant head injury. Your nose wasn't broken by the car, was it?"

"That happened before. A fist."

"I see. If you want, I can discharge you this afternoon. I would suggest, however, that you stay with us overnight. You're going to hurt worse over the next day or two."

"I'd like to go home," I said. "Sanders can pick me up."

"All right, tough guy," he said. "I'll have the hospital call Mr. Sanders."

He asked the nurse to bring a suture removal kit. As soon as she left the room, he bent close and said softly, "She doesn't like you, thinks you must be a gangster or something. Are you?"

"Hell no."

"Be honest with me, Mr. Morgan. Tell me how you feel, both physically and emotionally."

"What do you mean?"

"We both know you've suffered terrible violence," he said. "Violence yesterday and violence in the past. Stuff like that breaks a man. I need to know your real condition, so I don't spend all this time getting you well only to have you 'wander drunk' in front of a car again."

It took me a moment to catch his drift. "I see. You think I did it on purpose, that I tried to check out?"

He nodded.

"You'd think I was lying if I told you what happened."

He raised an eyebrow and tilted his head, curious.

"Okay, yesterday some cops tried to kill me. They grabbed me off Peachtree, made me drink a lot of whiskey quickly, so I would be drunk, then poured the rest on my clothes. After that, they pushed me out of the car into traffic. I was blindfolded when they did it. Did they find a red bandana on the road?"

He watched my eyes intently. "That sounds completely nuts."

"I'm sure. Nonetheless, it's true."

"The police sent a bandana in with you. A red bandana."

"I yanked it off just before the car hit me."

He took a moment, watching my eyes. "Do you want to talk to the police?"

"No thank you, Doctor. Given what happened, I don't imagine they would be of much help. Did anyone see what happened?"

"I only know what's written in the file. A taxi hit you. You were lucky. The driver said it was dark when you suddenly appeared in the road. He couldn't stop, but was going slowly. You might be alive because of the mayor's twenty-five-mile-per-hour speed limit."

"Well, that's one thing at least."

The nurse returned with a tray. She scowled while carefully tucking pillows around my head, positioning my scalp for the doctor. He snipped the stitches and then plucked them out with a hemostat.

"Do you have any memory of how you wandered onto the road?" the nurse asked while he worked.

"Oh, yes," I said. "I remember exactly."

Phil Sanders drove me home from the hospital. My blue suit was ruined, but he'd brought some tan trousers and a blue button-down shirt for me to wear. As I worked to get my arms in the sleeves, I suddenly laughed, then bent forward from the pain.

"It hurts?" Phil said.

"It does; it hurts like hell. But you know, I just bought three new suits, and in less than a week, all three are ruined. So much for my new wardrobe."

"Maybe you should think again about this job," said Phil.

It didn't hurt much when I walked slowly, but getting into his car was difficult. Phil drove a low-slung '37 Cord, a powerful two-seater, blue, with a convertible top and bucket seats. When the orderly opened the car door, I realized just how far it was down to the seat. I worked my way in slowly and then made the mistake of grabbing the top of the windshield frame with my bandaged hands. I nearly screamed at the bolt of agony across my ribs.

"Mark, take it easy," Phil said. "We're not in a hurry."

I almost told him to shut the hell up, but he was doing me a favor, so I simply grunted. Finally, I was in. My ribs and hip throbbed with pain, and even the bandaged abrasions on my hands, elbows, and knees hurt. Maybe going home was a mistake? The engine growled, and Phil pulled away, wove down a few side streets, and turned north on Memorial.

"Hey," I said. "We need to catch a cross street to downtown."

"We're not going to the Athletic Club," said Phil. "You'd have to go up a bunch of stairs. At my place, you can walk right in and go to the guest bedroom. Just one step up."

"Your place?"

"Martha can take care of you tomorrow while I'm at work. You need to rest."

"Phil, you don't have to do this."

"I know," he said. "But I'm doing it."

He cut over to Peachtree and continued north, out of the city. Night was falling, that time of magical twilight when everything looks soft and clean—just like it had the night before, when they'd grabbed me.

"I was pushed," I said. "Out of a car and onto the road. The cop who'd hit me on the head was there."

"What?" he said, glancing over. "The hospital said you were drunk."

"How often have you seen me drunk? They forced me to drink some cheap booze, then pushed me out onto the road."

"Mark, that's insane."

I told him everything that had happened, from leaving Duke Webster's office up through the doctor's examination.

"You remember?"

"I wasn't that drunk. They made me drink about half a pint, and it didn't have much time in my system. Oh, I remember their faces. When the time comes, I'll recognize them."

"God," he said. "Isn't this what happened to that Rubenstein fellow? People who bother the Germans get hit by cars. They meant to kill you."

"This was the Klan, or that new group, the Pioneers."

We drove in silence for a few minutes. As we approached Buckhead, Phil said, "Maybe Germans and the Klan?"

"Yep. But which Germans?" I grabbed my side; it ached with every jounce of the car.

"Mark, you cannot go back to the Athletic Club. They must know about you. You have to quit this job."

"Agreed," I said.

"Good," he said. We drove for a few minutes in silence. Finally, he cleared his throat. "I'd like you to come work at my firm."

"Phil, I can't do that."

"Of course you can," he said. "I need you."

"I don't know a damned thing about the securities business."

"Don't need to. I'll teach you. You were a good executive with Coke. You'll do important work for me on the road. I'm putting together mutual funds that will include dozens of different companies' stock. I need someone to visit those companies, find out their strengths and weaknesses. Ferret out hidden information. I need someone who can tell if the financials, the production data, or the forecasts aren't on the up and up. Someone who knows people, who can read them, tell me if they're dependable. Tell me if they're liars."

"Phil, I wouldn't make a good employee."

We drove along in silence, the long warm twilight engulfing us. "There may be a way to work past that. Until we figure it out, let me have some business cards printed up for you with my firm's name."

"I won't work for you, Phil."

"Just listen. The card will say 'of counsel,' like a lawyer. That way, my secretaries can handle your calls. If people ask for your card, it'll carry weight."

"That's very generous."

"Not really; it might cost me five bucks."

He slowed and turned onto Blackland Road, nearing his home.

"You need a title under your name on the card," he mused. "Something that communicates what you do."

"Consultant?"

"No, that doesn't really mean anything." He turned onto Valley Road. While I steeled myself for the pain of climbing out of the car, an idea came to me.

"I know," I said. "It should read, *Mark Morgan, Consulting Agent.*"

Phil's house on the hill glowed; all light and glass. We motored slowly up the drive and stopped in front of the cavernous entrance. He helped me out. His live-in maid, Martha, hurried to make up a guest bedroom. A cooling breeze blew through the house, stirring the white linen drapes that hung from a ceiling two stories high. Incandescent light shone golden on the moving drapes, weaving light and dark throughout the living room. The effect was delightful, magical.

A pedestal bed occupied the center of the guest room, covered with a textured golden spread. The back wall was a large glass block, looking into dark, thick woods. The other three walls were covered in fine ochre cloth. Cubist paintings, dominated by deep reds, oranges, and blacks, were centered on each wall.

"Hungry?" Phil asked.

"No." I sat slowly on the bed, aching all over. "Maybe I'll eat tomorrow. I don't need anything tonight."

Phil looked at his hands, methodically matching his fingertips together. Finally, he spoke. "Mark, forget about the rabbi's money. Forget about Packard and his promises. Stay here, lie low, and let Duke Webster take care of your police problems."

I chuckled. "When people find out I'm here overnight, tongues will wag."

"Let them," said Phil. "Besides, you're not exactly an eligible bachelor."

"Touché."

I began to pull the covers down on the bed, then had a thought. "Phil, I should make a phone call."

"Oh God, not the woman?"

"Yes. She may be worried about me."

"You're nuts, Mark. You shouldn't call her."

"Why not?"

"The conference ends tomorrow. Let her and her husband simply go away. That's the best solution."

"She's my friend."

"Really?" he said. "Every time I bring her up, you deny she's anything. Now, she's your friend?"

"I lied," I said. "I'm not sure exactly what she means to me, or what I mean to her, but there's something between us. We have a connection."

"Mark, you're an idiot."

"Idiot?"

"Haven't you figured it out?"

"Figured out what? What the hell do you mean?"

"Mark, you poor fool. She's one of them."

9

Friday, July 28, 1939

A loud shout woke me. Pounding, then the crash of breaking glass. I sat up quickly and gasped, my ribs on fire.

"You can't come in," Phil shouted.

A louder crash and the sounds of footsteps and of doors banging open echoed through the concrete and glass house. I'd fallen asleep fully dressed, except for my shoes. I bent gingerly to put them on. Before I finished, the door was thrown open, and the light switched on.

"In here," a deputy yelled. He pointed his gun at me.

I raised my hands. "What's going on?"

Detective Garret Hancock of the Atlanta Police Department followed the deputy in. There were dark bags under his eyes, and he looked like he'd not slept since I'd last seen him. Maybe he never slept? I glanced at my watch. It was after 4 a.m.

"You've gotta do something about your hours, Detective," I said.

"Yeah, you're still a funny guy," he said. "Come on, we're going for a ride."

"I'm calling my lawyer," Phil sputtered in the hallway.

"Do that," said Hancock. "But, if you get in my way, I'll take you downtown. Disorderly conduct, interference with a police officer, and, let's see, there're laws against sodomy in this state. Could get interesting." He leered at me.

I laughed. "That's what you think?"

"Can it, Morgan. You don't want to know what I think. You gonna come with us, or do we collar your fairy friend too?"

"Mark, don't go with them," Phil said.

The deputy grabbed me by the arm, wrenching me to my feet. I groaned; the pain was intense.

"He's injured," said Phil. "Leave him alone."

"Yeah," said Hancock. "You picked him up at the hospital, brought him all the way out here. God knows where he's been tonight. You should have stayed in the hospital, Morgan, and waited for us to come and talk to you. First thing I hear is that you were run down while drunk. Next, I'm disappointed to hear you're still alive. So then, we go to look for you, and you've disappeared with this fruit. I had to get these poor county deputies out of bed."

"Where are we going?"

"You'll come voluntarily?"

"I'm not in any shape to run. I'll do what you say and let the lawyers argue later."

"Stan, take him to my car."

The deputy marched me through the house and slid me into the back of a black Chevy sedan. Rawson sat behind the wheel, chewing on a toothpick.

"Nice to see you again, Morgan," he said.

"Wish I could say the same."

Detective Hancock swung into the passenger seat. "Let's go, Bill."

"So, where are we headed? Will the whiskey be better than the last time I rode with some cops?"

"Shut up," said Hancock.

We drove in on Peachtree. At Collier, we cut over to Howell Mill and headed south past the waterworks, then turned onto Huff Road. Crossing the railroad tracks, we stopped next to three other police cars. Was this where I would simply disappear? Was the wrecking crew waiting? Would they beat me to death? I gently lifted the door latch, but it didn't work.

Hancock spoke to a couple of cops. A moment later, a bright light stabbed into my eyes. I twisted away, my ribs screaming.

"Hold still, Morgan," growled Hancock. "Do I gotta come back there and hold your head?"

I quit moving, blinded by the light.

"Turn your head to the left. Now turn your head to the right."

"Yeah," said a familiar voice. "Different clothes, but that's him."

The light went out, though I stayed dazzled.

"When did you last see him?" asked Hancock.

"Wednesday morning. Seemed like a nice enough fella. Looks different in the back of a squad car."

Then, it hit me, the voice. Al Smith, the hobo. "What's going on?"

"Shut your trap," said Hancock.

The glow from the headlights swept over the road as Rawson made a three-point turn. I saw Smith briefly in the headlights, with two policemen holding his arms, watching us go. We continued up to Howell Mill and turned right.

"Downtown?" I asked, feeling some hope. They weren't going to kill me and dump me.

"Yeah," said Hancock. "Downtown."

This time, they handcuffed me in a holding cell. They took my wallet, keys, watch, and even my belt. The cell was Spartan, with a bench along one wall and nothing else. The odor of fresh urine and the reek of vomit filled the cell. My side ached as I waited. Finally, a jailer opened the cell and took me upstairs. He showed no sympathy when I grunted with pain, climbing slowly. He led me to the same interrogation room I'd been in before. "Sit down. You right-handed?"

I nodded. He removed the handcuff from my right wrist and fastened my left to the left leg of the chair. After that, he left the room and locked the door behind him. A few minutes later, Rawson and Hancock came in. Hancock sat at the table while Rawson stood by the door, just as before.

"Your act needs a change," I said.

"You don't want to see it change," said Hancock. "When'd you last see Paul Dittmer?"

"Dittmer? What the hell is this about?" The stuffing in my nose made me sound like I had a bad cold.

"Just answer the question. When did you last see Dittmer?"

I had to think; so much had happened over the past few days. I'd seen him through a window at the factory. "Tuesday. Tuesday night."

"Where was that?" asked Hancock.

"First, at his hotel. The Henry Grady. He and Wilhelm Kunst left the hotel together."

"First? When else did you see him?"

"At the Van Winkle Machine Works later that night. He and Kunst talked at a meeting of workers there."

Hancock and Rawson glanced at each other. "A meeting at the old machine works on Huff Road?"

"Yeah, that's the last time I saw him."

"Were you at the meeting?"

"Not officially."

"I bet," muttered Rawson.

"What about last night?" said Hancock. "You sure you didn't see Paul Dittmer last night?"

"Are you guys kidding? A car hit me on Wednesday. Klansmen trying to kill me pushed me in front of a car. I spent all day yesterday at the hospital. Around nightfall, I went to Phil Sanders's house. We probably got there a bit before nine. Broken ribs, broken nose—I'm supposed to be in bed recovering."

"Where were you between ten and midnight?" Hancock leaned toward me, his eyes hard.

"Asleep in bed. I'm sure both Mr. Sanders and his maid can confirm that. Besides, you might have noticed, I'm not exactly in the best shape. I wasn't out gallivanting around."

"Gallivanting," said Rawson, shaking his head.

"So, you were alone between ten and midnight?"

"In bed, yes. What, you think I had Sanders in there with me?"

"Might be better for you if he were," said Hancock. He stood and turned toward the door. Handcuffed to the chair, I couldn't move.

"Hey," I said. "Don't leave me here."

They said nothing, simply closed the door behind them. So I waited again. About half an hour later, the door opened, and Joe Packard came in.

"Why am I not surprised?" I said.

Packard sat. Hancock followed him. A third man I'd never seen before, with short, iron-colored hair, an immaculate suit, and a briefcase, followed them.

"No Rawson?" I asked. "What will we do for comic relief?"

"I'm damn sick of you, Morgan," said Hancock.

Packard held out a calming hand and turned to me. "You claim to know nothing about what happened to Paul Dittmer?"

"I told Hancock I last saw Dittmer Tuesday night. I was following him, trying to carry through on our deal."

"What deal?" said Packard, innocently.

I was furious, almost spitting. "Dittmer's dead, isn't he?"

"Yeah," said Hancock. "We're gonna burn you in the chair, Morgan. Sometimes they got to hit you two or three times with the juice before you die. The condemned try to scream, but the current paralyzes them. Freezes that look of agony on their faces. Let's see you make your cute cracks when they're strapping you in."

"Let me handle this," said Packard, putting his hand on Hancock's chest, moving him backward. I dismissed the idea that this was another good cop, bad cop routine. Hancock was truly angry, and I began to feel afraid.

"Look," I said. "You know I couldn't have killed Dittmer. But maybe I can help you figure out who did. Dittmer was a cold one, smart, but he was meeting with some rough people. Believe me, I know."

"You said Dittmer was at the machine works two days ago, last Tuesday?"

"I followed him there."

Packard sighed. "A Southern Railroad crew found Dittmer's body about two a.m. this morning. At the Howell Interlocking. He'd been dead for two to four hours."

"Howell Interlocking?"

"Hobo junction," said Hancock. "Next to the machine works. A witness identified you. We've got you, Morgan."

I was silent, unsure what to say. Hancock grinned in triumph. Suddenly, Packard asked Hancock to leave the room. Grumbling, the detective left.

"What's this about somebody trying to kill you?" Packard asked.

I told him about the car ride and being thrown into traffic. The man in the gray suit rolled his eyes and snorted.

"Who's Joe Brooks Brothers?" I said, nodding toward the gray suit.

"I'm Special Agent in Charge Marvin Hill, Federal Bureau of Investigation. Mr. Packard asked us to join him on this case."

"What's your problem?" I asked.

"Your story is hardly credible, Mr. Morgan. Klansmen kidnapping you, throwing you in front of cars? I hear all kinds of fanciful things, but this tops them all."

"Love the people you hang out with," I said to Packard, jerking my left hand against the handcuffs. It hurt. "Can't you at least take off the cuffs?"

"Not yet," said Packard. "You're still a suspect; can't have you slipping out on me."

"You know I didn't kill him," I said.

"You had connections to the victim."

"So do many people," I said.

"The Atlanta Police need someone, want someone, for these crimes. Let me tell you an interesting thing about the police. It doesn't have to be the right someone."

"Don't you want it to be the right someone?" I asked.

"After our last talk," Packard said, "I did a little digging. There were substantial files on your father and files on you, kept by Treasury. There were even more files kept by Mr. Hoover's organization.

"Files?"

"Interesting reading," said Special Agent Hill, opening his briefcase, taking out a notepad and pencil. "You seem to lead an exciting life, Mr. Morgan; plenty of money, travel, good schools. I had to put some things together between several files, but the gist was clear. You tell everyone your father was in the sugar business, but he really wasn't, unless rum counts."

He paused. "Would you like a cigarette?"

"No thanks," I said. "Mr. Hill, this isn't news. Some of it was in the newspaper during my divorce."

"Your father smoked, didn't he?" said Hill. "There's a photo in the file of him with a big, fat Cuban cigar. As his business grew, he could afford plenty, couldn't he?"

I stayed silent. He shrugged and continued.

"It wasn't just liquor," said Hill. "Prostitution and gambling were also mainstays of your family's business. And he defended it all with violence. How many deaths do you think your father caused, Mr. Morgan? How many lives did he ruin?"

"I'm not my father. I never worked for him, and I left that world behind years ago."

"Perhaps," said Hill. He made a note on his pad.

"Didn't you work for him after college?" asked Packard. "Isn't that why you came to Atlanta, so you could work for him near one of his best markets?"

"Your files must not be that good. I came here to get away from him. The job at Coca-Cola let me do that. I had to be independent, and Atlanta was good because it was never Dad's market. Liquor was already sewn up here by local interests. When he asked me to help him. I wrote and told him I would have nothing to do with his business. I wanted my own life, free of his control. That was over ten years ago."

"I see, so you quit on him," said Hill. "Right when he needed you most. Big competitors were moving in along the coast—organizations from New York, Baltimore, and Philadelphia. You stayed away because you had this great job at Coke. So, I'm trying to understand something: How did you feel when your dad died? They almost didn't find the wound in his eye, did they? The body was so torn up. But the coroner found it. Probably an icepick, all the way up through his brain. Pretty rough."

"You didn't even go back for the funeral, did you?" said Packard.

"If I had gone back, people would have thought I wanted something."

"Money?" asked Packard.

"Revenge," I said.

We sat in silence for a minute. Then Packard said softly, "You know, Mark, with your family history, admitting to following the victim, and spending the night with a known sodomite, hell, even just the way you look, a jury might be swayed. Maybe we can help you."

They were playing another version of good cop, bad cop, but a lot more sophisticated than Rawson and Hancock. Got to hand it to the Feds.

"Look, I'll do everything you want," I said. "I'll tell you everything I know. But I can't do any of that until I have immunity. Duke Webster has asked you for it. Ironclad. In writing."

The two men glanced at each other. "Can't give you that," said Hill. "It'd have to go all the way to an assistant attorney general on the federal side. We need to break this case now. I'll give you my personal assurance that you're safe if you help us."

"You must think I'm stupid. You need me. I know why the Huns have the counterfeit money, and I know what they're trying to do. I even know who they'll give the money to. If you want to know, get Webster in here and give me complete immunity."

Hill stared at me for a minute, then stubbed out the butt of his cigarette. Packard shook his head, smiled, and said, "I told you so."

"You really are tough," Agent Hill said. "I respect that. You know, the files include things you probably didn't imagine we knew. Most are in another file, one kept by the State Department. This guy, Philip Sanders, wrote twenty-six letters on your behalf, urging the State Department to help you when you were imprisoned in Peru. He must be a good friend?"

"Phil saved my life," I said.

"Yes, he probably did. Given what I read, I wonder if he's now a particular friend? Be a shame if we had to bring him in. If he went to jail and it was your fault."

"Go ahead and try."

Hill smiled. "Yeah, a tough guy because you're not really a man. Your ex-wife says you don't have any use for the ladies. Can't perform, not even a stir. Boy, that's got to be rough."

"Go to hell," I said.

Hours later, they brought me up from the cell again to a larger interview room. Duke Webster helped me to a seat. I was haggard, exhausted, and my ribs hurt so much I could only take shallow breaths.

"Did they do this to you?" he asked.

"I just want to go home," I said.

"We need to question him some more," said Hancock.

"Mark? Will you give them what they want?"

"Only if they make the deal."

"We still haven't heard from the DA," said Hancock.

"What about the federal immunity?"

"We've contacted Assistant Attorney General Stephens. Nothing yet," said Packard.

"Then I don't talk. Take me home, Duke."

"Charges?" asked Webster.

"Not yet," said Hancock.

"Let's go," said Webster. He turned to Hancock. "He needs his personal property back."

"That'll take a while," Hancock said. "Probably best if he goes back to his cell while we find it, process the paperwork."

"Garrett," said Joe Packard. "Why don't you fetch Mr. Morgan's personal property to hurry things up. I'll wait here with them." Hancock looked shocked, but left.

"He wanted to charge you," said Packard, "or at least hold you, but I told him no."

"You're a great guy," I said.

"You sound terrible, must be the nose. Look, we'll have the paperwork for immunity by this afternoon. Can you meet then, after your lawyer looks at it, to sign the papers and talk?"

I looked at Webster. He nodded. "Sure," I said. "Why so reasonable all of a sudden?"

"In my book, you're not a suspect."

"What happened? And why's the FBI interested? They don't do counterfeit."

"Later. When we talk."

Hancock came back with my wallet, watch, belt, and keys. I checked to make sure all the cash was there.

"It's all there," said Hancock. "You might want to check into something called a bank account, Morgan. It's not safe to carry so much around with you. Easy for cash to go missing, you know."

"That must happen a lot around here, huh?" Though it made my ribs scream, I pushed past him to the door.

Duke drove me to the Athletic Club. I hobbled up to the entrance and took the elevator to my floor. It was hot, almost noon, so I took a cool shower, trying not to wet the tape on my nose or the bandages on my hands. Afterward, I lay on the bed to think and fell asleep.

The phone woke me at five-thirty. I woke, soaked in sweat. It was Duke Webster.

"I got the papers from both the DA and the U.S. Attorney. You'll need to sign them. Also, Packard's here; he brought the federal papers over; says you agreed to talk."

I dragged myself out of bed and dressed in one of my old, worn suits. The pain was so bad that I shuffled like an old man, limping over to the Candler

Building. People on the street stared at my bandaged nose. Webster and Packard waited for me.

"The papers are good?" I asked.

"Better than I'd hoped," said Webster.

I read and signed four copies of two sets of papers. Webster took one copy of each and called in his secretary, telling her to file them. He handed the second set to me and gave Packard the remaining copies.

"My part's done," said Webster. "Do you want a room so you can talk? And, Mark, do you want me present during the conversation?"

"No, I'll talk with Packard alone."

We went to a conference room down the hall. Afternoon traffic noise from Peachtree Street filtered up through an open window. The lowering sun cast a golden glow on the surrounding skyscrapers.

"Okay," said Packard. "Did you kill Schulman?"

"I just found the body."

"What about Dittmer?"

"No."

"And this missing fellow, Goss. Did you kill him?"

"Nope," I said. "Is this just a fishing trip?"

"Shut up. In Peru, did you kill the guy there?"

I took a moment to think. "I don't think that's covered by the immunity grant."

"It can't be. The charges are in another country. But we agreed not to extradite you for any reason, so you're safe."

I thought about asking Duke Webster if that was true, but then decided, what the hell.

"Coke had a plant in Peru that processed coca leaves, removing the cocaine and leaving the coca extract used in the drink's secret formula. There were problems with the plant's product, and I was sent to figure it out. The cocaine was being diverted illegally. It was supposed to go for medical purposes, but instead went to criminal organizations. During my visit, I asked questions of the wrong guy. He sent a warning; some hoods shot me, breaking my leg, causing a compound fracture. They also broke my nose."

"So, you killed the guy who . . ."

"I didn't kill anyone. That dead guy worked for me. I can document that. They shot him in the gut, and he died next to me on the beach. I expected them to kill me too, but they didn't."

"Jesus. So, then?"

"The police took me to a prison hospital in Lima. There, a doctor set my leg and tried to fix my nose. The leg got infected; that's one reason the scar is so bad. After two or three weeks—how long I'm not sure—they moved me to cells for the condemned and scheduled me for execution."

Loud honking erupted below the window. We waited for it to stop.

"Yeah," Packard said. "*Sorry, Uncle Sam, we lost track of the prisoner, and he disappeared. We didn't mean to make such a terrible mistake with one of your citizens, but we're just a disorganized Latin American country. We'll try to do better next time.*" Packard lit a cigarette. "Then the diplomats share a drink, and the dead guy's forgotten."

"Only, I didn't die. And I got away."

"You ran?"

"Phil's money finally got some traction, bribes in the right places, and after five months, a judge released me to the custody of the U.S. Embassy in Lima. I was supposed to wait there until the trial, but I knew how that trial would go, so once I was strong enough, I slipped away."

"I saw the doctor's report made in Panama on your way home," Packard said. "Leg infection, internal parasites, malnutrition. Hell, you weighed less than one hundred and fifty pounds." He peered at me. "I think that doctor at Grady fixed your nose; it looks straight." He paused a moment. "No family to help you?"

"Father was dead. Mother and my brother, I don't even know where they are now."

"Germany."

"You know that?"

"Yep. You know that Hirsch and the Jewish Welfare Alliance thing doesn't check out?"

"Actually, some of it does." I told him about my call to the Temple and the meeting with the rabbi and Mrs. Jones.

"Rockefeller Center. We'll get someone to look into that. What about the counterfeit?"

I told him about Kunst and Dittmer at the factory meeting, the political aspirations of the Pioneers, and my hunch about the counterfeit money financing political campaigns.

"You never saw any money change hands?"

"They almost caught me at the meeting; I barely got away. Maybe if I'd gone back on Wednesday, I might have seen that."

"Going back would have been risky."

After a moment, I asked, "What happened to Dittmer?"

Packard stood and looked out the window. "The body was dumped on the railroad tracks down by Hobo Junction. Maybe the killer hoped a train would chop it up. A locomotive crew spotted the body and braked just in time. Dittmer's throat had been cut. Not just cut, his head was almost severed, the large arteries sliced. Pretty horrible."

"Someone wanted to be sure," I said. "Like with Schulman."

"The cut was similar, yeah. But Schulman didn't struggle. A blow to the head, according to the coroner, and then the killer cut his throat and bled him out like a pig. Dittmer was different. Lots of bruising and defensive injuries. There was a struggle before he was killed. Didn't happen at the tracks. Like Schulman, Dittmer was killed somewhere else and moved."

"You're pretty good at this murder stuff for a guy who chases counterfeit."

"I'm pretty good at a lot of things," he said, and smiled.

"Sure you're a Treasury agent?"

"Secret Service. We have a temporary office in the post office building. No secretary. You ought to visit my office sometime and see me in my glory."

"Sounds thrilling. How'd you get this job?"

"I'm a lucky guy. If you find the counterfeit, we'll both be lucky. How about this Anna Erlanger? Think she's involved?"

"Two days ago, I would have said no. Now, I'm going to have to ask her."

"That'll be tough to do," he said, closing his notebook. "She left on the train today for New York."

So, it was over. I stumbled back to the Club, called Phil, and told him I had immunity.

"Yeah," Phil said. "I talked to Duke. He says you're an interesting client."

"I hope to be an uninteresting client from now on."

"You should come back to the house. They know where you live."

"As long as I stay in the Club, I'll be okay. I'm too sore to drive."

"I'll come get you."

"No, Phil. There are things here I have to do."

"Okay," he said. "Look, I meant it about working for me. Come by tomorrow or Monday."

"We'll talk about it, but I won't be an employee."

"I have an idea for how we can work that out," he said, and hung up.

I tried to call Emma, but the WPA office had already closed. After heating a can of soup, I enjoyed a quiet, simple meal, then pulled down the shades and went to bed. The sounds of the trains at work, the noise of the afternoon traffic, and the buzz of the fan aimed at my bed were all the finest music. Even the heat didn't bother me. Exhausted, I slept like a dead man.

10

Saturday, July 29, 1939

The ringing phone dragged me slowly awake. It wouldn't stop. It rang and rang. The broken ribs burned deep inside my chest. Groaning, I turned on the light and picked up my watch. It was past 2 a.m. The phone still rang. I grabbed it. "Yeah."

"Where have you been?" It was the rabbi.

"The hospital, then jail."

"The meeting's over; the Germans are gone. A disaster. We need to meet now."

"I can't," I said, mentally exploring my body, seeking the extent of my pain.

"Breakfast."

"I'm hurt," I said. "It'll have to be later."

"Lunch. The French Room, next to the Winecoff Hotel."

"I know it."

"Be there at noon." He hung up. I held the dead receiver for a while, then slowly returned it to its cradle, turned out the light, and went back to sleep.

Later, the phone rang again.

"Morgan?" a whispery voice said.

"Yeah?"

"Clyde Berger. Remember me? We talked about the Germans?"

"Sure," I said, slowly sitting up and turning on the lamp. I grabbed my watch. It was 5:45 a.m. "We met at the Emerald Club; you liked my car."

"Yeah," he said softly. "Nice Buick." I heard the scratch of a match as he lit a cigarette.

"Shame to waste a match on a cigarette," I said.

"You've been there, brother," he said. "Look, I've got something for you. Really important something."

"Job's done; the Nazis are gone. I don't need any new information."

"Oh, you'll need this. You better believe it."

"Tell me more."

"You think it's free? Meet me at the Emerald Club. The parking lot, like before. You've got an hour. Bring a C-note." He hung up.

The Emerald Club looked different in the early morning light. Smaller, shrunken somehow. There was a black late-model Ford V-8 in the parking lot. Slowly, carefully, I climbed out of my Buick, fighting the pain. A man got out of the other car. His hat was pulled low, his jacket too big. He walked toward me. He'd made it halfway before I even stood fully upright. It was Berger. In the growing daylight, I could see he was a small man, rail-thin, sickly.

"Do you always work this early?" I asked.

"End of the day for me," he replied in his whispery voice. "You don't look so good. What the hell happened?"

I glanced down at the scabs on my hands, then felt the tape on my nose. "You really don't want to know. So, what's the emergency?"

"The money."

I gave him a hundred-dollar bill.

"You'll think it's a bargain," he said, carefully folding the bill and slipping it into a jacket pocket.

"So, is there a plot against the Germans?"

"Nope. The Germans are fine. No plot."

I was so surprised I couldn't think of what to say next. I'd expected something about a half-baked plot. Or, if I were lucky, about the Pioneers or the Klan.

"Damn it, so why'd you call me, have me drive all the way out here?"

He took his time lighting a cigarette. "I didn't say there wasn't no plot. I just said there's no plot to hurt the Germans."

A sick heaviness settled in my gut. I looked at him in the growing light, and he must have seen the thought in my eyes.

"Yeah," he nodded. "The Germans hired someone to kill you."

I had a bad moment. What if that someone was Berger? I'd made it easy; enough light, an empty public place, too early for witnesses, and there was no way I could run. He must have followed my thoughts, for a grin spread across his face, widening the split in his lip horribly.

"They asked me to set it up," he said. "I told 'em no dice."

"Thanks. Why?"

"I talked to some people; seems you're a hard-luck guy. Lost your job, your wife, and now they're out to kill you. I've got a soft spot for people who've had bad breaks. Let's just say I've had a few."

He tilted his head so that the morning sun shone under his hat. I saw that what I'd thought of as a harelip was part of a horrifying mass of scars across his face and mouth.

"Knife?"

"Yeah. They thought I had something in my mouth. Doctors say it can't be fixed, I just gotta live with it." He looked around the lot, scanning it. "You know, you've got to be more careful. When you got here, you didn't case the place at all. You just drove right up. Would've been easy." He took his hand out of his pocket, mimed a pistol with his fingers. His thumb fell. "Bang."

"Somebody already tried. That's why I'm beat up." I told him about the Klansmen dumping me out of the car on Spring Street.

"Hell, those boys are probably disappointed. Mayor's new speed limit has made their job harder. How you gonna kill somebody throwing 'em out at twenty-five miles an hour?" As he drew on his cigarette, he covered the gap in his lip with his finger. "You know, there's about a hundred murders each year in Atlanta, but they don't count the accidents. Seems to be a lot of accidents lately. But I'm talking about something different here. An offer to pay for your death. A contract, some would call it."

"You mean like the Brownsville Boys stuff I read about up in New York?"

He laughed. "More like what happened to the lottery king, Eddie Guyol. A fellow just stepped up after dark, said, 'you know you have it coming, Eddie,' then blew his head off."

"They caught the guy who did that," I said. "That Fluker fellow they keep trying to save from the electric chair."

Berger wheezed rhythmically, his laugh. "Fluker didn't do it. He was set up, but that's a different story. A couple of Germans, good Baptists, I'm sure, came to the Emerald Club two nights ago. When they asked me to off you, I told them no."

A car drove by, and he glanced at it for a moment. "One of 'em spoke real good English, flashed a lot of bills."

"He's got plenty, but it's all sourdough."

"You don't say!" He shook his head. "Just can't trust people these days, can you?"

He drew on his cigarette again, and I couldn't stand the delay. "Who did they hire?" I blurted. "Let me know what I'm looking for."

"Ever hear of Big Caesar?"

"No."

"Big Caesar used to work for Mr. Green."

"Mr. Green, the lottery king?" I asked.

"That has a ring," he said, chuckling, "especially with your stuffy nose."

"I'm not smiling," I said.

"Yeah, that Green. He took over The Bug after the Guyol murder. Some say he hired it. Green owns a lot of real estate too, including a bar called Spats down on Decatur Street. Big Caesar used to work there, sort of the manager for special problems, if you know what I mean. Well, last year, he quit. Takes on all sorts of shady business. Won't do it himself, though. What he does is put a bounty on ya."

"Big Caesar's a Negro?"

"That's what makes it so tough. Any skinny Colored kid could be the one. Slip a knife between your ribs at the bus stop, or shoot you in the back of the head when you're waiting to cross the street. Think about it; anybody, anytime. And you know how the Colored are; they're always there, but you don't hardly see 'em?"

"I can't live like that," I said.

"No one can. That's why you're dead. Unless maybe you blow town, check out the lights of Broadway, or gay Paree."

"Can I buy him off?"

"Who, Caesar?" Berger rubbed his chin, contemplating this idea. "Yeah, maybe. It won't be cheap, and you can't trust him. He might just take your money, then kill you, and collect on the contract too. But you'd never get that far. You'd have to meet with him, and one of these kids would nail you before you even got close."

I sat in the car for a long time. Berger was right; the rational choice was to leave. The train stations would be too dangerous, but I could drive north to Chattanooga or east to Augusta. I could sell the car, get a few hundred for it, and then catch a train to go far away. The seven thousand was enough for a new start. Phil would understand. I didn't know if Emma would, but I didn't know what our relationship was anyway. I hadn't seen her since I'd dumped Goss on her. By now, she probably hated me.

But I couldn't bring myself to leave Atlanta. It was my town. If I stayed, I'd need to avoid public places, places where I wasn't sure of the surroundings. The Club was too dangerous; I had to go somewhere else.

I fired up the Buick and drove back toward town, cutting over to Brookhaven, then down Peachtree to Buckhead. Near the intersection of Roswell and the two Paces, I parked.

Early on a Saturday morning, Buckhead Village was quiet. Wender and Roberts Drug Store had a sign in the window that said they were serving breakfast, but the door was locked. A trolley rattled by, and I saw the black faces of men and women headed to work. Further up the street, an older Colored man with a broom was sweeping the sidewalk in front of the Buckhead Five and Dime. Past him, I saw some men go into Minhinetts's Restaurant. I walked that way. The hair on my neck stood up when the Colored man with the broom spoke.

"Mornin', sir," he said. I mumbled something back.

A bell tinkled when I opened the restaurant door. A waitress turned at the sound of the bell.

"Morning," she said cheerfully. "Take any table you want. I'll bring you coffee in a moment."

I took off my hat and sat down. Like all restaurants in Georgia, it was segregated, whites only, so for the moment, I felt safe. I took a deep breath and relaxed. A handwritten menu held by a clip stood in the center of the table, but had no breakfast items on it.

The waitress put a cup in front of me and filled it with coffee. She was pretty, with thick curly brown hair and straight white teeth. Her smile gleamed. "Eggs, bacon, biscuits, and grits for breakfast today," she said.

"Sounds grand," I said, sitting back and blowing out another sigh of relief.

The waitress's smile grew bigger. "Darlin', looks like you had a rough night."

"You wouldn't believe."

"Well, you just relax, let Sally take care of you. How ya want them eggs?"

"Scrambled would be fine," I said. She had a cute figure, so I watched as she headed for the kitchen door.

"Breakfast with scrambled," she called into the kitchen.

"Yes, ma'am," said the Black cook.

And that's when it hit me: the poison of segregation. I imagined myself as a thoughtful, educated White man, despising how Jim Crow warped the lives of Negroes. Cosmopolitan, with a nuanced knowledge of the world. That made me feel like a good person. But segregation had warped my world, my life. I didn't see the Negroes who worked around me; I didn't notice the tasks they performed for my benefit. Worse, as Emma had pointed out, I'd never really known a Negro. Segregation created a curtain, and all I had ever seen were the faces they wore on this side. Who were they on the other side?

Sally dumped the breakfast in front of me and backed away quickly. The anger must have shown on my battered face. Anger at my naivety. Anger at my fear. Anger at the rabbi who had dragged me into this. I had a score to settle with that son of a bitch.

The French Room was a second-floor restaurant in an older commercial building in the theater district. Phil had called me reckless, but he'd seen nothing like the recklessness that took me downtown that day. I didn't care about the danger. I just wanted to see the rabbi one more time, to get my hands on him. The stairway leading up to the restaurant was sterile linoleum, while inside it was decorated as a French brasserie at the turn of the century. Wood paneling, brass fixtures, and white tablecloths, but it was all a bit worn. The waiters wore white shirts and black vests and had affected French accents. Maybe some of them were even French.

The rabbi was already seated at a table. With his hair awry, beard tangled, and dark circles under his eyes, he looked even worse than the last time I'd seen him. His suit had been inadequately cleaned of a large stain. He looked like a slob. In my worn suit and taped nose, I didn't look much better. The nearby waiter watched with a gimlet eye.

The rabbi put his hands on the table and pushed up in an arch, leaning toward me. "Refund all the dosh I gave you. Our relationship is at an end."

"That wasn't our arrangement."

"You're a fraud and a failure," said the rabbi. "I want the money back."

"I need to show you something," I said, standing. "It's out front. Come on."

I opened the door to the stairway, and the rabbi followed. When I reached the bottom, I turned. As the rabbi stepped off the last step, I grabbed him by the lapels of his jacket and slammed him against the wall. His head hit with a loud, hollow thump, and the old plaster cracked.

"Who the hell are you?" I said, shaking him. It hurt badly. Fire ran up my side, across the broken ribs, and down the back of my left hip. The pain fueled my anger. He said nothing, didn't struggle, didn't fight. I shook him, pulled him forward, and slammed him back into the wall, harder than before. "You son of a bitch, you almost got me killed. Hell, you almost got me killed twice."

"Death comes to us all," said the rabbi quietly.

I pushed him hard, toward the floor. He fell heavily and lay there, unmoving. "How would you like death to come right now, you bastard?"

"At least now we see your true nature."

"Gentlemen," said a waiter from the top of the stairs. "Is there a problem?"

"No problem," I said. "Just a spirited discussion."

"Will you be eating with us?"

I laughed. "Not likely."

I stepped through the door and began walking up Peachtree.

"Goss needs our help," the rabbi shouted, following behind me. "I know how to find him."

What if he found Goss, found Emma?

I stopped and turned. He recoiled. "How would you find Goss?" I leaned close, struggling to control myself.

"You are not the only person looking for him. We'll find him soon."

"Just tell me what's going on. Stop playing games."

I started walking again, and he followed. "Listen to me, Morgan." I ignored him, crossed the street, and turned into the S&W Cafeteria. There, Atlanta seemed to have returned to normal, with the usual Saturday shopping crowd of well-dressed women with bags from Davidson's and Regenstein's, and a few bored husbands along for the ride. The cafeteria had a large, open atrium with a second-floor balcony and chrome architectural touches that suggested a streamlined design. My bandaged nose and halting movements drew stares. I got in the service line, and damn if Goldstein didn't join me.

"We can eat lunch and talk," he said. I loaded up on standard American fare, paid, then climbed painfully to the second floor. I cut a piece of chicken and began to eat. The rabbi put down his tray and sat across from me.

"This is confidential," he said. "I'm only talking to you because you need to know."

"Cut the baloney. You're here because Goss is some kind of egghead, a scientist, and the British government wants him."

"Yes, of course. Goss is important. We also need to find Wilhelm Kunst. They are both SD agents. Neither was on the train yesterday."

"Kunst is dangerous."

The rabbi glanced around the balcony melodramatically. It was bad acting. "I am with an organization that's part of the Foreign Office. Kunst is a spy, and we have to keep tabs on him. Goss must go to England. I must find him, help him on his way."

"What's Goss's real name?"

"Don't you know?"

"I want to see if you know," I said.

"Best not to speak it, then. Safer for him, and for you."

"Do the Germans know about Goss?"

"If they knew," he said, "they would surely have killed him. That suggests they do not know. But what do they know now? Again, I had hoped you would tell me, but again you failed."

"Yeah," I said. "I weep over my failures."

"Perhaps you would if you understood what is at stake. Plus, Goss may not be a scientist. He may just be an SD agent trying to lead us astray. You must keep looking. Keep looking for them all."

I laughed and put down my forkful of green beans. "A moment ago, you wanted your money back. Now it's vague horseshit you're spouting. You're just a rat, a nasty, lying rat. Maybe I ought to beat the hell out of you and be done with it."

"It would be unfortunate if you did. Goss's knowledge is very important. Specific techniques, information, and experiments—I don't pretend to understand. We must find him, but I don't know if you are the best means of doing that. So, I may have said contradictory things. For that, I'm sorry."

"I don't care. People are trying to kill me. I need to leave town, and I need money. So, are we still on? If I find Goss, you will pay me five thousand dollars?"

"Four thousand, three hundred."

I leaned forward, put my face next to his, looking into his eyes. "You are a lying piece of shit. The seven hundred you gave me will be eaten up by expenses. I'll just go away, visit another city for some time. You're welcome to find the guy yourself."

He took out his wallet and gave me three more hundred-dollar bills. Crisp, clean bills; I almost hated crushing them into my wallet. Almost.

"Another advance," he said. "Four thousand when you give me Goss."

I ate some beans and took my time chewing. "It will be the full five Gs."

"Only if you give me both Goss and Kunst."

"Kunst? He wasn't part of our deal."

"It is now. I'll be in town until Tuesday night. I'll call you every morning at eight. Four thousand for Goss, one thousand for Kunst."

I glanced around the Cafeteria, scanning the crowd.

"So, you want to know where Wilhelm Kunst is?" I said.

"Of course. It's important."

I bent down close to the rabbi, close enough to smell his cologne. "Give me a thousand dollars."

"What?"

"Downstairs, over the rail. He's there, eating lunch."

The rabbi turned quickly, then smiled. "He's not alone."

I looked again. Anna Erlanger placed a food tray on Kunst's table and sat. They began talking animatedly.

"Anna? She left town. What's she doing with Kunst?"

"You fool," said the rabbi. "Haven't you figured it out? They're the ones in charge."

We followed Kunst and Anna outside. On the street, they split without speaking. Kunst crossed and walked south. The rabbi glanced at me, winked, and followed. Anna stood on the pedestrian island to catch the uptown trolley. Just before it arrived, she jaywalked quickly to the other side of Peachtree. The trolley pulled up, blocking pursuit.

On a guess, I turned north and spotted her headed the same direction. She glanced around, and I did my best to blend in with the crowd waiting for the light to change. She continued, and I followed, limping a little, trying to keep up. At Harris Street, she turned toward the Capital City Club, the meeting place for Atlanta's economic and political elite. I could not imagine why she'd gone there.

Suddenly, a big DeSoto sedan pulled up to the intersection. She was driving. I turned quickly and watched the reflection in the shop window behind me. She waited at the intersection while I stood conspicuously alone in front of the store. Finally, she pulled out, the locomotive nose of the DeSoto coming directly at me until she accelerated north on Peachtree.

I drove to Emma's boarding house, past the new Techwood Homes and Grant Field. Every jolt of the car made me catch my breath. Huge clouds towered in the west and soon covered the sun. Rain for sure, perhaps rough weather too. Rough weather in my head already. Confused and worried, I parked and knocked. Professor Wimberly answered.

"Professor," I said. "I need to see Emma. As soon as possible."

"She's not here right now." He stared at my bandaged nose for a moment, then opened the screen door and motioned me in. "You're Mr.

Morgan, her friend. Please, come in, and we'll wait for her. Besides, it may rain."

"No question it'll rain," I said, gesturing to the sky. He stepped out and looked west, shading his eyes. All you could see were thick, gray, and black towering clouds.

"Looks like a storm for sure," he said. "My wife's not home; she's visiting family. Her sister is ill."

"Sorry to hear that." I took off my hat. "When will Emma be back?"

"I sent her over to my laboratory. She should be back soon."

Inside the house, a perceptible breeze made it feel much cooler. The hum of a large fan came from somewhere in the back. I looked for it but didn't see one.

"Ah, yes, the fan," said the professor, who smiled. "I'll explain. I've built a whole-house attic fan." He gestured toward the noise. "It works wonderfully; pumps hot air into the attic, creating a negative pressure to bring in fresh air into the rooms below. Feel the breeze? My wife and I sleep with it on; she says it lulls her to sleep. You'll soon grow accustomed to the racket." He took out his pipe and began tamping tobacco into it. The whole scene was so domestic, so normal, that I began to relax.

"Makes sense," I said. "Hot air rises, so why not blow it into the attic?"

"Exactly. Simple physics, and much less expensive than air-conditioning."

I settled back in my seat and waited while he fiddled with his pipe. Suddenly, I thought of Goss. "Professor, what sort of physics do you do?"

"Well, I teach a basic class for engineers, and I teach statics and dynamics as well. That means I teach a lot of math."

"In your lab, I mean. What do you do there?"

"Well, students do the experiments that are part of the curriculum." He paused and looked at me. "Ah, I get it. What do I research? What am I interested in?"

"Yes, sir, exactly."

"My research considered rates of molecular diffusion as temperatures approach absolute zero. This is completely theoretical, of course; no one can actually reach absolute zero. In fact, zero Kelvin is, as far as we know, merely an approximation."

"You did experiments for this?"

"Some." He lit a match and took a few puffs until his pipe was going. "Can't do it all with equations, you know. I had to measure the rate at which diffusion decreases as the temperature gets lower, or increases as the temperature rises. Radium emits a radioactive gas, radon, which we could easily measure, so I used that for the experiments. Goodness." He stared off into space, waving his pipe. "That was more than twenty years ago. It was all fresh and new then; the cutting edge of science." He chuckled.

"You used radium?"

"What? No, that was the source of the gas. Radium emits radon; there are several theories why, but that doesn't matter here. We put the radon gas into a very cold environment, using liquid nitrogen. Essentially, we froze it. Then we measured the diffusion rate as the container slowly warmed. Because it was radioactive, we could distinguish it from the nitrogen. Had to be careful about the expansion of the nitrogen, though, that can happen explosively." He continued to look into a middle ground, smiling, puffing on his pipe.

"Do you do experiments like that here?"

"What? At Tech? Oh, goodness, no." He looked at me. "Do you know how much radium costs? It is one of the most expensive substances on earth, and this is just Georgia Tech. We do make liquid air and experiment with it. I wish I had time to do more experiments and the money to buy more equipment. There may be practical applications for the transmission of electricity that comes out of the low-temperature work."

"Ever do any atomic physics?"

He stared at me and slowly put his pipe down on the table. "No, not really, other than teach some theory. Why do you ask?"

"I read some articles in the library—simple stuff for laymen, but fascinating. Scientists are discovering how the atom works, how molecules are held together, and the nature of the atomic nucleus. Nuclear physics, some are calling it. They're unraveling the basic secrets of matter and energy, the nature of reality itself. Radioactive materials seem to play an essential role. I thought with your work . . ."

"I see, radioactive materials. Yes, they do play an important role, though I'm not involved in that sort of work. People like Niels Bohr in Denmark and Enrico Fermi are the ones doing it. Fermi won last year's Nobel Prize."

"Isn't Fermi in New York now?"

"I wouldn't know," said the professor. He picked up his pipe, realized it had gone out, and hesitated before lighting another match. His hand shook.

There were footsteps on the front porch. Emma called, "Mark, is that your car?"

The professor grabbed the arms of his chair, startled. I stood as she came in, holding the screen door for her companion. It was Peter Goss.

"I was really worried about you," I blurted. Goss looked startled, and so did Emma.

"Mark," she said, frowning, "jeez, what happened to your face?"

"A bad accident. I was worried about you."

"Worried about me? It's only been a few days."

"Ah," said Goss. "Mr. Morgan. Good'n - after - noon. How – do - you - do?" He smiled broadly, proudly. His English was terrible.

Emma peered at me, blinking. "Mark, goodness, your arms, your hands?"

"I was hit by a car and had to go to the hospital. It's a bit of a story."

Goss smiled and nodded. "But you are no dead."

"You understand more English than you speak, Mr. Goss."

"Mr. Morgan," said Wimberly, "you're mistaken. This man is Dr. Dirk Gellman, not 'Goss.' Gellman worked at the Kaiser Wilhelm Institute in Berlin. I've read some of his papers. He is a well-regarded young physicist."

"Yes, he worked with Otto Hahn and Lisa Meitner."

"You knew?" Emma asked. "How?"

"He told me. Not his name, but theirs. He was pretending to be a Baptist Messenger. When I talked with him at the hotel, he mentioned Hahn and Meitner. I looked them up. Hahn is famous, a chemist who works with radioactive elements. Meitner's famous too. There was a long list of those who had worked at the Institute. I just didn't know which one called himself Goss."

"We must be careful," said Wimberly. "Dirk and I have talked about this at length, and there are important issues here, issues you may not understand. Why don't we sit so we can discuss them? Emma, dear, would you see if there is any of the lemonade left in the icebox?"

With an irritated shake of her head, Emma headed back to the kitchen. Surprising me, Wimberly said in good German, "Dirk, please sit down."

"You speak German?"

"Any scientist worth his salt knows German."

"So, it is Dirk?" I said. "I'm flattered to meet you, *Herr Doktor* Gellman."

"I am sorry for the deception, Mr. Morgan, but I was afraid. The telephone call that night was the final straw, and you gave me little hope of help. When we saw Schulman's body, I thought you were part of a plot to kill me, so I fled. I left everything behind, except for what was in my pockets. After that, I wandered into the hands of thieves. They took all my money and locked me in a hot, dark room. Had you not come for me the next day, I do not know what would have happened."

"You'd be dead," I said. "That's what would have happened."

Silence followed, as if stating the obvious was embarrassing. Finally, Gellman spoke. "*Fraulein* Connor and *Herr Doktor* Wimberly have taken good care of me. I had read of this technical school, so I asked about the physics laboratory. It took a while for Emma to understand, but then she took me to Professor Doctor Wimberly, a good choice; he speaks German."

Wimberly smiled. "Dirk's been sleeping at the Lab. I have a cot there."

"Emma is helping me learn more English," said Gellman. "And they're hiding me."

I told them about the rabbi, the English woman, Miss Jones. "I think they want to take you to England. Perhaps your friends there could help you settle and find work?"

"I don't want to be in England."

"Why not?"

"I want to be here, in the United States. England, it's too close."

"Too close?"

"To Germany," said Wimberly. "Dirk's convinced war will come soon."

"The French, the English—they will not stop Hitler's armies," said Gellman.

"You think they can invade England?"

Gellman shrugged. "The English navy? Aircraft will just fly over it."

Emma returned with a pitcher and glasses. She poured four glasses and sat on the sofa. "Don't let me stop you," she said. "Besides, you're going to talk in German, aren't you? I won't understand a thing."

I turned to Gellman. "What do you know that is so important? Why do these people want you?"

Gellman looked at Wimberly, who nodded. "Tell him."

"I know how to make a special explosive. Or at least in theory," said Gellman. "Very much theory, but many have speculated on it, and most agree the theory is plausible."

"Lots of people know how to make bombs."

"No, Mr. Morgan," said Professor Wimberly. "This is something different. Dirk may know how to make a bomb that could end the world."

"Phil, we need to come to your place," I said into the telephone. "We have to hide."

"Mark, I have dinner plans."

"This is important, really important. We need a safe place, and I need to talk with you and get your advice. You don't need to entertain us. We need a hidey-hole, nothing more."

"So, I'm just supposed to turn my new house over to you and who else?"

"Phil, I'm sorry, but this is important. People really are trying to kill me and my friends. Besides, it's not as though we're having a party or something."

"Hey, that's a good idea."

"What?"

"A party," said Phil. "Why don't we have a shindig tomorrow? You know, a cookout? We can have steak and potatoes. Come on out tonight. I'll put you up; hell, stay Sunday night too. I'm just a lonely bachelor, you know. I'll change my dinner plans."

"Phil, thanks, but I'm not sure a party is appropriate."

"Sure it is. Nothing better than a party to deal with the willies, and you have definitely given me the willies. I'll tell Martha to get ready, and we'll have the party tomorrow evening."

He rang off. I put the phone down slowly.

"What'd he say?" asked Emma.

"He wants to host a party. A cookout."

"You're kidding?"

"Nope, boys and girls, we're having a cookout tomorrow. And he invited us to spend the night there."

Emma and Wimberly quickly put together overnight bags, and we all piled into the Buick. I put the top down. Emma and I took the front. Gellman and the professor squeezed into the rumble seat. The professor held his hat and clenched his pipe with his teeth as he leaned into the wind. Emma laughed, and the drive out to Phil's house was almost fun, except for my fear that a car full of Klansmen might cut us off at any moment.

We finally turned into Phil's driveway. "My God, Mark," Emma said, "this should be in *Architectural Digest*."

"An unusual home," said the professor dryly.

"For an unusual man," I said. "As you'll see, the house fits."

Phil's maid, Martha, came to the door as we drove up. "Welcome back, Mr. Morgan," she said with a hint of irony. She led the others inside as I worked to pull the top up on my car. A moment later, the storm broke.

11

Sunday, July 30, 1939

Sunday was a day of rest, and I slept a full twelve hours. When I woke, Phil and Emma were chatting by the pool. I took a shower, moving gingerly. Then I looked closely at my nose. It really was straight, and except for the purple bruising and swelling, it looked normal. The packing was driving me crazy, so I pulled most of it out. I threw the nasty stuff away. To my surprise, I could breathe through my nose.

Phil sat under an umbrella, smoking a cigar, with the Sunday newspaper spread out around him. "Sleep well?"

"Best I've slept in days."

Emma sat on a chaise lounge in the sun. She wore a broad hat and an ugly mustard yellow swimsuit. When she looked up from her book, she flashed a crooked smile. "Mark, your voice sounds almost normal."

Gellman was in the pool, splashing in the shallow end. "He doesn't really know how to swim," said Phil softly. "We have to watch him."

"I don't have a clue what he's been saying all morning," said Emma.

"Good morning, Dr. Gellman," I said in German.

"Ah, you are awake."

"Yes. We have much to talk about."

"Call me Dirk, please."

"Very well, Dirk. We will stay here all day and relax."

"This is a beautiful place. I've never seen anything like it. Please thank your friend for me."

I found a chair shaded by Phil's umbrella. He handed me the front section of the Sunday *Constitution*. "This may ruin your day."

I snapped the paper flat and looked at a headline under the fold. *Man found dead at Waterworks,* it said.

"Aw, hell."

"Told you," said Phil. "It gets worse."

A sanitation worker had found a body Saturday morning in one of the treatment ponds at the waterworks. The police identified him as Horst Hess, a German national who had visited Atlanta for the Baptist World Alliance convocation. Focusing on the backstory of another body found by the same man at the waterworks two years ago, the story emphasized his shock. The police called it murder and had detained a man.

Police say Al Smith is a homeless vagrant with a history as an agitator for the CIO. These agitators have been in Atlanta trying to organize the Exposition Cotton Mills, and Smith had been living in the woods near the mill. The police have not said whether Smith will be charged with the murder.

"This is absurd," I said. "Smith is no labor organizer, and he sure isn't a killer."

"Oh, great," said Phil. "You know this guy? I just got the glass in my door replaced from the last time the police visited."

"*Polizei*?" said Gellman from the pool.

"Nothing to worry about," I told him. From his expression, that didn't reassure him.

After a quiet moment, I said, "I don't think I understand anything anymore."

Phil put down his paper. Emma looked up from her book. They stared at me.

"We have to decide what to do about him first." I nodded toward Gellman.

"Why should we decide?" said Phil.

"The British want him," I said, "or at least the rabbi says he does. I don't like the rabbi, or trust him, but he'll give us four thousand buckolas for Gellman."

"Four thousand?" said Emma.

"Maybe more. He wants him badly."

"No. That would be like selling him," said Phil.

"Easy for you to say; you don't need four grand," said Emma.

"Dirk," I said in German. "Do you want to go with the English?"

He climbed out of the pool, and Phil handed him a towel as he took a seat. "From Germany, England looked attractive. From the United States, it does not. Professor Wimberly says that I may stay with him. I can work at the university laboratory as an assistant until my English is better."

"Wimberly says your work is important. Perhaps you could continue it if you went to England? Your friends are at the Cavendish Laboratory? That's a big deal."

"I'd rather be unknown and alive than famous and dead. I prefer working at the technical school here."

"He doesn't want to go to England," I told Emma and Phil. Gellman nodded his head. Phil snorted and sat back.

"But, Mark," said Emma. "Does he know about the money? Tell him you'll share it with him. Surely, going to England with two thousand dollars is better than sleeping in Professor Wimberly's laboratory with nothing."

I asked, and Gellman shook his head.

"I stay in America," said Gellman in English. He went into the house.

"But they know he's in Atlanta," argued Emma.

"I think he understands that," I said.

"You just want the money," said Phil.

"Of course I want the money," said Emma. "But keeping Gellman alive would be better. He'd be safer in England. If not there, somewhere other than Atlanta."

"Maybe," I said. "Whatever he does, he'll need money." I took out my wallet and gave Emma three hundred. "Take this for him; he'll need it."

"He needs to get out of town," she said.

"Emma, you may be right," I said. "But we have to respect what Gellman wants. If he decides to stay, he knows the risk."

"Humph," Emma said, and she returned to reading her book.

"We will have steaks, baked potatoes, corn on the cob, and Cokes," Phil said. "It'll be a blast."

"No Coca-Cola," I said.

"And red wine. Mark, you will have to taste this French red, a Rhône. It's perfect with steak. I have a case, but I don't think it's destined to last long."

"All right, I'll drink your Frog wine as long as you don't make me drink Coke."

Phil and Emma laughed. After such a terrible week, the normality of a cookout sounded wonderful.

"I'll call Sally Hemsted," said Emma. "Everyone'll like her, and she would appreciate a good party."

"Mark," said Phil. "Call that Treasury agent and have him join us. I'd like to meet him."

"He's Secret Service. And I'm not sure calling him is a good idea."

"Never hurts to cultivate people who can make a difference in your life."

"I don't have his number."

"I do. Duke Webster gave it to me."

I was astonished to see it was the main number for the Athletic Club. I called and asked for Packard's room. He answered.

"Packard," he said.

"Why didn't you just tell me you were staying at the club?"

"That you, Morgan?"

"Good voice recognition. Oh, and I didn't do it."

"Do what?"

"Whatever you're trying to pin on me now."

"You mean Hess? Cops already have a guy, the same fellow that fingered you for Dittmer. They think he did Schulman and Dittmer, too. Same method, same style."

"Someone cut Hess's throat?"

"Just like Dittmer and Schulman. Almost took his damn head off. The body had drained out, but not there."

"Smith didn't do it. He was a schoolteacher, for God's sake."

"Murderers are sometimes the quiet guy next door who grows roses. Anyway, it's not my case."

"Any word about Kunst? Maybe he did it?"

"Look, Morgan, you're asking too many questions."

"What about Kunst?" I pushed.

"I don't know about Kunst. He was with a group of Pioneers on Friday morning and didn't bother to go to the final Baptist meeting. Since then, he's vanished."

"I saw him yesterday at the S&W Cafeteria downtown. I'd bet he's still at the Henry Grady Hotel. Last I saw, he was headed that way."

"I've got a lot of irons in the fire; hard to keep track of them all."

"Well, that's not why I called. Tell me, Mr. Secret Service guy, do you have plans for this evening?"

"What on earth are you talking about?"

"I'm at Phil Sanders's, and he's invited you to dinner. I told him you're a bore, but he insists. Steaks and such, maybe a little wine. Any interest?"

There was a long silence, and I wondered if we'd lost the connection. Then he said, "Why the hell not?"

Phil rounded up rib eyes, Idaho potatoes, fresh corn, and ice cream for dessert. "There's always a way," he said. Martha cooked the potatoes and corn, but Phil presided over the grill. He refused to cook any steak beyond medium, and they were wonderful. We sat on the patio between the house and the pool to eat, and Phil brought out the French red.

"It's from the Rhône, in the south of France." He made sure everyone tasted. I glanced at Emma, remembering French wine and our evening at the Rainbow Roof. She smiled.

Wimberly and Gellman didn't care about the wine. They were caught up in a rollicking scientific conversation in German. When Joe Packard arrived, Gellman became more circumspect, sensing a policeman.

Sally Hemsted was a friend of Emma's from the WPA. Probably in her early forties, she was strongly built, athletic, with a long face and a sharp, pointed nose. She'd been a drama professor at Agnes Scott College in Atlanta before the college had retrenched, and she lost her job. She joined the Federal Theatre Project in '36, but they were on the road endlessly, and so to escape that, she moved to the Writers' Project. Emma mentioned that Sally knew Orson Welles, whose Mercury Theatre on the Air had terrified Americans the previous Halloween with their broadcast, *The War of the Worlds*.

"Orson's brilliant," Sally said, "but a loose cannon. Too smart for his own good, and worse, he knows it."

"Did you work for him on the radio?" Packard asked.

"Just some bit parts. The Theatre Project did Marlowe's *Dr. Faustus*, and my part included a blood-curdling scream. Orson was there, loved my scream, and had me come to New York and do the scream in a production of *The Shadow*. He paid me ten dollars, my travel expenses, and that was that."

"Nothing more?" Packard asked.

"A few small things. Ten dollars each time. I think Orson calls all his productions 'mercury' because he himself is so mercurial. Everything changes from day to day. One day, my scream was just what he needed; the next, he'd moved on to new things. He's just a kid, you know, twenty-two or twenty-three years old."

"But you were on the radio?" I asked, impressed.

"A few times." She turned back to Packard, clearly more impressed by someone from the Secret Service.

The other guest was a quiet young fellow named Arthur, who was Phil's friend. He worked as a draftsman for the architectural firm that had done the house, and they'd discovered each other during the project.

"Phil's a man of vision," he said, then reddened. "I mean, Mr. Sanders." He gestured widely at the sprawling modern house.

We finished eating about eight, then sat by the pool drinking. As the sky shaded toward indigo, a full moon emerged over the trees.

"Moon's great," said Phil, tilting back his glass of wine. "Magical, in fact. You never know how things will turn out, but I'm glad this went well."

Emma sat with me in companionable silence as we watched the moon rise.

"Tomorrow's Monday," said Phil. "Ready to come work with us, Mark?"

"I'm too beat up for tomorrow. I'll come on Tuesday."

"Tuesday it is," said Phil, holding up his glass. Emma, Phil, Arthur, and I touched our glasses together with a clink. We sipped and watched the moon. Suddenly, Phil said, "Mark, you gotta get rid of this price on your hide."

Packard sat next to Sally Hemstead. He poured another glass of wine. "Morgan has a price on his hide?" He laughed a bit drunkenly.

"Yes, and it's not funny; it's serious." Phil explained what Berger had said about the contract on my life.

"Sounds a bit dramatic, Mark," said Sally.

"Hell, that kind of stuff is real," said Packard.

"I wonder?" said Phil. "What if Mark put a contract out on Kunst? Offered twice as much money? What would happen then?"

Packard snorted. "If Kunst gets killed, Morgan goes to jail. Simple."

"You guys are pulling my leg," said Sally.

Phil ignored her. "Maybe, but would it keep him alive?"

"Explain what you mean," I said.

"Well, if you offered more money to kill Kunst, offered a lot more, killing you would be like killing the goose that lays the golden egg."

Emma giggled. "You're just joking," she said. She and Sally shared a smile.

"No," he said. "I'm serious. We haven't thought this through. Mark can't pay these guys off, because once they have his money, they will just kill him and collect on Kunst's contract. But if Mark offers more on a contract for Kunst, once he's dead, there will be no reason to kill Mark. Kunst won't be around to pay."

"Might work," said Packard, "but once Mark gives someone money for killing, he's a murderer too."

"But alive, and maybe he could beat the charge."

Silence fell.

"Joe, let's go see what the professor's up to in the kitchen," said Sally, leaping to her feet and pulling on his hand. Packard got up and wobbled inside.

"Were you serious?" I asked Phil when they were out of earshot.

"I'm serious. The only way to deal with ruthless men is to be ruthless yourself."

"Mark, you're not considering it?" asked Emma.

"Never," I said.

I couldn't sleep, so later that evening, lit by silver moonlight, I went for a swim. It was the first time since the car had hit me. The doctor was right; my overhand stroke caused agony to shoot down my left side, across the broken ribs. Anything other than a weak flutter kick tormented my hip. I soon found that a mild dog paddle didn't hurt too much, so I swam laborious lap after lap. It let me think.

Packard wasn't out to get me. He'd enjoyed the party a bit too much, and we'd poured coffee into him before he left. Sally had volunteered to drive him. Emma had smiled at me enigmatically. Maybe Packard got lucky? Professor Wimberly amazed us with a physics and chemistry show using kitchen chemicals and utensils. Gellman assisted. It was like watching a magician, and I glimpsed a wonderful teacher. All in all, a very successful party.

I paddled around in the pool, thinking of the others. Emma was asleep, and Phil and Arthur had disappeared. Gellman had fallen asleep on the couch, and Martha had vanished. So, it was just me and a midnight swim. Something splashed in the water ahead, and I rolled onto my side to avoid it, the rhythm broken. I grabbed what I thought was a towel, then realized it was Emma's ugly mustard-colored bathing suit.

Surprised, I spun around. She stood on the side of the pool, long and tall, like Saint-Gaudens' statue of Diana silvered by the light of the moon. Her skin shone like an iridescent pearl. I glimpsed champagne-cup breasts, a flat belly with a deeply indented navel, and lean hips. She dove into the water and swam under the surface, emerging directly in front of me. I laughed when she blew a mouthful of water into my face.

"Hey, you swim pretty well," I said.

"I'm glad you're swimming again, Mark," she said, treading water. "But you're so slow. I think I could beat you."

I paddled to the side and grabbed the edge. She joined me. She looked good, hair slicked back across her head, slim neck and arms, even her protruding ears fit. Perhaps it was the moonlight, but her lean figure stirred me. "You're gorgeous."

"None of that now. I want a race so I can say I beat an Olympic swimmer."

"I didn't make it to the Olympics. Just the trials."

"Close enough. Ready?"

"No." I turned to push off the wall. "Wait."

"Set, go."

She launched from the wall and beat me soundly to the other end. She laughed as I struggled up.

"Unfair. You don't have to fight the drag of a swimsuit."

"Then take yours off. It feels good to swim without one," she teased, submerging and then bouncing up out of the water, displaying her torso. I began swimming, and she launched from the wall, passing under me, pulling on my swim trunks, taunting me. I stood up in the shallow end. "Come here," I said.

She put her arms around my neck and wrapped her legs around me, pulling herself against me. Her eyes shone, lit by the moon. "I'm shameless," she said, and kissed me.

12

Monday, July 31, 1939

I woke with the sun, Emma sleeping beside me. The angles and planes of her face were lovely, and I watched her for a few minutes. How had I ever imagined I was not attracted to this woman? She'd made it all so natural, was careful of my injuries, and led me gently, so that my fears about performance vanished. Afterwards, I'd slept deeply, with no disturbing dreams. It was wonderful; she was wonderful.

I slipped out of bed and made my way to the kitchen. There, I found Martha cooking pancakes.

"Heard you moving around," she said, "so I started on these. Mr. Sanders left for work, but he told me to take care of you. He took that Tech professor home."

"Thank you," I said.

She brought me a plate with three pancakes, eggs, and bacon. I wolfed it all, followed by two more pancakes, a second cup of coffee, and then a third.

"It's good to feed a big man." She laughed.

"You didn't join us for dinner last night."

She ducked her head briefly. "I didn't know you people, so I stayed in the kitchen. We usually eat dinner together when it's just Mr. Sanders and me."

"How long ago did he leave?"

"Mondays, he gets to the office by six. That way, he has all his orders put together and wired to the floor of the exchange before it opens."

"Sounds like you follow his business. Do you keep up with the market?"

"Working for Mr. Sanders has been the best thing that ever happened to me. I've been living in his house, so I don't pay rent. I give what would be my rent money to him, and he invests it for me. No one I've worked for has ever been so generous. I'll soon have enough to buy my own house."

"Wish I could say that. It's Martha, right? I'm sorry I haven't introduced myself. I'm Mark Morgan."

"Oh, I know. And my name's Martha Washington."

I chuckled, and she smiled. "My father was deadly serious when he did that to me," she said. "And I haven't married. How could I mess up a name like that?"

"Maybe you could marry a man named Jefferson?"

She smiled. "Not good enough."

"Well then, Miss Washington, are the others up yet?"

"The scientist is still sleeping. Mr. Sanders's special friend went home late last night. The G-man and the lady went home too. It's just you, your lovely lady, and the scientist."

"You're well-informed."

"You better believe it. I have to run this house, so I'd better know what's going on." She smiled. "Will your lady be joining us?"

The telephone rang, and she excused herself to answer it.

"Mr. Morgan?" she said. "This call's for you."

Wondering who would know to call me at Phil's house, I followed her voice into a hallway behind the kitchen. She handed me the receiver. "It's that G-man."

"Packard?" I said.

"Yeah, it's me," he said. "Mark, you need to get down here right away. We've got a breakthrough on the counterfeit case."

"I thought you said it was too dangerous for me to go downtown?"

"You can park in the back lot of the post office; that should be safe enough."

"Safe enough? Thanks a lot."

"My office," he said.

Packard's office was on the second floor of the new post office building. It looked like a closet and had almost no room for a visitor's chair in front of the desk.

"Secret Service rates pretty high around here," I said, shoehorning myself into the chair behind the door.

"Screw you, Morgan. No wonder you don't have any friends."

"What's the big news?"

He tilted his chair back until it tipped and caught perfectly on the edge of the windowsill.

"Bet you spent a lot of time getting that just right," I said.

Packard smiled, laced his fingers together, and put his hands behind his head. "We've got an inside man. There'll be a transfer of cash from the Germans to the Pioneers tonight—one hundred thousand. In the parking lot at the Lakewood auto plant. East Point Klan will be there too. We ought to be able to nail Kunst, capture a bunch of the counterfeit, and get some of these Pioneers and Klansmen."

"That's a big break."

"Yeah. We'll need you to testify before a grand jury. Don't worry, that probably won't happen until next week." He pushed a piece of paper across the desk. "I need you to sign this statement so we can get a warrant. We might have to go into the Lakewood plant or the old Van Winkle Works; this gives us probable cause. I've got a U.S. Attorney and a judge waiting for this."

"What is it?" I asked, beginning to read.

"A summary of what you saw at the machine works, and what you were told about how the counterfeit was smuggled into the country. I'll get a notary to attest your signature, and we'll have enough to get the warrant."

"You'll nail Kunst?"

"Maybe. We'll need to find counterfeit money. Even then, he might suddenly come up with a diplomatic passport. If so, we'll have to let him go. But the Pioneers and Klansmen we sweep up are cooked."

I read the statement, and it was mostly correct. The notary came in, I signed, swore to the truth of the statement, and he attested to it. Packard was grinning and joking the entire time, then sent the affidavit off with a messenger when the notary finished.

"Well, that makes my day," he said.

"I thought last night might have made your day."

"Naw," he said. "She just took me home so I could sleep it off. Red wine hits me hard. Hope to see her again, though."

I squirmed in the chair, trying to fit my knees behind the door so I could close it.

"Hey," said Packard as the door shut. "That just makes it hotter in here."

"Joe," I said softly after closing the door, "I need to find Bill Cadwell."

"Who's that?"

"The newspapers say he's involved in vice here in the city. I have to talk to him."

"Then ask the police."

"Sure, I'll just walk in and ask cops who're on the take from Cadwell's organization. Or maybe the guys who belong to the Klan."

"I get your point. But why are you telling me?"

"I'm not telling you. I'm asking you to get me Cadwell's address."

Packard picked up his phone. "All right," he said. "It's your funeral."

Bill Cadwell lived on the west side, near Atlanta University. Fresh blue paint, a white picket fence, and a small, neat yard suggested the home of a quiet professor, not a criminal. It was 10:45 a.m. when I knocked on the door. A handsome, well-dressed Negro lady answered the door.

"Can I help you?" she asked.

"My name is Mark Morgan. I'm looking for Mr. Cadwell."

Her eyes shifted around, looking across the yard and at my car, then came back to mine. "Mr. Cadwell's at work."

"Then I'll talk to him at work. What's the address?"

"Sorry." She closed the door in my face.

I went back to my car and waited. The day was warm, I had the top down, and the sun made me sweat. I dozed a bit, then woke with something hard pressing into my neck.

"Bang," said a voice. It was Bill Cadwell poking me with his finger.

"You're the second person to do that," I said.

"I could've just made a thousand bucks."

"That's all they're paying? I'm insulted."

"You're a damn fool. If I'd been Junior, there'd be a nice car with a mess in it in front of my house. Now, how would I explain that to the newspapers? I'm a legitimate businessman."

"Glad you're not Junior. Look, I need to talk and can make it worth your while. You want a ride to work?"

"A ride to work?" He laughed. "Hell, I'm just getting home."

"But last night was Sunday? Everything's closed."

"We aren't, and people have to have fun."

"Okay, so you're done? Then you've got time to talk."

"Yeah, one whole minute, and then I need to go to bed. Got a little treat waiting for me."

"I met her." Then, I startled him. "How do I buy off Big Caesar?"

"Damn, you just get right to the point, don't you?" He walked around to the other side of the car, opened the door, and sat. "Radio, nice seats. Bet it has a good heater too. This is one sweet car, Morgan."

"I'll give it to you if you fix things with Big Caesar."

"What? Hell, I can have any kind of car I want. You see that '39 Cadillac Sixty Special? I don't need some pissant Buick."

"Okay, what would you want?"

"It'd be best if you just went away. You know, like China or India."

"I can't do that."

"I don't hardly know you. Why would I do anything to help you?"

"Because I know what kind of man you really are."

He sat for a while, running his hand along the dashboard, and then he laughed. "If you don't take the cake. Okay. A man offered Big Caesar a thousand bucks, but Big Caesar got it up to two thousand. Man said he'd pay when he saw it in the newspaper that you were dead, so he can't just make you disappear. There has to be a body. People have to know. Big Caesar won't do it himself; he doesn't work like that. Instead, he says anyone who nails you gets a thousand. He's greedy, keeps a grand for himself. Still, plenty of folks will do a lot of things for a thousand."

"He used to work for Mr. Green. Would Green be neutral in this?"

"Green runs The Bug. He's the biggest banker in the numbers racket now, bigger than all the others put together. The Bug makes a lot of money; the last thing he wants is something that rocks the boat."

"Then I need to talk to him. Can you make that happen? I'll make it worth your while."

Cadwell whistled. "Mr. Green's kinda hard to see. Doesn't exactly keep office hours, if you know what I mean."

"I need your help."

"Shit, first time in my life a White man asks me for help, and he's a crazy man."

I waited. Finally, he said, "Okay, I can get you to the right place, but I can't promise nothing. You'd be better off just moving away, a long way away. Maybe these Baptists will let you be a missionary in Brazil or something."

"I need to see Green."

"Okay, but if you go into the bear's den, don't be surprised if he bites."

We drove in Cadwell's black Cadillac Special, the car low slung with no running board. The ride was smooth, like riding in a boat on a calm lake. I preferred the sportiness of my Buick. Decatur Street was crowded with the normal business of the day. There was a lot of activity around the police station, which backed up traffic on a street already crowded with delivery trucks and cars. He stopped in front of a clothing shop. "Two shirts for the price of one," read the sign.

"Here?" I asked, surprised.

"Yep, this is where Mr. Green does Bug business. Dime Bug will be on today's stock market close, so they'll be doing the books, counting money, getting things ready."

The daily Bug cost a dime and paid ten dollars if you guessed the last three digits of the volume that day on the New York Stock Exchange. You had to bet before noon. A hundred to one payoff, with one thousand to one odds. Tens of thousands of people betting dimes. The odds were nicely stacked for Mr. Green.

We went through the front of the shop, surprising a clerk who quickly picked up a phone. We walked back through a tailor's workroom and knocked on a heavy oak door. A moment later, a mountain of a man opened it. He was one of the biggest men I'd ever seen, at least six and a half feet tall, light-skinned, and very broad. Though a bit of fat showed, most of his three hundred pounds appeared to be muscle.

"I'm supposed to see Uncle Lucius," said Cadwell.

I stared at Cadwell. He'd said nothing about Green being his uncle. Cadwell saw my expression and shrugged. "Don't like to brag about family."

"Who's that?" Man Mountain nodded at me.

"My uncle wants to see him too."

I smiled. Man Mountain scowled. "Nobody told me about this."

"Well, then, ask my uncle."

Man Mountain hesitated, then held the door open. Another guy armed with a shotgun stood to the side behind him. Shotgun Man motioned us in. Man Mountain closed and locked the door, then searched us both roughly.

"They're clean."

Shotgun Man opened a second heavy door into a small, windowless brick room. The air was stale, old. Harsh light shone from hanging bulbs. Shining silver coins covered a long table. Three guys, who were counting and bagging change, turned to look at us. Big men, Black, well-dressed, with hard faces and eyes. If I walked into a bar and saw them, I'd turn and walk out. There was also a fourth man. A shrunken geezer, wearing round glasses and an accountant's eyeshade, sat behind a desk with a ledger open in front of him and an ancient 81-key adding machine next to him. He ignored us, continuing his work, his pencil moving as he entered numbers.

Finally, he looked up. Lines in his ebony skin showed in the harsh light, and his short curly hair was turning from gray to white. Tired eyes regarded me flatly.

"Uncle Lucius, good morning," said Cadwell.

"Bill," said the old man. The men bagging change went back to work. The coins they were bagging clinked like rapid rain on a tin roof.

"Uncle, I'm sorry to disturb your work, but I'd like to introduce Mark Morgan."

The clink of money stopped. Everyone stared at me.

"I'm flattered to make your acquaintance, Mr. Green."

For several beats, Green said nothing. Then he chuckled and smiled broadly. "I can always depend on my nephew to make life interesting. Come on over and have a seat, Mr. Morgan. May I get you anything? A cup of coffee, perhaps?"

"No, thank you, sir." I sat in the chair next to his desk.

He closed the ledger. "You seem surprised?" He glanced around the room, then leaned back in the chair, watching me.

"I had no idea it was so big. There must be thousands of dollars here."

"More than forty thousand dimes a day," he said. "You know how the government keeps statistics on the economy to see if it is growing? Well, I know we're in economic recovery because the take grows every month."

I did the math. "Forty thousand every day?"

He smiled. "That's right, Monday through Friday, two hundred and fifty-one days a year. The net is about fifty percent. Keeps us busy."

So, a gross income of more than one million dollars a year on the Dime Bug alone. There were also nickel games, quarter games, and even a dollar game. My astonishment must have shown. One of the counting men chuckled, and then the clatter of pouring money resumed.

"Oh, I'm not the only one, just the biggest banker in Atlanta. There are more bankers; the total of daily business between them is probably equal to what I do."

"Mr. Green, normally, I would be fascinated. However, today I'm in a difficult spot."

"Yes, indeed, you are. It will be even more difficult once you leave this building."

"Ah," I said. "But why not here?"

"It would cause me too much trouble if anything happened in this building. The police station's just a few blocks away. Imagine the headlines. Bad for business."

"I can imagine."

"As long as you're my guest . . . well, I can control my people. Once you leave, and you will leave, I hope your estate plans are in order."

"I guess that means I can't go see Big Caesar."

"You want to see Big Caesar?"

"So I can make a counteroffer."

Green chortled. He wiped his mouth with a handkerchief, and the smile vanished. "Bill always brings me interesting stuff. Mr. Morgan, it doesn't matter how much you pay Big Caesar; as soon as he has your money, he'll have someone kill you and collect from the other fellow. You should've left town. Now, I just don't see how you plan to get out of this. In fact, why would he even listen to you?"

"Oh, he'll listen to me all right. You see, I'm offering five thousand dollars for him to kill the Kraut, Wilhelm Kunst."

Big Caesar turned out to be a short and slight man with a huge Roman nose. Easy to see where the name came from. He was confused by my offer at first.

"What, so you want me to kill him?"

"That's right," I said.

"Why don't I just kill both of you fellows?"

"Because you wouldn't get any money then. Think it through. I'm offering more than twice as much, so it makes the most sense to kill him. Once he's dead, it makes no sense to kill me since you'll get nothing."

Big Caesar took a moment to think it through. "Okay, but I made a deal. He gave me a hundred bucks to seal it. That's gotta mean something."

"A hundred-dollar bill?"

"Yeah."

"Then it's fake. Sourdough. Kunst's been passing lots of it."

Big Caesar looked shocked and took out his wallet. He pulled out a hundred and turned to Green. "Mr. Green, sir? What about this here bill?"

Green took the bill, laid it on his desk, and pulled out a magnifying glass. After a moment, he picked up the hundred and tore it in half. He gave the halves back to Big Caesar. "Paper's wrong," he said. "See how it tore, wrong type of thread in there. This is a fake bill."

"Shit," said Big Caesar, letting the torn halves flutter to the floor. "I ought to kill him for that."

I took a hundred from my wallet and gave it to Big Caesar.

"So, you'll pay five thousand?" he asked.

"Cash. Spread the word quickly. I want to be able to leave this establishment sometime today."

Big Caesar grinned, nodded at Mr. Green, and left.

Mr. Green asked softly, "Do you have more hundred-dollar bills in your wallet?"

"I do."

"May I see them?"

Unsure, I took out some bills and handed them to him. He took his time with the magnifying glass, looking closely at each bill.

"Bill," he said. "Let me see that other hundred."

Cadwell picked up the torn halves of the bill and put them on the desk. Mr. Green put aside his magnifying glass and took out a jeweler's loupe. He looked closely at all the bills.

"Is there a problem?"

"Afraid so." He put down his loupe. "I'm sure you've guessed; all these bills are fake. Excellent work, like the one Big Caesar had. In fact, exactly like the bill Big Caesar had. Identical, printed by the same process on the same paper."

"But that's impossible."

"I'm just telling you what I see, Mr. Morgan. A lot of bills like these have been showing up this past week, especially at the hotels."

"Big Caesar's bill came from Kunst, and I know he's been passing counterfeit. But those came from a different source, and you're telling me they're the same sort of fakes?"

"All of them. The same." He tilted his head and peered at me. "Perhaps that tells you something you needed to know?"

"Maybe." Where could the rabbi have gotten the counterfeit? Was he working with the Germans? That would explain his easy access to so much dough. How else could he have gotten the counterfeit bills? It made no sense. Why would he have me watching the Germans if he was one of them?

My concentration was broken when the door opened, and a young man hurried in. He whispered urgently to Mr. Green, who waved him to silence. "Mr. Morgan, you'll want to hear this. Tell him, Tommy."

"Well," Tommy said, "the police are all riled up. There must be at least two dozen cars in front of police headquarters. They got another one of them murders. You know, the slasher."

"The slasher?" I asked.

"That's what they's calling it. Over at police headquarters. Found another one an hour ago; one of them Germans. Just like the others, head almost cut off."

"A woman?" I asked, fearing the answer.

"Nope. A man. Some ofay called Kunst."

"Where the hell have you been?" Phil asked when I called.

"Trying to figure out a way to stay alive. What's wrong?"

"I've had two phone calls this morning for you. First, Emma called. Said she was sorry, but that she'd taken Dr. Gellman's fate into her hands."

"What? My God, is she selling him to the rabbi?"

"No, no. She says they're going to Washington, DC, to the Carnegie Institute. Apparently, there's a physicist Gellman knows there. They took the *Crescent Limited*. It left an hour ago."

"Damn it, what does she think she's doing?"

"Too late to do anything about that now. And that Treasury agent, Packard, called about half an hour ago. He needs you to call him immediately."

Phil gave me the number, and I scribbled it down.

"I tried your idea," I said. "You know, to reverse the contract."

"You're kidding? Jesus, Mark, I was drunk."

"Then get drunk more often. It might have worked."

"Might have?"

"Yeah, except Kunst was already dead."

"How did you know he was dead?" Packard asked after I squeezed into his office again.

"I have sources. They said it was the same way: a slashed throat."

"Good sources. Yeah, same technique, same style. The body was left in a field near Piedmont and Lindberg. Like the others, not much blood. Killed someplace else. No keeping this one quiet; there'll be photos in the papers. Newsies were there before the cops."

"Piedmont and Lindberg—you'd need a car to get out there and dump the body."

"That's right."

"Any witnesses? Maybe saw a big DeSoto sedan?"

"No one saw anything."

"Huh. Did you ever find Kunst's hotel room?"

"We're still looking."

I thought for a few minutes. "Is it a problem that Kunst is dead?"

"A darn big one. He was supposed to pay the Pioneers tonight. Now, we'll never trace the funny money."

"Humm," I said. "There might be someone else."

"What do you mean?"

"Don't know yet." I took out my wallet, removed a hundred, and handed it to him. "Tell me what you think of that bill?"

He held it up to the light from the window.

"It's fake. The paper's wrong; there's not enough thread, and it has one of the serial numbers used on others." He put it down. "Where did you get it?"

"That came from the rabbi."

"The rabbi? I thought you said he was British?"

"Maybe I was wrong," I said.

I went home to the Club. It was sweltering in my room, heated by the afternoon sun. I packed a suitcase and locked my room. In the lobby, I spotted the evening *Atlanta Journal*. Grabbing a copy, the headline was what I expected.

Slasher Strikes. Victim found near Piedmont.

A guy cutting grass had found the body. Nothing in the story about Kunst, other than that he was a Messenger attending the World Baptist Alliance meeting. The paper reported rumors of similar killings, while the mayor's office denied they'd hidden anything. Police detectives told the *Journal* they had leads, but they couldn't reveal them without compromising the investigation. An editorial speculated that communist union organizers might be involved. The police had detained a CIO leader with a Polish name as the edition went to press.

I suddenly remembered when I'd last seen Kunst. He was hurrying south on Peachtree, not toward the Henry Grady, but toward the Winecoff Hotel. I telephoned Packard's office, but it rang with no answer. When I went outside, I saw slow-moving rush-hour traffic clogging Peachtree. There was no reason to join the swarm, so I stowed the suitcase in my car and walked to the Winecoff.

It was smaller than the Henry Grady, older, but decently kept. I went to the front desk and asked if Mr. Kunst was in.

"I'll check, sir," said the young clerk. He picked up a phone and dialed a number.

"I doubt anyone will answer." I put the evening paper on the counter and pointed to the name in the first paragraph of the headline article. The clerk paused, read it, and then slowly put down the telephone.

"No one answered, sir."

"Detective Garrett Hancock," I lied. "Need to see the room. Now."

"Yes, of course, Detective. I'll get the manager."

The manager was older, with a long face and a white pencil mustache. He asked no questions, simply took me up to the fourth floor and opened a door. It was completely dark inside.

"This was Kunst's room?" He nodded. "We don't want to touch anything until we get a team here, but I need a glance."

He pushed a button, and a harsh yellow light flooded the room. The curtains were pulled tightly across the window. I checked the empty closet and the bathroom. There was just one suitcase, which was open on the bed, some clothes, and nothing more. I looked under the bed and under the mattress. Nothing. Beside the bed on the night table were a few business cards, but all were for restaurants. Then I noticed indentations on the notepad by the phone made by writing a number on the page above. I wrote the number in my notebook.

"Investigators will be here soon. Lock the door and don't let anyone touch anything in this room until they get here."

We went back down the elevator together. I saluted the clerk at the front desk and hurried out. For the first time, I felt certain that maybe I could do something right. Maybe I could make a difference. Crossing to the library, I used a public phone to call the cops. Wilhelm Kunst had been staying at the Hotel Winecoff, I said. The manager was keeping his room locked for their arrival. I hung up and tried Packard again, but there was no answer, so I tried the number from the notepad in Kunst's room.

"Georgian Terrace Hotel," announced a polite woman's voice.

I hung up. Gritting my teeth, I jumped into the Buick and joined the slow parade up Peachtree. On every corner, paperboys hawked special editions about the Slasher, and they were selling plenty. Atlanta had more than a hundred murders each year, usually family affairs, or acquaintances in a brawl. But this was different; an unsolved grisly murder, with a rumored connection to other murders, was a sensation.

The Georgian Terrace sat at the intersection of Peachtree and Ponce de Leon, across the street from the Fox Theatre. Though it was smaller than some of the downtown hotels, many travelers considered it Atlanta's best. The Georgian Terrace usually hosted Atlanta's notable visitors, from presidents to movie stars. When I pulled up, a valet hurried out to my car.

"Will you be staying with us, sir?" His name tag read Bobby.

"Just a brief visit, Bobby. I might want the car back any minute." I pressed a hundred-dollar bill into his hand. His mouth gaped. "Yes, sir. I'll keep it right out front."

The lobby had a large sitting area on the right and the front desk on the left. The clock behind the desk showed five 'til eight. I walked through the sitting room, but didn't recognize anyone. Farther back and to the left was the dining room. The maître d' looked up expectantly as I approached the entrance and smiled. I smiled back, and then I saw what I wanted.

She sat alone at a table along the left wall, wearing an elegant emerald dress topped by a short black Gaucho jacket with padded shoulders. Dark red lipstick, eyes expertly made up, and her blond hair tucked under a broad black hat. At first glance, she looked entirely different from the Anna Erlanger I knew; wealthier, older, more stylish. I sat at her table. Only her perfume was the same, herbal and dark. It hit me like a punch in the stomach.

"Good evening, Anna," I said in English. "I love your perfume. What is it?"

Surprise showed in her eyes, but she remained outwardly calm. A skilled actress. "How nice to see you, Mark. The perfume's called Tabu. It is lovely. French, of course." Her English was perfect, with an upper-crust northeastern accent, like Eleanor Roosevelt, but at a lower register. An excellent actress.

"I missed you. We were having such fun."

"Yes, weren't we?" She smiled and patted her lips with a napkin. "There's so much we need to talk about. Join me for a drink?"

"A drink? Sure." I snapped my fingers, and the waiter hurried over. "The lady and I would like a drink."

"Oh, Mark." Anna laughed, waving him away. "We can have drinks in my suite. I've finished eating; we may as well go up."

Her suite was on the ninth floor, at the top of the hotel, and we were silent during the ride with the elevator operator. She opened the door, motioned me in, and then closed and locked it behind us. The sitting room was in a round turret with windows on three sides. There was a fully stocked bar, and the view was magnificent. The evening sun hung just above the horizon, casting an orange glow over the city. I walked to the windows, admiring the sunset.

"So, that drink," she said, heading to the bar.

"A drink? You must be kidding."

"No, Mark, I'm not kidding." She turned to me, holding a black automatic pistol. "Please, sit down."

I sat.

"It's a shame you found me. How did you know I spoke English?"

"Oh, you made a few slips here and there. Especially the day you confronted my friend, Emma. They added up."

She crossed to the chair opposite mine and sat down, keeping the pistol trained on me. "Oh, Mark, why didn't you just sleep with me? It would have been so much easier. It always is. And it would have been fun. I like big men. My God, after that run at the factory, I wanted it so badly. You should have waited for me at the hotel. I would have slipped out to be with you, but you left."

"You'll always have to wonder why I didn't want you." I saw the barb strike home. "So, the money's here?"

"The money? You're still chasing it?"

"Kunst is dead." Surprise showed, and the pistol wavered for a moment. "Killed the same way as the others, throat slashed to the bone. No money in his hotel room. That leaves only one place."

"My God." Her eyes narrowed. "You're lying."

"It's in the evening paper. Shall we call the front desk and have them send up a copy?"

We sat quietly for a moment, with the gun still trained on me. Orange light from the sunset shone on it. Bigger than a .22, blue-black, it looked professional and deadly. Would she shoot me if I jumped her?

"Yes, Mark, I'll shoot you," she said, reading my thought. "This is a 7.62 Walther, not some popgun, and I'm a great shot."

"I have to commend you on your English; it's so colloquial. I'm impressed."

"Don't be. I got it the easy way. You weren't the only one with a foreign mother."

"So, what do we do now?"

"We wait. Some men are coming for the money. One hundred thousand of it. Your face, your history, the way you floundered about—well, I didn't expect you to work it out. You're a much better detective than I imagined. Kunst thought you were a government agent, but I could tell you weren't. God, that dinner, they were all such poor actors, weren't they?"

I smiled, but the tension in my gut made breathing short and shallow. "So, the Pioneers get their money. And then what, you leave?"

"We'll wait, maybe chat a little, until they get here."

"Charming. What if I just walk out?"

"Oh, Mark, I'm sorry. I'm afraid there's nothing I can do for you. I don't know how much you know, and I'm not sure I could force you to tell me. You may not be a government agent, but there's a chance you would tell someone who is. The easiest way to deal with a man who's a problem is to make the man go away. No man, no problem. I'm sure you understand."

"Well, then, can a dead man ask questions?"

"Don't waste your breath, Mark."

"Surely there's no harm in answering now? For example, Mendel Rubenstein?"

"That was Kunst."

"No, that was the Pioneers. They tried to kill me the same way. If you give them money, they'll kill more."

"Of course. Americans killing Americans. It doesn't bother me."

"So, we missed our big chance together. Isn't that how it always is?"

She smiled grimly. "You know, despite the tape, I can see your nose is straighter. A nice improvement."

"Thanks."

"Quiet," she said, extending the gun toward me, so I didn't say another word. We waited, and then there was a knock on the door.

"They're early." She stood. Keeping the gun trained on me, she moved over to the door and unlocked it.

"Come in," she said, watching me.

The door opened. The rabbi stepped through and took the pistol out of Anna's hand.

"Sit down," he said, training the gun on her. She sat in the chair across from me.

"Thank you, Rabbi," I said, standing. "You couldn't have come at a better moment."

He pointed the Walther at me. "Shut up. You think I came to rescue you?"

"Mark, you know this man?"

"He's the guy who hired me."

"Quiet," said the rabbi. "Miss Stossel, I've come for the money."

"Stossel?" I asked.

"That's her name," said the rabbi. "Anna Stossel. She's an Abwehr agent."

"What about Dr. Erlanger?"

"He's not her husband; surely you figured that out? Erlanger's real wife is in Essen; insurance for his cooperation, wasn't she, Anna?"

"Rabbi, I'm lost," I said.

"Yes, I expected nothing less. That's been your problem all along, hasn't it? You never knew what you were doing. Typical American, no experience whatsoever, but thought you could do it anyway. It was painful watching you flounder about, going nowhere."

"Why do you say Anna's Abwehr?"

"Because she is. Aren't you, my dear?" The rabbi stepped over to her chair and put the gun to her head. "Tell him."

"I'm an Abwehr agent, Mark."

"Good girl," he said, stepping back and pointing the gun at me.

I was flabbergasted. "But Kunst was SD. Your organizations don't co-operate."

The rabbi waved the gun. "Tell him," he said.

"It's better for him if he doesn't know."

"Why? Surely, you were going to kill him? Take him to a nice, quiet place away from the hotel and shoot him at the base of the skull. That's your trademark, isn't it? What is it, three men now? Quick and painless, at least for you." He licked his lips and touched Anna's chin with the pistol, lifting her head. "You're beautiful, truly beautiful. But a monster."

She looked down.

"So, tell him, dear Anna. How were you going to kill him?"

Anna crossed her arms. "I hadn't planned on it," she said.

The rabbi snorted. "Not yet, maybe. The whole story." He poked her with the gun.

"The Abwehr needed to place new operatives in the United States," she said, looking at me. "Last year was a disaster. We needed to bring in more professional agents, not just recruit amateurs who would be easily caught. Somehow, these plans came to the attention of Reinhard Heydrich."

"Who's he?" I asked.

"He's the head of the SD," said the rabbi. "He's been dying to develop overseas operations for the SD, wants the SD to replace the Abwehr as Germany's intelligence organization. Probably played a role in exposing several Abwehr agents here last year. He wanted intelligence and espionage controlled by the Nazi Party, not by the military. Tell him, Anna."

She took a deep breath and looked at me, her eyes no longer hard but pleading. "Heydrich has Hitler's ear. He foisted this half-baked plot on us. If we helped the SD with their operation, we would get the money needed to expand Abwehr operations. So, with that agreement, the SD got a million American dollars for their plot, and we got a million for our operation."

"And their plot was to influence American elections?" I said. "Support sympathetic political movements? Keep America out of the coming war?"

"I told them it was utter nonsense," said Anna. "They know nothing of America; their ignorance is astonishing. Just like their silly support for the Bund in New York and Chicago. It hurts us in America; it doesn't help us. Of course, no one in the SD would listen to a woman, so they sent the money and expected results."

"It's counterfeit."

"Most of it. We didn't know they would do that," said Anna. "Once the money arrived, we figured it out. The SD is truly incompetent. They didn't even fund us with real money, and they thought no one would notice?"

"So, Kunst brought the cash, but you were already here."

Anna was silent. The rabbi grunted. "She's been here for years, living in New York, a happy housewife. A simple operation, really, placing German agents with American heritage into American society. The long-term payoff could be dramatic."

"That's all the Abwehr was after?"

"Yes," said Anna. "That was all, until the crazy SD plot."

"You were never really interested in Peter Goss, were you, Rabbi?"

"No, but you were. I needed you to identify the security agents among the Germans. You did that for me. If you thought Goss was important, then I was glad to encourage it."

"And Eleanor Jones?"

"A do-gooder. All she cares about is rescuing Jews. She thought I was helping. It gave me legitimacy in certain circles." He smiled.

"Eleanor Jones?" said Anna, confused.

I ignored her. "You paid me with the same counterfeit money that Kunst carried. How did that happen?"

Anna looked shocked. “Harry Burchard?” she said.

“Very good, Anna,” said the rabbi. “The twenty thousand I took from him greatly facilitated this work, so I thank you. I used part of it for Mark’s payments.”

“Who’s Burchard?” I looked at Anna.

“He worked for us in New York and left with some funds. He vanished; we’ve had no word at all.”

“The Hudson is a big river,” said the rabbi.

“Rabbi, I don’t understand. Why would you kill all these men? Who are you?”

“I suspect he works for the Red Army Fourth Directorate, but has gone rogue,” said Anna.

“Anna, Anna, that’s unfair. I’ve not gone rogue, and this has nothing to do with the Fourth Directorate.”

“My God,” I said. “You’re not a rabbi. Who are you?”

“Who am I? I am judgement. I am vengeance. Call me Azrael; I am the Angel of Death.”

The Angel of Death watched while Anna tied my hands. She gently folded my fingers up so I could feel the knots. They were large and loose, and I could easily work on them. Then, she tied my ankles to the legs of the heavy chair. He forced her to bring the cash into the sitting room. She brought in a briefcase that held one hundred thousand dollars, which was intended for the Pioneers. Another large brown leather satchel held the remainder of the SD’s share—over eight hundred thousand, she said. Most of Anna’s million, intended to recruit and support Abwehr agents, was packed in the bottom of her steamer trunk. All three were placed near the door.

“Guns?” asked the rabbi.

"You're holding it," she said.

"Get the rest of the rope."

She slowly picked up the length of rope that lay at my feet. "So, how will it be? Will Mark kill me and then hang himself in remorse? Or will I shoot him and then hang myself? Perhaps some sort of lovers' death pact?"

"I'm not worried about Morgan right now. It is you who are dangerous, a viper. Throw that rope here, gently." She threw the rope at the rabbi's face, and he caught it with his left hand.

"Excellent. Now, stand in front of me with your hands behind your back."

Anna walked slowly over toward him.

"If you shoot us," she said, "the noise will attract attention. You'll be trapped in the hotel, and the police will find you."

"Perhaps," he said. "And you'll be dead. But if you do as I say, you may live."

Anna laughed and stood in front of him, defiant. The sun had set, and while the afterglow still lit the city below, the room had grown dark. I fiddled with the loose knots binding me, covered by the shadows. All at once, they gave way. I kept the rope wrapped around my wrists and waited.

"Turn on a light," he ordered.

Anna glanced at me, and I nodded. She bent toward a brass table lamp, then suddenly picked it up and swung. It hit his shoulder, knocking him toward me. I stood up, still tied to the chair legs, and grabbed him from behind. He reached back with the gun, but I slapped it away. My broken ribs parted with the motion, and I grunted in pain. He clawed at my eyes. I grabbed the rabbi's neck and squeezed. He twisted and fell, wriggling like an eel, trying to escape. I squeezed harder, and he elbowed me in the side. My vision darkened, and someone started screaming. The screams were mine. Then suddenly, he escaped from my grip.

I tried to stand, but tripped, still tied to the chair. He aimed a kick at my head, and I rolled aside, tangling my legs. He kicked at me again, but

I blocked it with my left arm. My watch shattered, the broken case and crystal scattered on the floor. Backing away, the rabbi drew a long knife from a sheath on his ankle. When he stepped forward, his foot slipped on the broken watch parts. I grabbed his ankle as he fell and held on. He bent forward and plunged the knife into my left forearm. The blade ripped into my flesh, and I screamed again. With my right hand, I grabbed his trouser leg and pulled. He raised the knife.

Anna hit him again with the brass table lamp. The thud echoed down through his leg. He continued to squirm, so Anna knelt, raised the lamp, and slammed it down on his head. She did it a second time, then a third. Finally, he was still.

Breathing heavily, I lay on the floor. My left arm was on fire. Breathing hurt. The ribs had shifted; I could feel them poking my skin.

Anna turned on a light.

"Oh God," she said. "There's blood everywhere."

She was right. It was welling out of the hole in my arm, and there were splatters all over my jacket and her dress. But the blood from my wound was minor in comparison with the growing puddle around the rabbi's head. His eyes were open, one oddly dilated, but the other seemed to stare directly at me.

"He has to be dead," I said.

"Oh, he's dead," said Anna without a second look.

I bit my lip as she lifted me to a sitting position, ribs grinding. She pulled the jacket off my right arm, then carefully off my left, then pulled back my soaked sleeve to reveal blood flowing out of the puncture in my left forearm. Pressing a towel on the wound, she gently placed my right hand on top to hold it. I couldn't tell how badly I was hurt, but I saw the knife, still in his hand, was long and thin.

"There's the knife." I nodded toward it.

Anna picked it up. It was a wicked thing, designed for slicing with a curved tip. My gaze shifted to Anna. Our eyes met, and she smiled before throwing the knife aside. It skittered under the couch. She spotted the Walther on the floor, picked it up, and pointed it at me.

"Aw, hell," I said. "We're back where we started."

The Pioneers arrived soon after. Three men, not at all what I expected. The leader was in his fifties, with a limp, short, grizzled hair, and a square chin. He was accompanied by a skinny young man with round glasses and the look of a clerk. A beefy third man, with broad shoulders and a barrel chest, stood in the doorway. All three wore gray slacks and matching open-collared white shirts. The body and the gore upset the skinny clerk. He stepped back when he saw Anna's blood-spattered dress. His companions calmed him down, but no one seemed to like it. Anna handed them the briefcase, and they sat down to count it. Each counted it fully on his own. Satisfied, they loaded it back into the briefcase.

"What about him?" said Anna. At first, I thought she meant the rabbi, then realized she'd nodded at me.

"Him?" asked the older Pioneer.

"You should take care of him. We can't afford any witnesses."

"What happened to him?"

Anna laughed. "That's just how he looks. He's had a rough week."

The men glanced at each other. "We're the Finance Committee."

"Then take him to people who know what to do."

They shrugged and pulled me to my feet. I gasped and bent over in pain. My legs were still tied to the chair, so the beefy guy pulled out a knife and sawed through the rope.

"Good bye, Mark," said Anna. "Think of me."

"Oh, believe me, I will."

She giggled. "Always so tough. Tough to the end." She turned and went into the bedroom.

"Let's go, buddy," said the older Pioneer. He put his hand on my back, but the touch was gentle, not rough.

"Hey, can you grab my bag?" I said, pointing to the leather satchel filled with Kunst's SD money. The youngest, the one who looked like a clerk, picked it up and carried it out the door. The leader swatted him, and he dropped it.

"What do you think you are, some sort of porter?" The leader kicked the satchel into a corner of the hallway, next to a steam radiator.

"Sorry," said the youngster.

The elevator operator stared, but oddly said nothing about me, splattered with blood, holding a bloody towel on my arm, hunched over in pain.

Out front, Bobby the valet smiled brightly. "You want that Buick now?"

"No," said the older fellow. "Bring our car."

"Oh, my God," he said, noticing me holding my arm. "You need a doctor."

"That's where we're taking him," said the older Pioneer.

"Bobby," I said. "Do me a favor. I left my bag on the ninth floor, at the end of the hallway next to a radiator. It's a brown leather satchel. Will you see that someone picks it up and puts it in my car?"

"Yes, sir, I'll do it after I get the car." He hurried away.

"Trying to pull something funny?" said the older one.

"No, just trying to act normal. You guys Pioneers or Klansmen?" I wanted to distract them.

"Both," said the youngster.

Bobby pulled up in the Klansmen's car. It was an old Nash, and squeezing into the back seat with the beefy guy was tight. The older fellow drove, while the youngster sat in the passenger seat, watching me. We headed south, into town.

"Larry, what are we going to do with him?" asked the youngster.

"No names, damn it. Gimme a minute to think."

"She said to take care of him," said the beefy Klansman next to me. "Does that mean we gotta kill him, or did she mean take him to a hospital?"

"I don't think that broad meant the hospital," said the older Klansman. "But we're the Finance Committee. Killing's not our job, and we don't got to do what that lady says neither. We're doing this for our country, for our children. I don't know nothing about killing no one, and I don't plan to."

"Fellows," I said. "I can get you money. Lots of money."

"Shut up," said the driver. "Did you kill the fellow who was lying on the floor?"

"Me? No, she did that. Beat his head in with a brass lamp."

"Damn," said the driver. "I believe you. She's one cold cookie. Talking with her this past week always gave me the creeps."

We bounced along in silence, the old car's springs overtaxed by four men. The towel on my arm was completely soaked. I lifted it off the wound, and blood flowed.

"Hey, fellows," I said. "This won't stop bleeding. Got anything that will help?"

It was almost comical how eager they were to help me, these men who Anna thought were carrying me to my death. They found some rags I used to press harder on the wound, trying to staunch the flow of blood. That hurt, and the pain made me woozy. Then I realized it wasn't just the pain.

I lost track of time. My vision narrowed. I felt nauseated, and I knew I was on the verge of passing out. I had no clue where we were. The drive seemed endless. We hit a big pothole, and the car bottomed out. I moaned loudly.

"What the hell's wrong with him?" said the driver.

"He's still bleeding," said the man next to me. The driver stopped, turned around, and shone a flashlight.

"Jesus! Blood's all over everything."

"Let's dump him and get the hell out of here," said the beefy guy.

"How are we ever going to get my car clean?" said the driver. "My wife will kill me."

Suddenly, the car door opened, and they pushed me out onto the curb. I fell heavily and couldn't get up. The car drove away. I vomited, then heard steps and looked up. Jimmy Brown, the guy who had been following me, bent down and lifted my head. After that, all went dark.

13

Friday, September 1, 1939

More than a month after the Baptist World Alliance meeting, I sat in New York's Pennsylvania Station cafeteria, coffee and breakfast untouched, staring at *The New York Times*. I'd known it was coming; we all had known, but it was still shocking. The British and the French had played a desperate game to delay the storm, but they'd finally run out of moves. Now, the storm had broken.

GERMAN ARMY ATTACKS POLAND; CITIES BOMBED, PORT BLOCKADED; DANZIG ACCEPTED INTO REICH.

Of course, we'd heard the news earlier, just after dawn. Arthur Godfrey's cheerful morning program had been displaced by H. V. Kaltenborn translating Hitler declaring war on Poland. But radio was ephemeral, and like music, its words evaporated into the air. Printed newspaper headlines were something else: tangible, lasting. Staring at the headlines did not change them.

Further down the page, another article discussed the Neutrality Acts and how they ensured the United States could not get involved in this war. *Good luck,* I thought. The cafeteria was full of late-morning commuters and long-distance travelers, all grabbing a quick bite, but unusually quiet. Most were absorbed in their newspapers. I wondered how many of them could possibly remain "neutral in thought and deed." The fascists were evil, a blight, and I wavered on my own commitment to neutrality.

I'd been in New York and New Jersey for two weeks, visiting companies for Phil Sanders, gathering information. Two companies didn't pan out, but I'd spent three good days in Bethpage, on Long Island, examining the prospects of the Grumman Aircraft Engineering Corporation. The numbers looked good, management had a clear vision of its goals, and the new F4F Navy fighter showed promise. They claimed it matched the fighter aircraft of the European powers.

As a businessman, the news of war in Europe should have pleased me. It enhanced the value of the Grumman stock we had bought. But it didn't please me, nor did the prospect of being a war "profiteer." I looked away from the paper and took a sip of coffee.

When I folded the paper to read page three, I felt a twinge in my left forearm. Thank God for Jimmy Brown. *Who knew he was still following me?* He saw me pushed out of the car and took me to the hospital just in time. The "rabbi's" knife had severed a vein deep in my arm, and only surgery and emergency transfusions had saved my life. It took a week to recover. Jimmy Brown had visited me at the hospital.

"Glad to see I didn't waste my time picking you up," he said. "Still haven't gotten the blood out of my car's upholstery."

"Thanks for saving my life. I didn't know you were following me."

"I'd switched to a beige Chevy. I'd been paid to follow you for two weeks, so I did."

"Why?" I asked. "I mean, who hired you?"

"Your ex-wife, of course. She wanted evidence of moral depravity so she could have the court terminate your parental rights."

"Sounds like Mabel. Did you find any? Moral depravity, that is."

He smiled broadly. "It's pretty funny, you know, me being able to help you like that. That nasty crow, your ex, saved your life by hiring me."

"Yeah, I laugh about it while enjoying my moral depravity."

"Well, you do have some odd birds as friends."

On hearing this, Phil had sent Brown two hundred bucks and some flowers. "Replace your upholstery. From an *Odd Bird*."

I glanced at my watch. My beloved Hamilton Cabot had been destroyed in the fight, but that may have saved my life. First thing on leaving the hospital, I'd visited Reiser and Wassermann Jewelers for a new watch. They had some interesting Swiss pieces, but I settled on another American-made Hamilton, called the Gilman; 14-karat gold and a cool one hundred bucks. A watch says a lot about a man, goes the radio ad. When I check the time, I like what a solid gold watch says.

While the "Finance Committee" had gotten away with their hundred thousand counterfeit bucks, no Pioneer political campaign developed. I figured the "Finance Committee" might have simply split the haul and gone their separate ways. But Phil thought the money went to Gene Talmadge's political machine. And Talmadge was suddenly before the public as never before. After two defeats running for the Senate in 1936 and 1938, with his campaign organization bankrupt, his political career seemed at an end. Then, his fortunes turned. Ol' Gene looked like a sure bet to win the governor's office again in 1940.

As for me, I'd gone down to the Secretary of State's office and registered my own company, the Morgan Information Consulting Group.

"Group, huh?" Phil said. "Who else?"

"A group of one. I'll work for you on a fee basis or a retainer. Maybe work for others eventually. This way, friendship doesn't get entangled with business."

"I'm hurt you didn't think you could work for me?"

"Sure, I'll work for you. Just hire my company." We laughed.

This trip to New York was the first test. I thought I'd done well.

There was an unexpected bonus from the disaster of the World Baptist Alliance meeting. When I retrieved my car from the Georgian Terrace Hotel, I found that, as I'd asked, Bobby had put the brown satchel in my car. It held $750,000 in counterfeit one-hundred-dollar bills, along with $60,000 more in smaller bills. I turned the bag and all the counterfeit hundreds over to Joe Packard. He was ecstatic about recovering three-quarters of a million in counterfeit, praised my honesty, and insisted on buying me a drink. We went to the Athletic Club bar, and I drank a scotch and soda, guiltily aware that just below us, hidden in my locker, was sixty thousand dollars in tens, twenties, and fifties. But, as my mother once said, lying is the way of the world.

Packard told me the police had searched Anna's suite the next morning. Not only was she gone, but so was the fake rabbi's body. There was blood on the floor, a ruined rug, a blood-splattered green dress, several blood-soaked towels, and a long-bladed knife. No sign of the dead man. Packard suggested that he might not have been dead, had perhaps recovered enough to escape. I knew better.

"She cleaned up and dumped the body. Or someone did it for her."

"So, this bastard is really dead?" Packard took a sip of his drink and looked at me.

"I saw his eyes, Joe. Glassy. Fixed. Dead as a doornail."

"Who the hell was he?"

"Damned if I know," I said. "Anna said he was a commie, but Nazis always scream commie. In the hospital, I wondered whether he was with some sort of British spy outfit. But that doesn't make any sense. I think he was just an unhinged nut."

Packard fiddled with his glass, letting the quiet burble of conversation in the bar flow around us. "You know, this whole thing is awful, his using you to identify his victims."

Until that moment, I had not really thought about it, but Packard was right. I'd been used. He saw the shock on my face. "Ah, so the light dawns?"

"Yeah," I said. "Thanks a bunch for helping me feel better about it."

He laughed. "How about this? Anna disappeared. She left the Georgian Terrace about an hour after you, driving a DeSoto sedan with Tennessee plates."

"I saw the car earlier. What happened?"

"The DeSoto was found at The Read House Hotel in downtown Chattanooga. Betty Smith from Memphis had stayed there one night, then vanished, abandoning it. No one saw her leave, but the rail station's just a block from the hotel."

"So, she's still out there?"

"A Nazi agent, somewhere in the wind."

I was glad to leave Atlanta on the trip for Phil Sanders, to focus on something new. After my time at Grumman, I returned to New York City and chased down the address of the Jewish Welfare Alliance on Fifth Avenue. The secretary at the Temple in Atlanta was correct: Rockefeller Center, but an empty office. The tenant had been something called The Antipodes Insurance Association.

"They cleared out a couple of weeks ago," said the secretary in a neighboring office.

"What did they do?"

"I guess something to do with insurance. There are companies from all over the world here."

"Did you ever meet a woman named Eleanor Jones? Heavyset, looks a bit like Kate Smith. British accent?"

"I'm busy with work most of the time."

"Ever hear of something called the Jewish Welfare Alliance?"

"Didn't notice any Jews, if that's what you mean."

I called Packard long distance to see if he could help.

"That's just how it is," Packard said. "Sometimes, you never know. The point isn't to figure everything out; if you try, you'll only go crazy."

"So, then, what's the point?"

"You and umpteen philosophers have asked that question since the beginning of time. All I can say is that for me, the point is to stop the bad guys. Or at least throw a stick in their spokes. That's all you can do."

"But who are the bad guys?" I asked.

At that, he laughed.

Then there was Emma. She had written a long letter explaining what happened after she left Atlanta, delivered to me while I was in New York. She and Gellman had arrived in Washington without incident and went to the Carnegie Institute. Within hours, Gellman was offered a position, and they promised to work out immigration for him. Emma then stayed in Washington, DC, for a few days, sightseeing.

Saw the sights in Washington and used up all that money you gave me! After that, I went to the family farm. Spent five days there. My mother is fine, though my little brother says he'll do anything to get off the farm. He begged me to take him to Atlanta, but he has school to finish. I'm now back at the WPA, working on the Georgia Guide. I wrote an article about that ex-slave, and the Constitution published it! I'm going to try writing more for the paper. Wish you were here. Come home soon, and call me. CALL ME!

Yes, there was something there, and I didn't want to lose it. Just thinking of Emma made me smile happily. I'd sent her a telegram, saying I'd be home on Saturday, the second.

I ate a bite of cold eggs and checked my watch again. Fifty minutes before my train. I turned to the sports section, refusing to read any more war news. Scanning the box scores from Thursday's games, I drank my coffee and picked at the eggs. Behind me, two women chatted in annoyingly loud voices. I didn't turn to look.

"Ingrid, that hat is lovely," one woman exclaimed in a harsh, nasal New York accent.

"Thanks, Meg. I found it at Macy's," said the other woman with the same accent.

"Oh, did you see the sale on stockings?"

"No, I missed it. Show me." The rustling of paper was followed by exclamations of delight and more discussion of the sale.

"Oh, look at the time."

"We better hurry."

I sat for a moment, wondering what had possessed me to listen to their conversation. I'd never looked at them, but something felt familiar. Then it hit me. The perfume. Dark and herbal. *Tabu*. Anna's perfume.

I turned around quickly to see two women headed for the grand concourse. Leaping up, I grabbed my bag and hurried after them. They were lost in the crowd until I glimpsed them descending a stairway across the concourse to the Long Island Railroad. I ran down a similar nearby stair, hoping to catch up, only to discover it didn't go to the Long Island platforms. I ran back up the stairs, wove through the crowd to the other stairway, and hurried down it, pushing past people.

"Hey, bud, where's the fire?" one guy called.

At the platform level, I looked around wildly. A guard was closing a scissor gate across the entrance to one platform. I hurried over and looked through the gate, but the platform was empty. I then turned and saw two women far down the opposite platform. They stopped, and the first stepped up into the train car. I hurried across the corridor. The second woman handed up her shopping bags. Her hair was brown, but her figure and her stance screamed Anna.

I pushed through the turnstile, but suddenly, my jacket pulled backward. I heard it tear. I looked back; it was caught in the mechanism. I pulled again, and the jacket ripped further. A new suit I'd just bought.

"Hey, buddy, let me help you." I glanced up. The platform guard came over and began to work on the turnstile, trying to free my jacket. I looked down the platform and saw the second woman had one foot up to board the train.

"Anna," I yelled. "Anna, it's Mark."

She paused, one foot on the step, and looked over, startled. It was definitely Anna.

"Where does that train go?" I asked the guard.

"That train? Hell, half the length of Long Island. Stops at every little burg."

"Anna," I yelled again.

She stepped up into the doorway of the car, shook her head, and disappeared into the coach. The conductor's whistle blew, and the train doors slammed shut.

I stopped struggling. It was finished. Stopping her would accomplish nothing. She was a Nazi agent, but that was people like Packard's problem, not mine. At least I could give him an idea of where she was living.

The guard untangled my jacket. It was ruined.

"What was that all about?" he said, handing me some torn cloth.

"I wanted to talk with that woman," I said. "But she's not who I thought she was."

With a chuff and a clash, the train pulled slowly away into the darkness under the city and was gone. I let her go.

That was my last Neutrality Act.

14

The Consulting Agent: Cash and Carry

Volume Two of the Mark Morgan and Emma Connor Saga

15

Wednesday, December 13, 1939

I'm a consulting agent on retainer for Sanders Securities, an investment company based in Atlanta. Uncovering corporate malfeasance and financial fraud is my business. Sometimes, it's just numbers work, much like what Frank Wilson famously did in the Al Capone case. Sometimes, it's a bit more. The information I uncover helps Phil Sanders avoid bad investments, but in this case, I found more than bad business. I found trouble.

Phil sent me to Miami to gather information on two companies, Pan American and Flamingo Limited. Inside Pan Am's modern terminal on Dinner Key, a huge globe illuminated the world-spanning operations of the airline. Pan Am's executives openly discussed its management, operations, finances, and problems. The Latin American routes were growing, profits had increased, and new routes to Europe and across the Pacific held great promise. However, the war in Europe and the spreading conflict in China threatened the company's opportunities. All this was well documented in numerous memoranda and audited reports. I'd photographed these materials with the help of friendly Pan Am secretaries. On the whole, Pan Am was a solid bet.

Flamingo Limited was not. The company had air cargo routes across Florida and the Gulf states all the way to New Orleans. They'd recently added flights to Cuba and planned a public stock offering on the Curb Exchange in January. Sanders could get in "on the ground floor," they said. It was all smoke and mirrors and the projected profits were a bunch of hot air. In fact, I found no provable profit in their operations. No one at Flamingo was open, friendly, or forthcoming. At noon, they asked me to leave.

At the Miami airport, I chatted with the guys who handled air freight. None had anything good to say about Flamingo, and several made dark hints. I'd spent much of my youth in Havana, so I telegraphed acquaintances there, asking about Flamingo's Cuban routes. They replied quickly. Flamingo worked with some very unsavory people. That tore it. No way in hell we would invest in the company.

Returning to the Hotel Victor on Miami Beach, I dropped my things in the room and went down to the bar. With my gin and tonic, I walked out to the swimming pool. Guests gathered there in the evening as they waited for the first dinner seating. Torches cast a flickering light on the small, well-dressed crowd surrounding the pool. But I wasn't there to meet people; I was there because the pool deck offered a spectacular view out over the Atlantic. To the east, the darkening sky melded into the ink-black sea. I could just make out the faint rhythmic hiss of gentle waves on a beach.

I toasted the scene before taking a long pull on my drink, the scent of lime balancing the tart tonic. It's hard not to be philosophical when looking at the ocean, to reflect both on future possibilities and on death. I raised the glass for another sip when the world exploded.

Off balance, I reached blindly behind and grabbed a shirt as I fell into the pool. Pain enveloped me, and it took a moment to realize I'd pulled a guy in with me. He pushed my head underwater. That was a mistake. I've played a bit of competitive water polo, so we scuffled until I got a good grip and held him under instead. After a minute, he quit. I let go and swam to the shallow end, where I pulled myself onto the steps and tried to make sense of things. A woman stood near the side of the pool, both hands over her mouth, clearly shocked. The man beside her was yelling.

"I saw what you did, you son of a bitch," he said, pointing at the guy in the pool and turning to other guests for support. One fellow dashed off toward the lobby.

I gingerly touched the back of my head, finding the beginnings of a large lump behind my right ear. As my heart slowed, I started to feel nauseated. At that moment, the hotel concierge squatted next to me.

"We've called the police," he said. "Do you need help getting out of the pool? A guest who's a doctor can look at you." I climbed out, my suit soaked and heavy. He guided me to a chair, where a man examined my head.

"What's your name?"

"Mark Morgan."

"Do you know today's date, Mr. Morgan?" He felt around my skull.

"It's the thirteenth, of course." And then I laughed.

Bright lights switched on, illuminating the pool deck. The milling crowd quieted as my attacker levered himself out of the water and began stalking toward me. I stood. I'm six feet, one eighty, with broad shoulders from years of swimming. This guy was bigger. Oddly, he was dressed for tennis: a white shirt, white trousers, and what looked like white Keds. Dripping black hair was plastered across his face, but it didn't hide his long, narrow nose and sneering, thin lips. As he approached, the sound of a siren grew. The guy changed his mind and trotted past, toward the lobby. No one got in his way.

"Damn," said the concierge. "Did you see the look he gave you?"

I saw. His meaning was clear. The guy wanted to kill me.

The cops found a lead-filled sap. "He probably hit you with this, Mr. Morgan. Wanted to knock you cold; maybe thought you'd drown in the pool."

"Hit me a little too high." I touched the growing egg behind my ear. "My ex-wife always said I was hardheaded."

The cop smiled. "Yeah. You were lucky." He peered at me. "Ya look kinda familiar."

"Tommy," said the other cop. "That's 'cause he's a ringer for Max Schmeling; you know, the guy that fought Joe Louis. Anyone ever tell you that, Mr. Morgan?"

"That's a new one," I said, having heard it a hundred times.

They moved me indoors, and I answered their questions. I couldn't tell them much. Andrew Stevens, the man who had shouted at my attacker, told them a bit more. The crowd had been waiting by the pool for the first dinner seating when the big fellow suddenly appeared. Stevens noticed him because he was so large and not dressed for dinner. Then, the guy pulled something from his pocket and swung it at my head. After that, all Stevens saw was a struggle in the water.

"May I ask some questions?" I said.

"Sure," said Tommy, the cop.

"Mr. Stevens, what did your wife see?"

"I'm sure the same thing I saw. The guy just walked up and hit you. He said nothing, did nothing; he just hit you."

"Maybe she saw something more. I think she was nearer than you. May we ask her?"

Mrs. Stevens was still a bit rattled. "Yes, I was right there. So close that when he swung that thing, it brushed me. Scares me just to think of it."

"Do you remember anything else?"

"Well, let's see. He said something when he swung; you got hold of his shirt, and then you both fell into the pool."

"What did he say?"

"I'm not sure I can repeat it. It's not nice language." She looked at her husband.

"It's okay," he said.

"Well, I heard it clearly. 'Take this, you fucking snoop.'"

The two cops looked at each other. I looked at the floor and rubbed my head.

"Mr. Morgan," Tommy asked, "why are you in Miami?"

"Just a business trip. I spent yesterday with the Pan Am people."

"And what's your business?"

"I work for Sanders Securities in Atlanta. Investment counselors."

My mind began to churn. The thoughts made my stomach churn, too. Maybe the attacker was from Flamingo Limited? That opened a real can of worms. Knowing who they were connected to in Cuba suggested who they were connected to in Miami. The name at the top of that list was Meyer Lansky.

I didn't know Lansky, and I didn't want to know him.

"Do you need some water, Mr. Morgan?" said Tommy, peering at my face. He'd caught my unease.

What I needed was the first train out of town. The Royal Palm usually left around 10 p.m. I glanced at my watch. The second hand was not moving. I shook it and saw water behind the crystal.

"Damn it," I said. "That goon killed my watch."

The Consulting Agent Series

The Consulting Agent Series

Over twenty years ago, a photograph awakened my curiosity.

https://digitalcollections.library.gsu.edu/digital/collection/ajc/id/10882

I found this photo in the Georgia State University Library in 2005. The picture, taken in July 1939, showed Peachtree Street and what was then called the theater district. The Davidson's department store, Capitol Theater, and Roxy are on the right; farther down the street on the left are the Paramount and Loews Grand theaters. Hanging over Peachtree is a Nazi flag, with the iconic Coca-Cola sign behind it. The Banners on lampposts welcome the Baptist World Alliance to Atlanta.

Bizarre and interesting, so it stayed in my mind.

A bit of newspaper research (the hard way back then: microfilm) revealed that the Baptist World Alliance met every five years in different locations around the world. In July of 1939, 40,000 *Messengers,* representing more than sixty countries, assembled in Atlanta. Given the date, a central concern of the meeting was world peace, justice, and the prevention of war. Perhaps, I thought, an academic article could come out of this story?

The meeting was remarkable for 1939 in Atlanta, Georgia. Early in the proceedings, the Alliance leadership, given permission by Mayor William Hartsfield, removed the legally required segregation signs from meeting venues. In tandem with this, a vigorous debate erupted over Nazi

Germany's racial policies and the spread of totalitarianism. Despite the protests of almost 300 German Messengers, a resolution condemning Germany's race laws passed. There was even a strong anti-imperialist element in the resolution.

"We condemn all racial animosity, and every form of oppression or unfair discrimination toward the Jews, colored people, or the subject races in any part of the world."

Soon, however, I was caught up in the research and then the writing of *Dark Places of the Earth: The Voyage of the Slave Ship Antelope*, and I put the article idea aside.

About this time, I began working with fiction writers at Georgia Southern University. Not just to improve my style for *Dark Places*, but also because of my lifelong interest in writing fiction. Fiction allows you to address truths and illustrate the human condition in ways that are impossible while constrained by the sources used in writing history. Influenced by the image of Peachtree Street with a Nazi flag, I sketched out an espionage novel set in Atlanta. But I didn't have time to write it.

Then came the pandemic.

Archives and libraries closed, and I put aside my research project on the case of *Fletcher* v. *Peck.* I began work on a novel about the illegal slave trade, inspired by my research on the slave ship *Antelope*. The result was *The Slaver's Apprentice*, which won a Royal Palm Literary Award from the Florida Writers Association and will be published by Northampton House Press in 2026.

After writing *The Slaver's Apprentice,* I returned to the Atlanta story. Market trends showed readers love genre series. Perhaps this book was more than a one-off; perhaps this could be the first volume of a noir crime and espionage series set in Atlanta? Tales in the tradition of Joseph Kanon, Philip Kerr, Robert Olen Butler, Alan Furst, and most recently, Thomas Pynchon. Books I enjoy. So, *Neutrality Act*. Then, I sketched out the next three volumes in the series: *Cash and Carry, Lend Lease,* and *Atomic Age*.

In my naiveté about the fiction world, I didn't know that I had set a very high mark.

Thus, the stories of Mark Morgan and Emma Connor emerged. Not simply of them navigating the dangerous world of organized crime and spies, but also building an investigative partnership amidst the fits and starts of a budding romance. In the noir tradition, a first-person narrator, Mark, carries the burden of telling the stories.

Despite his privileged background, nothing is easy for Mark Morgan. He's not only ignorant of the seamier side of Atlanta, he's sometimes quite dense, impulsive, and haunted by recent devastating events. A man who was on top, but now he's broken and increasingly cynical about his world. Yet, he maintains some sense of justice. He needs work to survive, and will thoughtlessly take on some truly odd commissions.

Emma, a former librarian, works for the WPA Writers' Project, though that will soon come to an end. Bright and remarkably knowledgeable, she's cautious and deliberate in her actions: a steady hand in the developing relationship with Mark. She is quite conscious of her modest background and intimidated that a man as attractive and connected as Mark is interested in her. Of course; she has a hidden past not yet fully revealed.

How will these two very different people deal with gangsters, phantom killers, and Nazi spies?

What could be more noir than that?

A book is only as good as the people and resources that contributed to it.

First, I must thank my patient partner, Miriam. There is no way I can fully express the love she showed by reading and commenting on endless versions of this manuscript. My friends Elena Albamonte, Bill Allison, Valerie Davis, Gary Edwards, and Jimmy Griffin all read versions of the story and provided many helpful suggestions.

Both David Poyer (https://poyer.com) and Tina Whittle (https://www.tinawhittle.com) gave me well-developed critiques, editing suggestions, and advice about the pleasures and perils of writing fiction. Many thanks to these professionals for their help.

The March 2025 Ossabaw Island Writers Retreat and the Amelia Island Writers Work in Progress Group both freely offered critiques and ideas for the book. Henderson Library at Georgia Southern University, the archives at Georgia State University, and the Atlanta History Center were essential to working out the historical context for the story. Anonymous judges for the Florida Writers Association Royal Palm Literary Award also provided helpful critiques that contributed to the final manuscript.

My thanks to all these and other individuals, groups, and institutions for their help in creating not just this book, but the idea for a continuing series: *The Consulting Agent*.

www.ingramcontent.com/pod-product-compliance
Ingram Content Group UK Ltd.
Pitfield, Milton Keynes, MK11 3LW, UK
UKHW041635190726
13854UKWH00006B/2510